Lucy
and

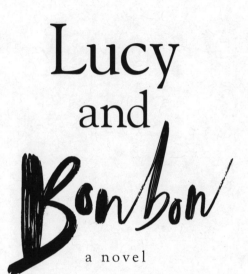

a novel

MIROLAND IMPRINT 35

Guernica Editions Inc. acknowledges the support of the Canada Council
for the Arts and the Ontario Arts Council. The Ontario Arts Council
is an agency of the Government of Ontario.
We acknowledge the financial support of the Government of Canada.

Lucy and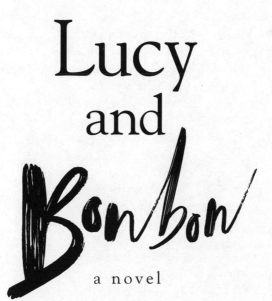

a novel

Don LePan

MiroLand
publishers

MIROLAND (GUERNICA)
TORONTO • CHICAGO • BUFFALO • LANCASTER (U.K.)
2022

Guernica Founder: Antonio D'Alfonso

Connie McParland, Michael Mirolla, series editors
Julie Roorda, editor
David Moratto, cover and interior design
David Chidley, cover photograph
Guernica Editions Inc.
287 Templemead Drive, Hamilton, ON L8W 2W4
2250 Military Road, Tonawanda, N.Y. 14150-6000 U.S.A.
www.guernicaeditions.com

Distributors:
Independent Publishers Group (IPG)
600 North Pulaski Road, Chicago IL 60624
University of Toronto Press Distribution (UTP)
5201 Dufferin Street, Toronto (ON), Canada M3H 5T8
Gazelle Book Services
White Cross Mills, High Town, Lancaster LA1 4XS U.K.

First edition.
Printed in Canada.

Legal Deposit—First Quarter
Library of Congress Catalog Card Number: 2021952014
Library and Archives Canada Cataloguing in Publication
Title: Lucy and Bonbon / Don LePan.
Names: LePan, Don, 1954- author.
Description: First edition.
Identifiers: Canadiana (print) 20210387084 | Canadiana (ebook) 20210387092 |
ISBN 9781771837187 (softcover) | ISBN 9781771837194 (EPUB)
Classification: LCC PS8623.E63 L83 2022 | DDC C813/.6—dc23

To Alex
(1976–2007)

Preface

The story of the hybrid variously known as Bonbon Gerson, Bobo Gerson, and Beau St. Clair is one of the defining narratives of the first part of the twenty-first century. Any reader will be familiar with it at least in outline, and many will be familiar too with the great arguments it has given rise to. Has the existence of a hybrid "changed everything" in terms of how we define what it means to be human and what it means to be animal? Has it, in effect, moved the line that we draw to separate ourselves from other species? Has it even eliminated any such line? Or is the case of Bonbon simply a one-off—a strangely freakish case that we need not take much account of when we generalize about what it is to be human, about the so-called sanctity of human life, and so on?

This book will not settle those questions, and it offers no dramatic new information as to the outline of what happened—either in the Congo or in North America. Nor can I promise to take the story to a conclusion that will fully satisfy the curiosity of many readers as to what finally became of Bonbon; this book makes no attempt to answer all the questions, lend support to any of the wild hypotheses, prove or disprove any of the unsubstantiated claims. What it does do is bring together in a single volume, for the first time, the first-hand accounts of the participants in the story. Some of those accounts have already been published; others are unpublished or little-known. Many are perhaps better known to those north of the border—where so much of this story unfolds—as they are to most of us here in America, or to the millions around the world who are acquainted merely with the more sensational aspects of the story. I hope that, excerpted and brought together as they are here, these bits and pieces will provide a coherent account that will give readers a real sense not only of what happened, but also of how it felt to those who were involved.

1.

Lucinda Gerson

[The following is from the first section of a transcript of the handwritten notebooks in which Lucinda Gerson provides an account of her son's story—and her own. The publishers of the full account have generously allowed me access to the handwritten original—and generously allowed me to include substantial excerpts in the present volume. I should make clear that they have not divulged to me—any more than they have to the general public—how the notebooks came to be in their hands. This volume will thus not put to rest the controversy over the publisher's behaviour—any more than it will the ongoing controversy over the actions of Lucinda herself. But the notebooks have now been indisputably verified as having been written in her own hand, and they remain the necessary starting point for anyone who wishes to make an informed judgement concerning her behaviour in the past—or to speculate as to her whereabouts in the present.]

So there's two kinds of kind, right? There's, like, *what kind is it* and all that—*kind* like *type*, OK? Or *what kind of book is this?*, ha ha. And then there's *kind* like in *kindness* and *being kind*, and we all know about that even if we don't do it. Not near enough of it, any-ways—we got to work on that, right? And if we got to work on it maybe it doesn't so much come naturally. So what about *human kind*? Which kind is that?

And then there's *mankind*, but I'm not even going there, ha ha.

Anyways, I can tell you what kind of people my family is. We come from Comber, originally, all of us—that's near Detroit but on the Canadian side, on beyond Windsor. *Comber* rhymes-with-*sombre*, not *bomber* or with some guy running a piece of plastic through his hair. No bombs going off in Comber, I can tell you that much for sure—it's flat country and there's not a whole lot that people would call interesting, if you want to know the truth. Some people, anyways —the older I get the more I think there's interesting stuff any-wheres. But that's where we lived all the time we were growing up, 'cept for the year when I was five, that was when Dad "tried his luck" in Montreal, but it turned out there wasn't no luck there. Not for him, anyways, or for us, and we were back in Comber by the time I turned six.

My older sister, she loved Montreal and it pissed her right off that she had to move back with the rest of us. 'Course she didn't say it like that, Susie's always used good language, but that's how she felt. She was always restless after we moved back, she wanted to move *anywhere*, and she started getting a lot of ideas about what anywhere was like from flipping through all the old *National Geographic*s that had been sitting in the garage since our grand-father died. I say *flipping through* but that's not right. Susie was a smart kid, she was reading them too, and not just the words under the pictures neither. Dad kept saying that he wanted us to be im-proved by those magazines, that he didn't want us growing up and not being able to do anything 'cept working on the line at R&R Rubber Trim like he did, *nothing 'gainst the car industry but there should be something better'n R&R*, he'd always say. My mom would never say much when he went on like that, I think she was OK with dad making his eighteen dollars an hour at R&R, it was a lot more than she made at the Superette. Anyways, I reckon Susie got herself a lot more improved than I did, every which way. By the time she was nine she wanted to go to Africa like other kids wanted to ride a horse or have a dog to look after. And Africa for Susie had to be jungle. Not the desert, not the—what do they call it, the plains—*savannah*, ha, I looked it up just then. None of that: it had to be jungle, had to be the real Africa.

Africa didn't fade away when Susie hit the teen years, neither. She skipped a year in high school, she did a four-year anthropology degree in three, and whatever else she needed beyond that she did in no time, it seemed like. There she was at 29, already with her professor job and the doctor degree she says most people don't get until they're halfway through their thirties (most people? Ha!), writing us from some camp near Lake Mai-Ndombe, near Inogo, near Kinshasha, yeah, I looked up those spellings too. Near a lot of other places I bet nobody's ever heard of. Trying to figure out if these chimpanzees who aren't really chimpanzees—bonzees, they're called—if they're what she calls a matriarchal society. If the women dominate the men, basically. They use sex to do that, that's the theory; they have it all the time and they seem to have a lot of fun doing it, but a lot of times one of them is using sex to control other ones, that's what Susie's thesis was. Like, as if it would be news that some people use sex to try to control other people. But anyways.

Alright, I was 27, OK? I'd spent a lot of time trying to figure out other things, including how not to be controlled by a man. And how not to control one too, I guess. *The personal is political*, as Susie use to say; she got that one right, but now she says it's sort of an old fashion thing to say. Anyways, the personal was still political for me—I guess I was old fashion, some ways. When my mother was going to throw out all the long loose skirts and dresses she'd worn in the 60s—*hippie clothes* she called them—I said *no, give 'em to me*, and I started wearing them a lot. Somebody said the other day that I still look pretty good in a long skirt and a tie-dye T, but that's another story.

My mom used to say that she'd been just about the only working-class hippie, she used to tell me that she sometimes wished she'd either had less of a brain so she wouldn't of seen no wrong in the

Vietnam war or any of that, or more of a brain so she would of gone to university and been more like—more like what? Like a regular hippie, I guess. She always wished she'd been able to go to all those places too—Kathmandu and San Francisco and New Orleans and them, all those places that weren't part of the regular world. Specially New Orleans, she'd watched *Easy Rider* a bunch of times and she'd keep singing that song, *All I want is to be free, and where that river flows, that's where I want to be*, something like that. But she never did get to none of them, not even New Orleans.

She was pretty happy when Susie went to university, I can tell you, and when Susie did so well. She sure smiled a lot about that and she'd tell anyone who'd listen all about Susie and how well she was doing.

Make love not war was another thing I picked up when my mom was about to throw it out—she had a couple of old posters as well as a few buttons with slogans on 'em like that. I think she still believed what was wrote on them but she never talked about it. Seemed like she was happy enough to get rid of the stuff. I didn't have any more space than she did, or any more money, neither. (I was mostly working summers at the Gas 'N Go, they always needed more help in the summers, but it wasn't like they paid more when they needed more help, I was just scraping by.) Anyways, there was something in me that would rather of gotten rid of cell phones and GPS gadgets than throw out that old junk from before I was born. Actually I think Susie would have felt the same way if she hadn't of been halfways round the world. Maybe not the old clothes—you never could get Susie into a skirt or a dress—but the buttons and the posters anyways. She had all of that book learning, but take that away and we thought a lot alike, the two of us, that's what I told myself.

I guess legally I was as much an American as a Canadian, but neither me nor Susie never thought we was American or Canadian. It wasn't so much that we thought we were both. It was more like we didn't think of ourselves as either. *I want to be a citizen of every-where,* she'd say. *Or of nowhere at all.* I wasn't as political as her, but I guess I sort of felt the same. Course she didn't get to be a citizen of anywhere except Canada, but she was always going over to Detroit to see some show or other, or join in some protest, or hang out with some guy she'd met in some bar on the Canadian side. She'd even go over to take in a Tigers game with people she hardly knew, and she didn't care a whole lot for baseball. That was the way it was for a bunch of years when I was growing up and it's not like I blame her. Like I say, Comber was pretty quiet.

I got to be American 'cause I arrived early. My mom was thinking she probably had just a few good nights left before I arrived— back then people didn't go all bananas if you were a woman and you wanted to go out and have a drink or three when you had a little one on the way. Most people, anyways; Dad didn't like to see a woman drinking if she was pregnant, not even a drop, *if she's got a bun in the oven, the mom has to be eating for two, and the dad has to be drinking for two*, that was what he'd always say. But Dad wasn't there that night, he and Mom had actually broken up, ha ha, they did that a few times, it was only after I arrived that they patched it up again. So anyways, Mom had left Susie with a friend and she was over at Chassy's in Detroit with a couple other friends taking in some band when her waters broke, and next thing you knew there I was, 20 inches long and six weeks early. And American. *Born on American soil,* they love to say that. *We* love to say that, maybe I should say.

You want to know something funny? After Chassy's closed down they put a zoo in there. I'm not kidding, that's where they put the zoo, right where Chassy's used to be on East Congress, right next to the Benevolent Society. The Benevolent Society's still there, maybe you know that. They fixed it up a little but it's still shabby and it's still selling second-hand stuff to people who need it. Maybe they sell just as much to people who *don't* need it, ha ha. But the zoo, right where Chassy's used to be? Like I say, that's funny. I guess maybe you don't know why that's funny until you've heard a little bit more of this story, but I'm telling you it's funny.

It was after Uncle Harry died that I started to think that maybe I could travel a bit too. Some people used to say Harry hadn't been really rich, he'd just been *well off*. Eff off to that one, I say. Call it what it is—Uncle Harry had money, and he left a bit of it to us, and that was great.

Alright, so it wasn't *only* Uncle Harry leaving each of us some money that made me think of going somewhere. Things weren't exactly great the last year or two I spent in Comber. The only work I could get was shit jobs in the Gas 'N Go, or else Dave and Joan's Price Chopper Food Mart.

Me and this one guy—Estes Danby was his name, you wouldn't think anybody'd be called Estes in a place like Comber, but there was, and he had a decent job at the plant—back then Chrysler and them had that big car factory in Windsor. Estes was my guy—*Estes is the bestest* I used to tell him. And we were going to have a kid, maybe a few of 'em. We weren't going to get married and that wasn't going to matter, you didn't need to spend a fortune on a big day and a piece of paper. We were right for each other and we were going to stay with each other always and we had a nice little apartment over top of the jewellery store, Sellars' Jewellery, maybe you've heard of it? That Danny and Sylvie Sellars used to run—on Main Street? It was a nice little apartment, not so little, really, it was a two-bedroom, there would have been lots of room for the two of us and the kids. I mean, kids can share a room, does 'em good, I think.

But it all went wrong, didn't it? First he got me pregnant—and that was a good thing, don't get me wrong there, I wanted kids as much as he did and I didn't have no morning sickness or nothing, hardly any. But then his friends and his parents got to him about marriage and respectability and all that garbage. We had a few arguments about that but finally I let him buy me a ring from Sellars', 'course everybody always jokes about buyers and sellers and a girl going to the highest bidder, ha ha, but I didn't think it was too funny. Anyways we picked a date when we'd make it official at the registry office; turns out he thought it would be a good idea to have a name change too. Not him, of course—he wanted *me* to change *my* name and be a Danby, and I didn't want to be no Danby. I wanted to keep being me. It was a big deal, that fight, but this time I didn't give in, *I'll marry you but I won't do nothing to my name*, I told him, *I'm not going to be you*. I guess it was never the same afterwards, though we made all nice for the wedding, and we went through a lot of the motions of loving each other, and some of it wasn't just going through the motions neither. I don't mean just *that* way. I can think dirty just like anybody, but I'm talking about feelings too. Anyways, it didn't last. How do you effing know what's going to last?

So then there was the morning when I did have a lot of pain down there, but it was only nineteen weeks—it wasn't time yet, that was the thing—and Estes was at the plant so I got a taxi and then I called him on his cell but he wasn't picking up, and at the hospital it was hours and hours and then they told me no, the little one hadn't made it, there was no little one. Not then, anyways. Somehow that was the last straw for Estes. Of course he said *don't worry it's not your fault* and all those things—well, damn right it wasn't my fault, who put it into his head that it could have been my fault?

You don't want all the details—trust me, you don't. All that happened was the sort of thing that happens everywhere every day; it was just a shame that we'd gone and gotten married. Now we had to go and get separated and go and get divorced, and go and get two lawyers, 'cause they always say both sides have got to have their own effing lawyer, who has the money for that?

So you can see that I had a lot of reasons to be happy about Uncle Harry, not about him dying and all, but the money. The money and the being able to get away. Really get away, that was the thing. Not Toronto or Detroit or Toledo like I went to once. See something of the world, maybe find out some stuff. Maybe be happier. Being happy's overrated, but it doesn't totally suck, either.

Go to India, I thought, like Mom had never been able to. And maybe go to Nepal—and for sure stop in and see Susie in the Congo. *Stop in*—that was literally what I thought to myself, can you believe it? And then of course I started talking to people. Dad was dead by this time (what with his smoking and that, and all the nights he'd *just stop in after work* at the Dominion House and not get home till eight or nine; he never made it to 50, not that I blame him for that, like Mom used to do all those years. I'm just saying), and so was Mom—that had been the shocker, a heart attack right out of nowhere, age 58—but I talked to just about everybody else, my friends, my ex-boyfriend Matt (the only one of my boyfriends who *had* turned out to be a friend), the travel agent in Chatham, and of course Aunt Ellen, since it was going to be her Harry's money that I'd be spending, 'course I talked to her too.

Anyways, you know what every last one of them said about the Congo part of the idea? They said I was crazy. *Just crazy, you don't just go there like that, not to the Congo, it's not for tourists, it's not for visiting of any sort, people get raped there, people get killed there, it's a wonder your sister ...* They went on and on, but like I told Aunt Ellen, I'm just about as stubborn as Susie is. Or as Uncle Harry was—she got a good laugh out of that. So I went ahead and booked a round-the-world ticket, first stop Kinshasha, except of course for the bazillion stops you had to make in airports before you could get to a place like that. And next thing you knew I was on a crapped-out old bus that somebody said they thought they'd heard might get to Inogo before dark. Every few moments there'd be a thump when we hit a pothole and you'd bounce up and then down again hard on the seats—they were hard and cramped, my rear end started to be sore in about five minutes, I can tell you that. The old woman beside me seemed to know where we were going but I couldn't make head nor tail of anything, she kept smiling and making motions to the chicken she was keeping down round her feet, and that chicken kept fidgeting the whole time, she was quite a character—the woman I mean, not the chicken. Both of them, I guess.

At first I'd thought I wouldn't actually tell Susie I was coming. I'd just show up out of the blue, wouldn't that be a surprise? But everyone gave me a lot of reasons why that would *not* be a good idea, and it sounded like one of those times when what everyone says is right. So I'd wrote ahead, and the letter must have gotten there 'cause when the bus finally pulled in to Inogo, Susie was ... —it was pitch dark by this time, and I'd asked the driver about that, *are you behind schedule or what?*, but he'd just said *everything come soon soon, madam, you will be seeing*, and he laughed a big, hearty laugh, so maybe they were on schedule after all. And then after a pause he said, *you go see those people at their ape station?* I told him I was, and I asked him what he knew about the place. *The place? I am knowing it well*, he said. *But the people?* He shook his head. *These people—they selves is who they stick to.* He paused again, and then he added one more thought. *These people—they stick to they selves, and their apes. They maybe think* we *are the animals, what? We people of the Congo!* And he laughed his big laugh. After I'd been to the station, I think I would have thought of something to say to that, but not then I didn't. I just smiled and tried to laugh a laugh too. And then I went back to my seat and tried to look out again, into the dark night, but for a long time, all I could see was my own face reflected in the glass.

Dark or no dark, it wasn't hard to pick out Susie from all the others, she was wearing jeans and a white top like she always did, and of course her face is white too, I shouldn't say *of course*, 'cause I didn't even say what colour I am, did I? We hugged and all, and she smiled, but you know what? I actually wasn't a hundred per cent sure she was glad to see me.

It didn't take more 'n a couple of days before I could start to see why it bothered her to have me around. There she was, living way out in the bush, but it didn't feel like bush, not really. There were five of them in all—it was *university-this* and *research-grant-that* and *post-dock-the-other-thing*. It must be some sort of embarrassment to have a visit from your kid sister who hasn't done any more than finish high school, really.

Of course I wanted to try and fit in. I told everybody I'd been to college and that wasn't a lie, not really, I just didn't say it had been a stupid little community college that nobody'd ever heard of, and I only went for less than a year. But people know when you're faking it with shit like that. Truth is, I reckon I embarrassed Susie just by being there.

Plus, it had been her thing all along in the Congo, and here I was, the little sister, come to horn in on her. "I know it's hard for somebody from outside to understand," she kept saying, "it's hard for somebody from outside to get much out of it. You'll probably find a lot that's more interesting in India."

And maybe I would. But this was plenty interesting too, living in little round houses with grass roofs—huts with hats, I called them—and spending all your time watching bonzees. You got to figure big apes would be big meat eaters, right? Meat, plus a lot of bananas. And Susie says chimps are just like you'd expect—they'll eat rats, monkeys, whatever. But not gorillas, and not bonzees neither. Basically, it's fruits and veggies they eat—vegetarian. No, more like that weird one—vegan, that's it. But not like, strict—I mean, they'll eat bugs sometimes. Worms. Don't see no human vegan do that, do you, ha ha.

OK, so maybe it's nothing special watching apes eat fruits and veggies. But the sex? They did it all the time, that was one thing. It'd be hard to count how many times a day they did it, and you could see every bit of it. And, whatever people say, who doesn't find that interesting? That was the obvious thing, of course people got off on all the sex, no matter how much they dressed it up in their fancy language. I tried reading some of the sex parts in Susie-style fancy-language books—*Males are nearly always sexually receptive; whereas most other animals copulate only as an act of reproduction, bonzees appear to derive continual physical pleasure and emotional satisfaction from sexual contact, both heterosexual and homosexual ... That bonzees often copulate face-to-face has been widely observed, but bonzees engage in an extraordinarily wide range of sexual behaviours—they are by human standards quite adept and profligate in their sexual endeavours.* So on and so on, just like us except they do it a lot more often. And except with them, seems like the women always have the final say, even if the guys do a lot more strutting around.

Visitors weren't supposed to "interact" with them too much—even researchers weren't supposed to; this was, like, the opposite of Jane Goodall and them, you weren't supposed to "taint the research" by disrupting the bonzees' social lives. You were supposed to just watch them, mainly from this observation hut that was just bamboo and thatch built over a gigantic hill they said was made by termites, except I never heard of termites that would want to build a mountain. They must not be like any termites you get in Comber—Detroit even, or some of the other places you hear about, New Orleans and that.

You'd sit there and the bonzees would sort of know you were there but usually they couldn't see you and usually they'd forget about you and go about their business as if you weren't there. That was the theory anyways. And I've got to admit it was pretty neat, there were two groups of them and they were all interesting. Didn't take long before you could tell who was who, how they acted differently, had their own personalities. Of course Susie and the others had to give the animals names, you wouldn't want to call an animal like that K9 or R2-D2 or whatever. But they didn't want to give them normal names like Tom or Liz neither. So they'd started giving them the names of cities—they thought that was funny when they were in the middle of nowhere. And because it was bonzees, people started thinking of all the "B" names. There was a cute young one they called Berne and a slow-moving older guy they called Bilbao, Bill for short, and there was a Bonn and a Brisbane, they were none of them places I'd been, I can tell you that.

There were two babies, one in each of the little groups that would come to this open area in the trees, and the bonzee babies were Bathurst and Buenos Aires. Bathurst was named for Bathurst, New Brunswick—one of the researchers was from right near there. For some reason they always called that baby Little Bathurst, not just Bathurst.

And there was one grown-up called Beirut, Bei for short, he was beautiful but troubled, maybe they'd been thinking of all the trouble when they named him. Bei loved to put on a show and to give a good time to anyone. He was 'specially good with Little Bathurst, he would play with him and carry him anywhere, so much that you got to thinking Little Bathurst was a little spoiled. But you could see that Bei suffered too; he got picked on by one of the bigger males, one they never found a city for, they called him Udie, after some of the sounds he made. Udie was the biggest one and a few times I saw him rape Bei; they don't call it that, *between males, forced mounting has been known to occur* is what they say. Like I mentioned, bonzees are always having sex and most of the time it's friendly. Almost *all* of the time, in fact—which is a lot more than you can say for humans, right?

But not absolutely all of the time; sometimes you would get a male like Udie who was just—well, rape is what it was, and every time it happened Bei would be left screaming.

That was pretty hard to take, but you know what was almost worse? The way Susie and them just accepted it. Calm as could be. They didn't get upset by it, they didn't even seem to feel anything for Bei. Sure, they'd given Bei and the others cute little names, but when it came to *feeling* anything for what Bei must have been suffering—well, it was like they'd turned off their sympathy taps.

This was research, and if you started feeling anything for the research subjects, you had to stop yourself, you had to distance yourself. I almost wrote *you had to stop yourself having any human feelings*, but that's the thing about humans, isn't it? We've made it so's it can seem natural to be distanced. To be unfeeling. We've made it so's it can seem natural not to care. It's not just that, neither. We've made it so's it can seem natural to be nasty. Can't it? Natural for us humans to love nobody but ourselves and our own group and be nasty to everyone else. To hate everyone else.

And then I thought of all the human nastiness that happened in the Congo a hundred years ago, the people who'd been raped and killed and mutilated, going back to when that Belgian king had ruled it like it was all his and he'd had people's hands and legs cut off if they didn't do what he said and he had millions of them killed as well, I mean really, ten million people or something like that. And all the nastiness from less than ten years ago—all the killers and rapists and all of them, coming over the border from Rwanda and the refugee camps and whole villages being... I read up on it when I was eight miles high coming over here, I got a book, how other countries piled on, and how in the end there were maybe five million dead and who knows how many raped. It was just ended when Susie and them set up their research station, but stuff was still going on in other parts of the country, that's what everyone said. And everywhere there were people suffering, people who lost their parents, their children, who've been raped, who've been beaten, who were always going to have the scars. And Susie and them? I'd asked her about it all and she said yes, yes it had been a problem, in some ways it was still a problem, but she was talking about how hard it was for *her*, problems setting up a research station and running it, not about how hard it was for all the people who suffered through everything. It was like she didn't see them—what mattered was the research. All that nastiness, she just didn't feel it—just like she didn't seem to feel anything about what was happening to Bei.

Susie and them weren't hating Bei—it wasn't *their* nastiness—but they sure weren't loving him, neither! And the more I saw them just accepting what Udie was doing to Bei, the more I started to feel something like hate inside me. Hate for Udie, and hate for us humans—not specially for Susie and them, but for all of us humans. Yeah, I know it was stupid, but that's what it was and I couldn't help it. What I was feeling was something like love for Bei, and something like hate for all of us humans.

But I couldn't say that to Susie, could I? It was her life, it was what she'd dedicated herself to … —well, I just couldn't, not even on the night before I was supposed to leave.

Susie had opened a bottle of wine and then another bottle and we stayed up late and at first it was alright, it was good, even, we were talking about Mom and how great she'd been but how big of a pain she'd been too, and how strange it was to have both of them gone, Mom and Dad, I mean, so that there was just Susie and me in the family, no parents and no children neither—she and me didn't have our own children and we weren't really children ourselves now that we didn't have parents, ha ha, you know how it can get when you're drinking. And then suddenly it seemed like Susie couldn't stop asking me questions but they weren't really questions. It was, like, *what are you going to do with your life, Lu?*—that sort of thing. When she started nagging me she started calling me *Lu*—that's what I used to like to be called when I was a kid.

When she'd picked me up in Inogo she called me what she's always called me since we were teenagers—*Luc*. As if I was a guy, *Luke Skywalker* or something, but I've never minded that, maybe I've always had a part of me who wanted to be a guy, ha ha. Lots of people call me different things. Lots of times people call me *Luce*, you spell it L-U-C-E but you say *Loose*, it could mean *running loose and wild and free* but it could also mean what Mom used to call *a loose woman*, ha ha. I never minded that neither, maybe I should of.

But now? Susie was using a name I hadn't heard since we were little. I didn't know what to think of that. I sure didn't like all these questions: *don't you really have to think about some big issues, Lu? You could go back to college and train for something. Or get a proper job. Is travel really going to help?* And really she was saying *you're stupider than me and you've been wasting your life, if you're not getting a graduate degree, you better get a job in the Ford plant like everybody else in Windsor,* except she didn't have a clue, the Ford plant was closing and everyone was being laid off and she didn't even think to ask. People don't ask the real questions, do they? At least hardly ever. We go on in our own little worlds and we—alright, what the fuck do I know about it?

Anyways, thinking like that made me sadder than I'd been in a long time and when we finally went to bed I couldn't sleep. I kept thinking about all the things that Susie had said and all the things that I *hadn't* said but that I should have said, about her and her whole research project and about what humans are like, all of us, and about how Bei ... More than anything I kept thinking of Bei. I knew I would be going in to Inogo and Kinshasha the next day and then off to London and then to Mumbai, but it wasn't any of that I was thinking of, it was the other stuff.[1]

Finally I got up, very quietly, and I crept out. I closed the thin little door ever so quietly, and then I was on the path to the observation hut. When the moon was out you could see everything and suddenly there was a figure coming into the clearing on beyond the observation hut. He turned and saw me and he started to come

---

1. [Editor's note] Readers are advised that the next few pages are taken up with Lucinda's description of her encounter with Bei. The description is frank—some might say graphic. It is not to my mind obscene in any way, but some readers might well, for entirely understandable reasons, find it disturbing. It may readily be avoided by simply skipping past this section and resuming the narrative at the next line break. (For those who choose not to read the description of the encounter itself, its nature and its outcome may readily be inferred from subsequent references.)

closer. Now he was walking on two legs just like a man would except they are so short, the legs of a bonzee. I froze up for a second, I mean, here I was, late at night in the middle of nowhere in the middle of Africa, and here's this strange guy coming towards me, who wouldn't be a bit scared? But then I thought *no, he's a bonzee, there's never been no human attacked by a bonzee, daytime or nighttime, everybody says that*, and then I thought *maybe he's a little bit sad and a little bit lonely, sort of like me*, and then I thought that I wouldn't of thought that if I hadn't of been drinking a fair bit, but I had been drinking a fair bit, so there you go. He wasn't much more than four foot four, four foot five, maybe, and as he got closer I could see that it was Bei, he was all alone. And then I could see that that he was rubbing himself and for a second I was, like, *what is this?* but we all do it, we're all animals, and I thought of what Udie had done to Bei and how nasty animals could be and how nasty human animals could be, especially, how it was us humans who were the nastiest so much of the time and how we had to learn to be more loving, more like bonzees were, almost all of them, almost all of the time, we had to learn to be more like Bei. And I felt something in my heart, a warm feeling came over me, *it feels good, doesn't it, Bei?* I said to him, *what you do to yourself, what you do …, and if people—well, who are any of us to say it's wrong? It doesn't need to be tied in with having children, does it, Bei? Or with competing with all the other boys, or with competing for anything, you don't need any of that, do you, Bei, you don't, you're a sweetie, aren't you?*—that's some of what I said, something like that. Maybe some of it I wasn't saying I was just thinking, maybe all of it. Anyways he couldn't understand anything I said if I did say it, could he? But those were the sorts of thoughts I had— no point in denying it.

And then I looked into his face and I thought of Matt and I thought of Estes and I thought of Rick and Joe and Sandy, I thought of all the boyfriends I'd had and I thought, did I even know any of them? They would look at me, all of them, when they wanted something, when they wanted pleasure from my body, and they would look as if they were caring for me, as if they wanted pleasure *for* me, as if they ... —*love*, that was the word they all used. Did they feel it? Did any of them feel it, feel the ache that I would feel at night when I was falling head over effing heels for one of them? That longing, and then the ache in the end when they'd say *we're just not right for each other, that's all—its no one's fault*, and now here was Bei's face in front of me, innocent like a child and not trying to make me think anything about how much he cared for me, just wanting pleasure, wanting to give pleasure, wanting to be loved. When Susie'd talked about how only bonzees and bonobos and humans make love face-to-face, what were the words she used? Did she say *make love*? Maybe words don't matter, but the feelings matter.

We touched each other then, I touched him on the shoulder first and he touched my arm, and then we touched each other's cheeks, all the books say their faces are closer to the face of a human child than they are to the face of a chimpanzee, or a bonobo, or a monkey, any of them. He moved his face towards mine, and he had the nicest smile. I know you're going to think that doesn't sound right, *he's just an animal*, you're thinking. But I'll say it again—we're all animals, aren't we? And I'm telling you, and it's true, he had a smile, he had a sweet, sweet smile. *Had* or *has*? I don't know. Is he living now? I wish I knew.

And then we touched each other again, I didn't mean to touch him down there, I don't think I meant to. I had just brushed against him and he was making soft little sounds, he was so hard and he was making these soft little sounds and then we held each other close and his arms were around me and then we were lying down somehow beside the termite mound and my wide skirt had ridden up, high up above my waist and then he was inside me, and I think I really did want him to be there, though I never would of expected that'd be something I'd want. I know I didn't *not* want him to be there, anyways. And I know tears were streaming down my cheeks but I didn't feel sad. I don't know what I was crying for, it was some sort of release, I guess. Anyways, I didn't push him away, I didn't tell him *no*. I held him closer, I held him very tight. Even now I can't think it was wrong. I can't think he did wrong, I can't think we did wrong, I can't think any of it was wrong. We held each other afterwards and he was still making those soft sounds.

You're thinking it must be gross, he must have been so hairy, but I didn't notice none of that. I might as well tell you, I'd pretty much been there already so far as hairy guys were concerned, I remember how thick it was all over Rick, not just his chest and his armpits and between his legs and the face he never shaved, but all over, heavy on his arms, his legs, over almost all his back. He wasn't the best lover, Rick, but it wasn't because of the hair, I can tell you.

I blew him a kiss, Bei I mean, as he loped away, and somehow I felt as light as the night sky, with all those stars and the moon. My feet took me back to the sleeping huts and I don't know where my mind was taking me.

∾ In the morning I had to go. I didn't say anything after breakfast but then when Susie was driving me in the jeep to Inogo—I don't know why but I thought I had to say something, and I said to her *they're not just dumb animals, are they?* Sort of as a question but I guess it came out wrong, anyways she was sort of angry with me, *you've been here this long and that's all you've learned?* And she told me about some of the bonzees in zoos and places where they were studied in captivity, she had told a lot of it to me before, all about another Sue who was a researcher and another bonzee, Zanzi, who had more or less learned to read, and all that. *The dumb animals are the human animals,* Susie said, she was raising her voice now, *those human animals who won't recognize that humans are not the only ones with thoughts. With feelings. With lives that matter*, and she went on like that for quite awhile. *It's not just these animals that matter*, she was saying, *it's all animals, but these ones are so close to us, so close* and then I could see her face straining and see how much it all mattered to her, and somehow that ended up being the moment when I *could* say what I'd really wanted to say.

Could there ever be one that was both? That was what I asked. *Could one be born that was half human and half* ... —*Like a mule, I mean*, I finished, and she stared at me like I was stupid. *Don't be ridiculous*, she said, *of course there couldn't be, the science just isn't ... And besides, can you imagine some guy getting it in his head to—it's too crazy, there's no way in a million years that ...*

I interrupted her. We would be in Inogo soon, and my bus would be there, and I had to know. *It could be the other way*, I said. *It wouldn't have to be a guy who ... It could be ...*, and I guess there was sort of a funny pause in what I was saying and then she looked away from the road.

She looked right at me. *Lu*, she said, *sometimes you have a weirdly dirty mind. I mean really weird ...* and she almost missed a curve, and the jeep swerved and skidded but she gripped the wheel tight and she stayed on the road and she started to drive faster and I didn't tell her anything more. She'd always thought I slept around too much—she was never proud of me. More like ashamed, really, and I just looked ahead and finally I said it wasn't a big deal, I was just curious was all, a person had a right to be curious and a person couldn't be expected to know all the things that Susie knew. *I* couldn't be expected to know all those things, anyway, and maybe she found it hard having me there but I was glad I had come, really glad, and really grateful too. A lot of that was true.

I missed my period in Mumbai. And then I missed it again a month after that in Kathmandu and that was just when I was about to come back home. It was time to come back, anyway. I'd discovered I wasn't the sort of person to wander for months and months in places like that, though you can meet a lot of interesting people that way. One time I spent the night with one of them, I mean we had sex, it was more like that than making love. Nari Singh, he was, and I made silly jokes about his Singh thing. He took it really well. I liked him. But we were pretty different—I mean, he was training to be a police officer, how weird is that?

Anyways, that night with Nari happened after the first time I'd missed my period so I knew it couldn't of been him. Whatever, I had to find out, so of course as soon as I got back to Comber I figured I would head off again, and find a way to say *bye bye* to Bei's kid before it even was a kid. I was going to just drive into Windsor where I knew there was a clinic but then I thought *what's the thing going to look like? Even at 15 weeks is it going to look a lot different than a normal fetus, I mean a normal human fetus?* And if it was, like, different, there would maybe be a lot of talk about it at whatever clinic I'd had it done at. And maybe I didn't want all that talk to be happening in Windsor, where there was a lot of people who knew me, and there was a lot of people who knew a lot of people in Comber too—if you could ever say there *was* a lot of people in Comber. So maybe it would be better to go across the border and have it done where there was nobody that knew me. Nobody at all.

2.

Susanne Gerson

[The following is an excerpt from Susanne Gerson's narrative of her interactions with her sister Lucinda during and after Lucinda's visit to the Lake Mai-Ndombe Research Station near Inogo. The account was leaked to the media in the months after Bonbon's birth; Gerson eventually gave unrestricted access to the material to all news media, stating that she did not wish the *Post* to be in a privileged position in any way with regard to this material.]

It must have been at least a month after Lucinda left before she and I were in touch again. I had emailed her a couple of times to ask about India—and I had asked something else too, in a postscript to one of the messages—whether there was any significance to that strange bit of conversation I'd had with her in the jeep on the way to Inogo at the end of her visit. When she'd started talking about mules, I mean, and I'd thought maybe she was making some weird joke about bonzees having sex with humans. Of course I hadn't taken it seriously, but something about it kept nagging away in the back of my head; I told myself it was all ridiculous, but the nagging thoughts wouldn't go away. So I added a *were you serious?* PS to my next email.

It was a week or more before Luce wrote back with the shocking truth:

> You might as well know sooner rather than later. Yes, Susie, that conversation meant something—and yes, I'm

pregnant. I know you won't believe it, but Bei's the father. You're going to go ballistic over this, I know that. I wish I could do something to make it better. I'm sorry, Susie, I'm really sorry.

And that was it. Of course she was right—I did go ballistic. I was furious with her, and I sent her an email that maybe I shouldn't have. But I also couldn't entirely believe it, even as I was going ballistic. Even if she and Bei could have ... —I didn't know what verb to use. Even if they had, it seemed utterly far-fetched to imagine that she could be pregnant by him. And even if she truly were pregnant by him, you would not expect a viable fetus to result.

But if it did? Immediately I started to see the consequences. The media would turn it into a circus; it would be horrible for her—and horrible for the infant as well.

And for me, and for a research station in the middle of nowhere. Publicity of the worst sort, and publicity that would go on and on. Reporters and photographers would manage pretty quickly to find the middle of nowhere, you could be sure of that. And they wouldn't be interested in any story about an endangered species of great ape in an extraordinary environment, or about the nuances of the behaviour patterns and cognitive abilities of one of our closest cousins. It would be sensationalism, pure and simple. It might well end up being almost as distressing for Bei and for the others in Inogo as it would be on the other side of the ocean for Luce and her freakish offspring.

And for science? No doubt the linguists and the geneticists would salivate at the thought of doing research on a hybrid, but it wasn't hard to foresee the effect of all the excitement over a hybrid on ongoing research into great ape behaviour. The distraction would be complete. Who would think to start making monthly donations to a cause so tarnished as the Lake Mai-Ndombe Research Station?

If we managed to survive at all, it would be only with the greatest difficulty.

If Luce really was pregnant in the way she said she was, she had to be persuaded not to give birth to the creature; it was as simple as that.

* * *

Lucinda Gerson

[Following is the continuation of the transcript of the handwritten account by Lucinda Gerson of her son's story—and her own.]

If I'd of known everything I know now, maybe I wouldn't of worried 'bout anybody thinking anything and I would of just gone ahead with it in Windsor. I don't know. But I know there was a hell of a lot of things I didn't know, I guess that's true of all of us sometimes.

So what I did is I went over the bridge to where no one would know me, to the Planned Parenthood Detroit Health Center on Cass Avenue. That's *center* with an *-er*, not an *-re*, Canadians make a big deal about that sometimes. But other than that, it's not so different on the other side of the river, it really isn't. 'Cept of course on the other side the people are mostly black. I'm good with that. And 'cept of course as well you sometimes got to pay—no "socialized medicine" like they keep calling what we got in Canada. But I was good with paying too, I might not have had the cash but I had a credit card, ha ha.

Anyways, that's where it gets complicated again, 'cause I never actually made it inside the clinic. I think you might of heard some of the story from here onwards—this is when it started to get in the news with the lawsuit and all, the Choose Life people suing me for false pretences, whatever. But I didn't pretend nothing, and I never said nothing that wasn't the truth.

There were people with signs outside the clinic, and two of them came up to me, Maggie and Linda they said they were, though I didn't take in their names right at first. Their signs were about saving lives and that's what they wanted me to do, they said. They totally understood where I was coming from, that's what they said and I thought *how the fuck could you understand? You don't even know me!*, and I said exactly that, all of it except the *fuck* part. It didn't put them off. What they had was a proposition, that's what they said. It was just a proposition, a suggestion, and of course I didn't want to take a life, that was what they told me, nobody who thinks of having an abortion *wants* to take a life, that's what they said, even a *sort-of-a-could-be-a-life* like a fetus, people do it 'cause they don't see a better way. And Maggie and Linda were here to help me find a better way—that is, if I wanted to see if there *might* be a better way. That's pretty much all of what they said, but then they said it again with different words. They kept pestering me, and half stepping in front of me.

It wasn't anything they said or did that stopped me from going through the door to the clinic. But all the talking made me wonder what I'd tell the people inside if I did go in. Was I really going to tell them that I'd had it off with a bonzee in the Congo and now I wanted to end the pregnancy? Ha ha.

What I did then was stop talking to Maggie and Linda—stop listening, more like, 'cause they weren't letting me do too much of the talking. But I didn't go in. All I was thinking was I'd better do some more thinking. But there's not anywheres to think right around a clinic with protesters outside of it. So I went all the way back home to Comber. That was when Susie called.

* * *

Susanne Gerson

[Following is the continuation of Susanne Gerson's
narrative of her interactions with her sister Lucinda
during and after Lucinda's visit to the Lake Mai-Ndombe
Research Station near Inogo.]

I must have called her number a dozen times over the course of five
or six days before she finally picked up. Even then it was only after
the fifth or sixth ring. It had never been any good leaving messages
for Luce; she never responded to them—never even listened to them,
I don't think. With her latest phone there wasn't even a voicemail
option, no matter how many times you let it ring; she must have
disabled it.

"Hi Susie." She hadn't disabled the call display.

"Luce." Now that she was on the line I couldn't think what to
say. "I been thinking 'bout you." This was what happened whenever
I'd start talking to Luce—or to anybody from back in Comber. I'd
start acting as if I'd never been to university myself, never moved
away. I'd say 'bout for about and I been for I've been, and might of
for might have. I told myself to stop right there. "I've been thinking
about you and the baby."

"If there's going to be a baby. Susie, I know I could of acted
different. I should of acted different."

One part of me heard what she was saying and what she was
feeling, while the other part of me was hearing the of's instead of
have's, and thinking for the umpteenth time how far away from
each other we had grown. But if I was to have any influence over
her now I had to humble myself; I knew that. "Yeah. Sure. I guess
you should have acted differently. But I guess I should have acted
differently too. That email. I should have thought before hitting
send; I should have ..."

"What I did was no worse than what anyone does when they have sex with someone who maybe they wouldn't have if they thought about it a bit more. It was strange, and it was sad, *he* was sad, Bei was, and all I did was …"

"All you did was everything. They're not like us, Luce. You can't just …" I guess I couldn't help getting into it with her.

"Susie, it's you who keeps saying that they're people too, people with thoughts, with feelings. And that they matter just like we do, that they're so close to us, that they're …"

"No, Luce. I never said they were close to us like *that*." Did I really have to explain all this to her again? "Close to us in evolutionary terms. Maybe sometimes close to us emotionally—or with something like emotions. But not like *that*, Luce, not like what you did. Not close, like, to let them put their thing right inside you, for God's sake. It's disgusting. It's …"

"If you talk about it like that, Susie, it's always disgusting. Sex, I mean. That's how you talked of boys when you were fourteen and I was twelve, *Jennifer's going to let him put his thing inside her.* I remember." Ever since we kids she'd done this—constantly interrupting me. I let her go on; I even tried to listen. "You can always make it sound gross if you want to, Susie. But why should it be disgusting? Why should it be disgusting if …, if …, when you feel close to someone if …"

"We feel close to our brothers and our sisters, Luce, and our *children*, for God's sake, and we know they feel close to us, but that doesn't mean we … " But I knew I had to say more; I knew I had to steer things away from what had happened to what was going to happen—or what might happen. I took a deep breath. "Whatever I feel about any of that, I have to get beyond it, Luce. I realize that. And I realize I shouldn't have said what I said in that email. I'm sorry—really I am. I have to forget what happened and think of you and where you are now, and of what's best for you. And I'm trying, Luce—really I am. I want to help you. I want to help you do the right thing now. Have you found someplace where they ... someone who will?"

"Give me an abortion? Yeah. I guess I have. But Susie, I'm not sure ..."

"I'm so glad, Luce!" I couldn't help breaking in. "And of course everyone feels a little unsure before going through with it. But it's totally safe, really it is, Luce. You'll hardly feel a thing—honestly."

"But I'm not sure I'm going to do it, Susie. I'm not sure I *can* do it ..."

"Anyone can do it, Luce. Anyone. Trust me, I ..."

"But you don't understand. I'm not sure I *want* to do it."

"Luce, Luce, Luce." I couldn't think of anything else to say.

"Luce what? Why shouldn't I have the kid if I ..."

"For the *sake* of the kid, to start with. What sort of life is he going to have if you go ahead with this? Or she. There's not going to be any happiness for a kid like that in the world we live in. He probably won't even be allowed to live in the world; they'll take him away from you, Luce, and they'll ..." I didn't want to say all the things they might do. But I shouldn't have said what I said next. "Is it to get attention, Luce? Is that why you're even thinking of going through with this? I'm sorry, but I have to ask." Of course I wasn't sorry, not then—and I didn't have to ask. But that didn't stop me. Sometimes you have to tell people the truth. "You know you always wanted to be the centre of attention. Ever since you were little. I remember when you were six years old you ..."

"When I was *six*! Everyone wants to be the centre of attention when they're six goddam years old!" We were silent then, but we could feel each other seething on the other end of the line. I took another deep breath, and I waited a good ten seconds before I said anything else.

"I can help you, Luce. Financially, I mean. I know it hasn't been easy for you. I could ..."

"I don't want your money. I don't want any hand-outs, I don't ..."

"That's not what I meant, Luce. I'm not trying to bribe you. I'm just trying to say that I ... —well, I make more than you do, probably more than I should. And anybody who works at the sort of jobs you work at gets paid less than they should. I should have been offering more help to you than I have been—I can see that now. I want to start doing more to help. Better late than never, I hope."

"Yeah. Right. Susie, we better not go on like this. I won't have the kid. OK? I won't have the kid. I'll get an abortion—just like I said I was going to do. No problem."

That was just like Luce—if she ever gave in, she'd do it suddenly, and she'd pretend it had been what she'd been going to do all along.

"You won't regret it, Luce. And I will help—really I will. Whether or not you need it, you deserve it." Did I mean that? I don't know; it just felt like the right thing to say.

"Yeah. Right. So long, Susie."

I put down the satellite phone—it was the only way you could phone out from the research station. Luce wouldn't have believed how much that one phone call cost. But it was worth it; if she was going to terminate the pregnancy, it was most definitely worth it.

3.

Lucinda Gerson

[Following is the continuation of the transcript of the handwritten account by Lucinda Gerson of her son's story—and her own.]

'Course I would tell her I was going to get rid of it. That was always the only way to get Susie to lay off—tell her what she wanted to hear. But I can say to myself what I could never say to her—I sort of thought she was right, too. Not maybe for all the reasons she said, but how often are we right for exactly the reasons we give for what we do, or for what we try to get other people to do?

So a couple days later I went into Windsor again and I went back over the bridge, and I parked near that same clinic on Cass Avenue, and I could see the same protesters standing outside. Were they exactly the same ones? Two of them sure looked like Maggie and Linda. I thought I'd just stroll around for a few minutes before going in, just to sort of steel myself. So I just started walking. At first I didn't think of anything, I just walked. South, down Cass, they called it the Cass Corridor where all the drugs and the gangs and the murders used to be years ago but now it was supposed to be one of the signs of a new Detroit, everything all fancied up or whatever. Except it didn't look fancy to me. There'd be an old building and then an empty space and then another old building that might have gotten some fresh paint, and then another empty space. Maybe it was a little fancier than Sandwich Street in Windsor, but that's not saying a whole hell of a lot. Anyways, I turned a corner and there

29

was this place called Honest John's with what looked like a vacant lot on each side, and another vacant lot on the other side of the street. You could see it was a bar, and when you walked inside—I don't know why I'm writing "when *you* walked inside," it was *me* who walked inside—it was all pretty dark. There was one neon sign that said *Sobriety Sucks* and another neon sign that said *Men Lie*, well ain't *that* the truth?

I ordered a Bud and I started thinking some more 'bout what I'd tell the people at the clinic when I'd say I wanted to have an abortion. *If* I said I wanted to have an abortion. I would never have minded having a kid, not at all, even on my own. But it scared the hell out of me to think of having a kid that was half human and half something else. It wasn't just the fact of it that scared me. There was all the specific stuff too, like how you'd raise a kid like that, what you'd feed it, what you'd do for school and that, how you'd—OK, wouldn't you think of this? Can you get bonzee sizes for diapers? Long story short, there'd be a lot of crap to think of, including crap like that. Damn right it was scary.

Alright, what about other people? My folks always raised us to think of other people first, let's be honest, it's pretty hard to do that, isn't it, but you've gotta try. The most important other person in this case would be the kid, I was thinking. What would be best for him? It wouldn't be no easy life, I figured, there'd be all sorts of other people giving him a hard time—that's if they even let him mix with other people. Who knows? People might freak out once they knew he was a hybrid. 'Course if I had an abortion I'd be ending him before there *was* a him, you could hardly say that would be best for him. Or could you, if he was going to have a life that was just miserable? How could you tell for sure?

Why was I thinking *he* all the time? That's the way we're trained, I guess. But I decided to start thinking *she* instead. Could it be for the best to have an abortion, if the life *she* would have would be miserable? Just miserable.

"It's fucking miserable for a lot of folks, ma'am. Bud can help."

"I said *fucking miserable* out loud?"

"You did, ma'am."

"OK then. You better get me another Bud."

"Yes ma'am."

Maybe I didn't even have no right to bring somebody like this kid into the world. Maybe what I'd done wasn't natural and the kid wouldn't be anything natural, and there shouldn't be any place for any living thing like that in the world. But what's so special about *natural*? If we really believed in keeping everything natural we'd still be living in caves or jungles and there'd be no hospitals and no wonder drugs and no jet planes. And no Budweiser. Ha! Anyways, bringing some bonzee blood into the human world'd be a good thing. Bonzees are good. Simple as that. Better than humans. You think I'm joking—I mean it. You don't see bonzees starting wars and bombing the crap out of other people because they've got different politics or a different country or a different god. Or telling other people they can't have a job or a place to live because they're a different colour. Or beating the crap out of other people—some guys, it just gives them pleasure to do that. Bonzees, not so much.

All right, so I guess no one can be a hundred percent sure it'd be a good thing to bring a bonzee into the world; no one can be a hundred percent sure what'll happen with your genes. With a *g*, the *genes* you inherit with the DNA and that, not the pants one—though you can't be too sure what'll happen with them neither, can you?

So you can't be sure, and maybe she wouldn't be a good person. If I have her, that is. Maybe she'd be a monster. Or he'd be a monster. He, she, it.

But it's not like I planned this, did I? I'm not trying to play god here and change the human race. I'm not some mad scientist like Frankenstein making some creature in a lab, doing something that couldn't ever happen in nature. Sex happens all the time in the world of nature, sex *is* the fucking world of nature. Sure, we call some sex natural and we call other sex not natural. But the stuff people used to call unnatural back in the day? Everybody these days calls it natural. Most of it, anyways—and vice versa. Just think of what they say in the bible you're supposed to do if you're a widow and you don't have children. You're supposed to let your dead husband's brother fuck you—him and no one else—and you're supposed to have kids with him. Not just allowed to, *supposed* to! Didn't matter one bit if you hated the thought of having him inside you making babies—you had to do it, 'cause that's what Moses and the rest of them thought was natural and right and good.

So much for Moses! At least what happened between me and Bei was OK with the both of us. But all I'm saying is that with what him and me did there wasn't nothing happening in no lab, there weren't no test tubes and there wasn't no cloning or any of that. It was natural. Maybe it was a funny sort of natural, but a lot of funny sorts of things can happen in nature.

So maybe I should let it happen, go ahead and have the kid, just see what happens, and maybe it'll be good. Maybe it'd be like playing god to *stop* it happening, to go into that clinic and ask them to do the suction or whatever.

Suction. I didn't like the sound of it.

Sobriety sucks, the sign kept saying. I kept sipping my Bud.

What's wrong with playing god, anyway? He did some pretty shitty things but he did some OK ones too. If there is a god, I mean.

"You want another Bud, lady?"

Sure I wanted another Bud. *Want to get wiser? Drink Budweiser.* They should put up a neon sign with that on it.

I'd been reading up on bonzees, like anyone would. I mean, anyone who's had it off with a bonzee in the Congo and they're trying to decide if they should end the pregnancy.

I made jokes about it all the time. To myself. There was no one else I could make jokes with, was there? But it didn't ever feel like a joke. Not ever.

By now I knew about how bonzees were different from chimps or bonobos—I didn't know how to say *bonobos* at first, you say the *no* stronger, bo*no*bos, not *bo*nobos. And I didn't know how, way back in the nineteen-twenties or whatever, everybody had thought that what we call bonobos and bonzees now were all just chimps, a little different in looks and a *lot* different in behaviour, but still chimps.

Then a lot of years later they figured out how that was all wrong; the bonobo was a separate species. And then, a few years after that, they finally figured out that they had to subdivide again what they'd thought were all bonobos. There were three groups, not two. Chimps, bonobos, and this other group that was sort of like bonobos, but sort of not. The bonzees—that's what they decided to call them. Quite a bit taller than the bonobos, most of them, and with lighter hair and less of it. And their legs a little less stubby—they walk upright way more often than they do on all fours. And their lower faces don't stick out quite so much. Anyways, everybody nowadays recognizes the three as different species. And all three sharing something like 98 % of their genes with each other—and with us.

So eventually bonzees got to be called a different species, their own species—everybody who does biology is sure about that now. Maybe not so very different from bonobos, but different for sure. Just as friendly, just as into sex. And the females running the show, just like with bonobos. But bonzees maybe a little bit stranger in the head—maybe that makes them more like us, eh?

And lighter, on average. Not the fur—the skin. Lighter skin. 'Course chimps have that when they're young; even some bonobos have pretty light skin when they're young. But not as light as bonzees, with their light brown skin under their fur.

Giving birth didn't scare me none. Like I say, it was the thought of raising the child that scared the shit out of me. But I wouldn't be able to tell people why I was scared. Not my friends, and not the people at no clinic, neither—they'd never believe me, they'd think I was some sort of wacko.

I'd just have to say I didn't want to have the child and not give any reasons.

∽ No, I didn't need another Bud. I came out into the sunshine. It always makes you squint when you do that after you've been in the bar or whatever mid-day.

I walked back a different way, up 2ⁿᵈ past some vacant lots and then the Tom Boy Super Market that was all boarded up, but there was some big community garden on the other side of the street with all these vegetable boxes. If you can't buy it you better grow it, I guess.

And then a couple minutes later I was talking to Maggie and Linda again on the sidewalk on Cass outside the Planned Parenthood, *just asking*, I said. What would they do if I *did* have the baby? Would they make sure it would be well taken care of? Would they guarantee it? *Yes yes yes*, they just about fell over themselves saying they could do everything, they would do everything, they could guarantee this, that, and the other.

But would it have to be in America? That was another thing, I might have been born in Detroit but I felt Canadian a lot more than American, and I'd like to think my kid would be brought up in Canada. What a mistake that was, but back then I couldn't have known, *home and native land* I was thinking. *Sure, sure*, they said, *the child can be brought up in Canada but it'd be better if it were actually born in America, the paperwork's a lot easier to arrange in Michigan in cases where the mother has decided not to have an abortion but to give the child up for adoption.* Once the paperwork was in place, they said they'd work with their sister organization just over the river to find a Canadian family to adopt the child, *no problem at all*. I kept asking them questions, *what's the name of your organization, what's the name of your sister? I mean, you know, your sister organization?* Could they write all that down for me on paper—write that if I had the baby and gave it up they would make sure it was well cared for, and in Canada. No matter what happened, no matter what sort of baby it was, no matter if it had Down syndrome or if it had anything, whatever I gave birth to, would they swear to that, sign papers about that, make sure it was cared for just as well as any human baby would be cared for?

And then somehow I was back in my car and I'd never gone inside the clinic, had I? Did I know what the hell I was doing? How the hell does anyone know what the hell they're doing? I shook my head and put the key in the ignition but then I thought of the Budweisers and I sort of felt them too. Maybe I better have a little nap, I thought. So I did that, and then I woke up and I wasn't feeling any of the Buds any more. I wasn't feeling much of anything as I drove back to Comber.

Sure enough, by the end of that week there were documents from Choose Life in the mail. They were signed by people in the Detroit Choose Life and people in their sister organization across the river in Windsor. I waded through the wording, and then I waded through it again. There's no way you can figure all that stuff out, but by the end of the next week the papers had all been signed and double signed. Notarized is what they call it, makes everything effing legal. *An Agreement between Lucinda Gerson and Choose Life*, blah blah blah.

I didn't send any emails or make any phone calls to no one, not even to Susie. Especially not to Susie, I guess. Everyone's got a right to change their mind; she knew that. But I told myself that I would tell her—for sure there'd be a time when it would feel right to tell her. Just not right now.

And from there everything was just like a normal pregnancy, so far as I knowed. I'd been pregnant when I was with Estes and, like I said, that didn't work out. Who knows what would of happened to my life if that little one had lived?

This time everything went fine, I hardly got no morning sickness at all, and the Maggie and Linda people arranged for medical care on their side of the river so's it wasn't going to cost me nothing to have the kid in Detroit. I might of liked just to hole away some-where until I'd had the baby and then no one would know nothing about any of it, but by this time I'd pretty well gone through Uncle Harry's inheritance money, and I had to pay the rent and I had to eat—I was eating for two, like they say. I went back to the Price Chopper 'cause Dave and Joan really liked to have women working there who were *in the family way*, that's what they called it, Joan said when she'd been young she'd lost her job 'cause you weren't allowed to be pregnant where she worked and she didn't want that to happen to no one, not ever.

So, like I say, the stuff that went on in my body was just like what goes on in a billion other women's bodies all the time. And the stuff that went on in my head? Maybe that wasn't too much differ-ent neither. These days everyone who has a baby gets all stressed out. Rich people get told how dangerous everything is, and they stress out about it—*am I drinking too much coffee?, am I getting enough calcium?, how guilty do I have to feel for that one drink I had three weeks ago?, what if the kid is born with one of those conditions?* What if, what if, what if? And poor people don't get told nothing and they don't have nothing, and they stress out about that, they don't have no money and they don't have no regular doc-tor, and the doctors and nurses at the clinics poor people go to haven't got no time for the people they're supposed to be caring for, and all a woman knows if she's pregnant and she hasn't got her family to help her is *I could die, my baby could die*, and all they say to her is *calm down, calm down*, et cetera, et cetera, and all they give her is drugs. I'd been there—that first time with the miscarriage—and I knew a lot a people who'd been there.

This time I didn't worry 'bout hardly none of that. What hap-pens is what's gonna happen, I kept telling myself, and then I'd tell it to myself again, and then if it didn't seem to be sinking all the way in I'd have myself a couple Budweisers. Not five, not six, not eight—a couple. Like folks always used to allow themselves a couple drinks before it was the twenty-first goddam century. And their kids turned out fine. Like my kid was gonna turn out fine—I kept telling myself that too. Fine. Just a little different, that's all. Just a little bit half-human.

OK, so sometimes I worried.

Anyways, there's not a lot to tell about the next few months. Basically, I tried not to think about everything that might happen once it was born, and mostly I did a pretty good job of not thinking. Anybody can do a pretty good job of not thinking about something if they put their mind to it.

* * *

Susanne Gerson

[Following is the continuation of Susanne Gerson's narrative of her interactions with her sister Lucinda during and after Lucinda's visit to the Lake Mai-Ndombe research station near Inogo.]

I couldn't help but pay more attention to Bei after Luce had told me everything. Not that I treated him any differently—I don't believe I did, at any rate. But I paid more attention to how he was interacting with the others. He was still as playful as ever, especially with little Bathurst, and he was still getting a hard time from Udie.

All right, I did treat him differently from before in one way. There was one time when Udie was about to mount him and you could tell Bei didn't want it and I yelled out, loud enough and harsh enough to make Udie back off. One of the junior researchers looked at me sharply.

"Alright, alright," I said. "I just couldn't bear to see it happen to him again, that's all. It doesn't seem right. It *isn't* right."

"But that's the whole thing, isn't it, Susie? We're scientists. We don't get to say what's right or wrong. Not when it comes to bonzees, anyway." I knew she was right and I promised her it wouldn't happen again.

I watched Bei in another way as well. It sounds stupid, but Mom always said that you could tell once someone was no longer a virgin. That they looked different, they had a different look in their eyes, a different spring in their step or whatever. I knew it had no foundation in fact whatsoever, but still, I couldn't help looking at Bei to try to see if having made love with a human had changed him in any way. Of course there was nothing to see, but I kept looking.

One other thing I did: I spent quite a bit of time in the evenings Googling research that had been done on the topic of hybrids, and theories that had been formulated about hybrids. There had been a hybrid ape produced by the chance mating of members of two different ape species in an Atlanta zoo in 1979; that actually happened. (Researchers apparently tried without success to impregnate the hybrid, a female; she proved to be sterile.) Then there had been the work of Ilya Ivanovich Ivanov and of Robert Yerkes—the rumoured creation of a "humanzee" in the 1920s—but in fact it had been a failed attempt. Something similar happened in the 1980s in China, apparently. I read about all that, and I read the musings of Richard Dawkins (that a hybrid would "change everything") and of Stephen Jay Gould (that creating a hybrid in the lab would be the most interesting but also the most ethically unacceptable experiment he could imagine).

I couldn't help but be struck by the fact that all the science—or pseudo-science, some of it—had focused on the possibility of creating a chimp-human hybrid. Nobody talked about the possibility of creating a bonobo-human hybrid or a bonzee-human hybrid. Why would the researchers have looked at interbreeding with members of a violence-prone species dominated by alpha males, and never at interbreeding with a species dominated by strong females and prone to addressing conflict through sex rather than violence?

This whatever-it-was hadn't been created in a lab; it was no experiment. Did that change the ethics of it? And what about the creature itself? If Luce weren't going to abort the pregnancy, what would her offspring look like? How would it grow up? How would it behave? The questions ate away at me, but of course I knew it was all just idle speculation; none of it was relevant. Luce was going to have the abortion, and that would be that—and thank god for it.

4.

Lucinda Gerson

[Following is the continuation of the transcript of the handwritten account by Lucinda Gerson of her son's story—and her own.]

A bonzee's gestation period is just a little under eight months, so you had to figure it'd be somewhere between eight months and nine for my little one. And sure enough, it was just under 38 weeks when I started to feel it was going to happen. Like they arranged, I'd have it at Mercy Hospital, but of course the old Ambassador Bridge was always overloaded with trucks even when it wasn't rush hour, and when the contractions started coming it *was* goddam rush hour, and the cars were barely moving, and I was thinking my waters were going to break any second. I got pretty stressed on that bridge, I can tell you. And it was only me in the car. I couldn't ask no friend to help me through—that would mean they'd see what the little one looked like once he came into the world. Why I didn't want that I don't a hundred percent know, but I didn't.

I figured the Customs & Immigration guy would ask me where I was heading, like they always do, so I was ready.

Where were you born?

The hospital!

Lady, I pretty well figured that. I mean what city …

I got to get to the hospital. I gotta get there fast, officer, I'm in labor …

I guess he could see when he looked close that I wasn't lying— he waved me through and next thing I knew there were police cars

40

on each side of me, and sirens screaming, and then I was at Mercy Hospital. Not a lot of people ever wanted to go to that part of town in those days, but I can tell you I was pretty glad to arrive. And then I was in a hospital bed and they gave me something for the pain and it wasn't too bad, they gave me drugs and I pushed and I pushed, and of course I swore, and then I pushed and I pushed again, and it went on and on and on—just about any mother can tell you what it's like, and it wasn't no different for me, 'cept maybe when one of the nurses said *what a shame the father isn't here!* and I guess when I heard that I snorted pretty good between pushes. And then I swore some more and screamed some more while I pushed, and then I stopped to breathe deep and then I pushed and pushed until there was no push left, and then the nurses said they knew I could do it and I said *how the fuck can you know that?* but of course they were right 'cause they got me to breathe some more and push some more and push some more—and then it was over, and he was there.

He was only four pounds and he was the sweetest little one, with his sweet little eyes and his wide mouth open to me. I held him close and hugged him and right away I started to cry, and right away I was thinking *I'll have to give him up, I can't give him up, I can't give him up.* But I made myself not think of any of that; I made myself think just of now, and the funny warm thing I was holding, all warm and alive.

And hairy! *Lanugo, it's called*, said the nurse, *all babies grow it in the womb. It should disappear soon*, but then she shook her head and added, *he sure has got a lot of it!*, almost like she knew he wasn't normal. I didn't care about his hair; his sweet little mouth was making sucking motions like he wanted to suck on a candy and I thought of candies, *bonbons* they used to call them when I was little in Montreal, and I thought of bonbons and bonzees and his sweetness and I knew he was Bonbon, and that was what I named him. "Little Bonbon," I cooed at him, "little good-good, you're a good little Bonbon, aren't you? I'm your Lucy, Lucy who brought you into the world, little Bonbon." I don't know where that *Lucy* came from—no one had ever called me Lucy before, and I'd never thought of myself as a Lucy.

And then Bonbon made that sucking motion again and I thought of the suction, of what I'd been going to have them do to me and to what was going to be him, and for a second that made me feel all empty. But only for a second. What I'd done felt right. Little Bonbon felt right.

Maybe I shouldn't of said I'd give him up for adoption. Maybe I shouldn't give him up. Not for anything, not for anyone. He was so warm and so little and so wonderful.

Everybody at the hospital looked worried and they tiptoed around, and then the doctors came and they told me *the baby is very vigorous.* Well, anybody could see that much. But the doctors and nurses, they said it as if it were some kind of disease, *vigorous.* And then they said they didn't want me to be too concerned, *there's nothing life threatening,* they said, *though there is some concern about the health of the child.* And then they paused and didn't seem to want to say more; *we'll need to do some tests,* they said. I kept crying and crying and it wasn't tears of joy any more, they must have thought it was because of what they were telling me, and because he didn't look quite like the other babies. But it wasn't that. It was feeling that now he wasn't a part of me anymore. And feeling that it wasn't going to be as it should be, with a mother and a child. He wouldn't be mine—how would he be brought up? I hugged his little body closer and suddenly I ached with fear for him. I'd signed all those papers and I'd done all that thinking and I still hadn't thought it all through. Maybe I hadn't *felt* it all through. With him looking like he did, of course there wouldn't be no family that would want to adopt him; it didn't matter if it were Detroit or Windsor or Comber or anywhere. No one would want a baby who looked like that, would they? And when the tests results came back, no one would be able to figure it out at first and then there would be more tests, and they'd start asking questions. It would have to come out in the end, all of it. How had I ever thought it wouldn't come out?

What would happen to him? Who would take him?

Sure enough, the Choose Life people were at my bedside that evening, and they said that there seemed to have been some second thoughts on the part of the couple that they had expected would adopt the child. They said that they were "working on things," and that none of the fundamentals in our agreement "appeared to be affected"—that's how they put it. I had to understand that their appointed people were still official guardians of the child. But I would have to understand as well that there "could be some slight delay," and that in the meantime, if I were agreeable, the child could stay with me. *This will only be temporary, I must understand, ...*

Well, that was fine by me. I hated the uncertainty but I loved to have my little one all curled up on top of me, his little mouth sucking on me and his little body all warm.

They'd said it should be only a couple days before they had the test results and then they would know everything they had to. But it must have been three or four days went by with Bonbon and me still in that Mercy Hospital and him still hairy and still "vigorous," and everybody looking at me more and more strange every day. You could tell the Choose Life people didn't know what to think, but the doctors said mother and child had to stay together until they had the results of their tests.

On the fourth day, spur of the moment, I told them I changed my mind. I told them that they could forget about the adoption, that I would take Bonbon after all. Every day I'd been feeling a little more how much I loved that strange little thing. One of them said how lovely that was and how she knew it was for the best—she was the one who was there every day and saw Bonbon and me so close, Cynthia was her name, she was sweet. But the others said that was no good, I could of done that right after the birth, or the next day, or the day after that, but now it was too late. More than three days after the birth was too late, that's what Michigan law said; after 72 hours you couldn't change your mind. When I heard that I cried, you don't want to know how much I cried.

It was still a couple days more before there were preliminary results of tests that looked like they showed something no one had ever seen before. They said the only way they could explain the results was if the child was part human and part something else. And then they were all over me, doctors and administrators and who-the-hell-knows what, asking me how I conceived the child, where I conceived it, who was the father? And they made it so I couldn't just say *father unknown* like I did when I filled out the forms. They made it seem like I'd just been screwing a bunch of guys and I didn't know which one made me pregnant.

And so I told them—I told one of them. I said I wouldn't tell it to all of them together, they had to all of them get out of there except for just one person. I would tell Cynthia if she would listen.

She listened all right, but then she had to tell everyone else, and then everybody started looking at me like I was weird and sick, and suddenly the Choose Life people were appealing to this principle and that principle, *provision 3 on page 9* or *clause 4, subsection 3 on page 27*, there were 43 pages of that thing we'd signed, 43 goddam pages. Whatever. They were trying to make out that they hadn't said to me what they said to me. They were trying to make it so they hadn't lied when they promised he'd be adopted by *a loving Choose Life family.* A couple days before, they were saying I couldn't get out of the deal, and now it seemed they wanted nothing more than to get out of the deal themselves.

They could see it wasn't going to be easy to find no loving family to take *this* particular little one. That was part of it. But pretty soon they must of figured out as well that they might not *want* no loving family taking care of Bonbon and treating him like a son. Treating him like a human. Not if they wanted to keep all their fundamental goddam values intact. You got to remember where these people were coming from, animal-wise. Christians, right? They've got their lamb of God who's also Jesus somehow, and you can kill him and eat him in some sacrifice, don't ask me to explain it. But that lamb of God ain't the product of no horny farm boy humping a sheep, I can tell you that much. It'd mess up their ideas big time if some kid who was half human and half ape got to be treated just like any regular human kid. And Choose Life held responsible for the whole thing? They didn't want any of that, I can tell you.

So they wanted to figure out some way of keeping control of the situation—not having Bonbon stay with me forever and be accepted as a human being, but not having him adopted neither. They didn't know how to do it at first, they just knew they had to control the situation. So they kept to the letter of the agreement, which said that the child would have to be raised in Canada, under what they called their auspices—that meant they'd somehow be responsible. Bonbon and me would have to check out of the Mercy Hospital— there was nothing wrong with either of us, not anything the doctors could fix, anyways. Bonbon would stay with me in Detroit until he was a month old—the Choose Life people had an apartment where we could stay, *everything will be all nice for you*, they kept saying. And then when Bonbon was a month old they would transfer him to their facility on the Canadian side, *awaiting Canadian adoptive parents*, as they put it.

They had their people stay with me and him right through the whole process; there was always two of them in the apartment with the two of us, that whole month. I kept thinking that Bonbon would be different from a human baby. I'd never been a mother but I'd knowed lots of human babies in Comber. Bonbon wasn't a bit different. Not that every baby's the same as every other baby, but you know what I mean. And he just wasn't no different. I know what you're thinking—that I wouldn't be the best judge. But it's not just me, and it's not just where it's a half-half baby. You listen to

Suzy Kwaytenda on the TV like I did; she's taken care of bonzee babies and she's taken care of human babies, and they ask her straight up, *what's the difference?* and she says, *there's no difference*, and they ask her again, *you really mean there's no difference between a human baby and a bonzee baby?* and she says it again, *there's no difference. None.* And that was between babies that were all human and all bonzee, not between a human and a half-half.

The more time I spent with him the more I loved my little half-half, my little Bonbon. But it was only for a month! I thought of trying to make a break for it with Bonbon when we went out for a breath of fresh air or something, so we could stay together not just for that month but for always, but I didn't have none of the papers saying he was mine, so what was I going to do?

When Bonbon slept I would turn my back on the Choose Life people and look out the window for the longest time. The apartment was way up high and you could see the whole of downtown Detroit, the skyscrapers that had been at the heart of everything in the 1940s and the 1950s and that had stood there empty with all their broken windows since '67; everybody still talked about '67 and all the burned-out buildings, you could see right through everything, but there was a lot that had happened the last few years, it wasn't as bad as it had been, that's what everybody said. Detroit was where me and Bonbon should of stayed, but I couldn't of known that then.

You could see across the Detroit River too, south to Windsor and beyond. I could almost imagine I could see Comber, it was that clear some days. Everybody always thinks Windsor is north of Detroit. I won't say they don't know their ass from a hole in the ground, but they don't know nothing 'bout those bends in the river, that's for sure. There can be a bend in so many things, so's they turn out like you don't expect.

That's what I would be thinking, but then Bonbon would start to gurgle and whimper a little and I'd go to him and feed him and I'd try not to think about nothing anymore.

∾ At the end of the month we all crossed the border together; they said that was part of the agreement, and I had to say all the right things at the Ambassador Bridge so it was all official that the child had crossed with the parent, never mind that the parent had signed an agreement to give up the child. And then I hugged little Bonbon once more, *maybe it will be the last time*, I was thinking, *I can't stand this*, and then the Choose Life people took my little Bonbon and I took myself and my stretch marks and my aching breasts and the ache in my heart back to Comber, back to work at the Price Chopper. They said they'd finally found a fine mom and a fine dad all ready to take care of my little one, a Mr. and Mrs. Cherney, they didn't even give them first names, and Bonbon would be with the Cherneys starting right now, even though it might be a few weeks before all the paperwork was done and everything was final.

You know what they never told me? That Michigan law is different from Ontario law. That on the Canadian side I would of had 30 days after he'd been born to change my mind. Now maybe they would have taken Bonbon away from me anyway, on account of how he wasn't human. But I bet they wouldn't of been able to: how's it going to look if they take a child from his mother? Any child, even half a human.

Whereas this way they could say that *I'd* said I didn't want it, that I'd given it up.

Given it up—it sounds like surrender, doesn't it? But I never did surrender, not even when I was all confused about what to do.

I bought one of those pumps and I started expressing my milk two, three times a day. I guess that somewhere inside of me I must have kept thinking I might somehow get little Bonbon back again. I sort of felt that keeping the milk going was like keeping alive some hope. I know that sounds stupid. Sometimes we *are* stupid. People, I mean—all of us.

It was another week before they had final results of all the tests, before it was official: Bonbon was half human and half bonzee. The

Choose Life people had all their PR people ready, all their cautious statements honed, all their *aren't we good?* words ready.

I didn't have nothing ready. I'd been doing what maybe I do best, just trying not to think.

Those tests didn't stay private long. A CBC reporter heard something from some of the Choose Life people. She told me later she filed a *you're not gonna believe this!* sort of report that the producers decided they sure weren't gonna believe, and wouldn't put on the air neither. But then somebody who knew the whole story told somebody who knew somebody at NBC, and suddenly it was everywhere. You couldn't turn on a television or look at a newspaper without it screaming it out at you, *Woman Gives Birth to Hybrid; Half Human, Half Ape—a World First; Baby or Monster? —You Be the Judge!* And the reporters, and the would-be reporters —*I'm a blogger and I'd like to know ...*, they'd say when they emailed me, as if they'd given themselves some license to—to do I don't know what. They found me at the place I'd rented in Comber, down the end of Main Street, and they found me at the Price Chopper, and all I could do when they turned the cameras on me was turn the other way. That, and cry.

At first a lot of people were saying what a miracle it was, *it's a miracle* they kept saying. Even a lot of people who didn't believe in no god would say it—and a lot of the news people wrote that down too. But you could tell from the start that quite a few of the people who *did* believe there's a god thought this was the devil's work.

Of course a lot of the science people got all excited, they were falling all over themselves, they'd be able to test him for language skills and for his thinking skills and all of that, it was a big deal. And everyone had their own view of *the ethical questions involved*, those were the sort of words they always used. As soon as they were onto all that, you knew they weren't going to think of Bonbon and me. Not for real. Not as real people.

And of course a lot of people couldn't help thinking of the sex, couldn't help thinking of a woman being fucked by some ape. Or, as they would put it, they couldn't help thinking of *how it had happened*. That way the words sounded more delicate, but the thoughts weren't, you can be damn sure of that.

And my name. There were a lot of people who'd say something about my name. *Lucy—that's the name of a famous ape, isn't it?* and blah blah blah. Sometimes they'd say *ape*, sometimes they'd say *Neanderthal,* sometimes they'd say *sub-human*. Sometimes they'd add something else just to drive it home. *Like attracts like, I always say*—that sort of thing. I'd tell them as loud and as angry as I could that I was *Lucinda*, but of course I'd always been other things too— *Luc*, and *Luce*, and whatever else. Some days I didn't know what all I was. I read a book once called *Lucy*, it was by someone whose name was *Jamaica* but she wasn't from there she was from some other island, and the woman in the book is living in America and she's a very angry person and she's not very nice to a lot of people. It's hard to like her—but you *do* sort of like her—maybe because you see things through her, right the way through. The book, I mean. And near the end she asks her mother why she'd been named *Lucy*—with her mother and her there was sort of a love-hate thing. And her mother says *I named you after the devil himself. Satan, whose other name is Lucifer. Lucy for short*. That was in a book— that was her, not me. But it's stuck in my memory, hasn't it?

Then there were the people who you always hear saying a fetus has just as many rights as a woman, even when it's just one tiny cell. 'Cept of course, in *this* case, most of those people didn't think the same principles applied. In *this* case the woman should have had an abortion. In *this* case I had some sort of weird obligation to end the pregnancy. If anything made me a hundred percent sure a woman should have the right to control her own body, it was those people and the crap some of them screamed at me.

But some of the so-called "pro-choice" people were almost as bad. More than a few of them said they would absolutely always fight for a woman's right to choose, but in *this* case, they'd make an exception. That was one thing you could of gotten a lot of the so-called "pro-life" people and a lot of so-called "pro-choice" people to agree on; in *this* case, I should have had an abortion.

Then there were the real wackos and weirdos. For a while there was at least one death threat a week—people saying they'd kill me, people saying they'd kill Bonbon too. And people saying they'd rape me, with all sorts of twisted logic as to why I deserved it. They'd teach me what it was like to be properly fucked. Some guys. Go figure.

Even the people who were normal, you could hear the outrage in their voices in so many of the interviews—*how could she?* was just under the surface of every single shitty thing they said. And I got to hear it often enough over the phone, from a lot people I'd thought were my friends and from a lot of people who were total strangers, they'd somehow get hold of my phone number or they'd stop me on the street and they'd keep asking it, *how could you?, how could you?* Even in the middle of the night there were the phone calls, *how could you do such a thing? How could you foist something like that on the rest of us? It's just not natural, it's just not right. It's disgusting!*

And what could I tell them? It was just a strange moment on the other side of the world and things had gone wrong between me and my sister and I'd thought about all of us, all of us humans and all of us animals, and I'd felt like a bit of a lost soul and I'd met a bit of another lost soul. What the hell's that going to sound like?

Of course I had to talk to Susie as well. A bunch of times I didn't answer when I saw it was her, but then I finally did, I figured it couldn't be any worse than a lot of the other calls. But was she angry! There was a whole lot more of *How could you?, Luce, really, how could you?*, and then on and on about the last time we'd talked on the phone, *you promised me you were going to have an abortion, for fuck's sake*—she actually said that, and Susie never swears. She was just about losing it, *How could you? How could you?* again and again. What I couldn't do for the longest time was get a word in edgewise. I didn't let her know I was crying. Susie never could guess that type thing over the phone, not the way some people can.

"I never promised, Susie. Yeah, I said it, but I never promised. Sometimes you just don't know what's going to ..."

"You could have told me you were wavering, Luce. You could have phoned, you could have ..."

"I had to work it out, Susie. Besides, the charges—it costs a fortune to ..."

"I would have paid the damned satellite phone charges! How can you think I wouldn't..." And off she went again. "What are you going to do?" she finally asked. "How are you going to bring the thing up? *Are* you going to bring it up? What's going to happen?" And so I told her all the ways in which I didn't have a clue what was going to happen. But she answered sort of mechanically. All the air had gone out of her. Eventually we tried to say nice things to each other for a few minutes, nice normal things, and it started for a moment to feel as if maybe she wasn't quite so far away. Then we hung up, and she was still a very, very, long way away. Goddam Inogo is where she was. If I couldn't make my own sister understand what had happened—I mean, understand it in some way that was really *like* what had happened—how could I hope to make anyone else understand it?

∾ The Choose Life people were pretty unhappy, I can tell you. And the Cherneys—soon as they heard what had happened, they were fighting mad, *you promised us a child, a real child!* and all that, and Choose Life had to assure them they wouldn't have to go through with it, wouldn't have to adopt Bonbon—but if they could just keep him for a short time while they sorted things out. The Cherneys weren't happy but they went along with that—I think Choose Life had to pay them a big whack of money in the end.

Choose Life really, really didn't want to let me have Bonbon, that was the thing—if anything proved someone was unfit to be a mother, it was having it off with a bonzee. So Choose Life would do just about anything not to let me have my little one—but they sure wanted me to have all the blame. For a while they said they were considering a lawsuit, *it would be deemed breech of trust in a court of law*, their person told me—of course it wasn't Maggie and Linda and Cynthia any more, it was some guy in a suit.

"You can't expect the baby to be adopted if it's not a human baby. Not by any normal family. Not if it's ..."

"Bonbon. Call him by his name. He's Bonbon. And he's a *he*, not an *it*."

"Whatever we call him, Mrs. Gerson ..."

"Ms ..."

"Whatever we call him, he's only half human. The clear implication of the agreement was that you would be turning a human baby over to Choose Life to be put up for adoption."

"You show me where it says 100% human. It says *child*!"

"A child is a human child; it's implied, Ms. Gerson, it's definitely implied. And that can stand up in a court of law. No judge would expect us to be able to find adoptive parents to raise something like that—or foster parents, for that matter. And even if they were willing —think of the risk. What if he turns out to be violent? Or sexually aggressive? Or both? Does he go to school with human children? What if he starts exposing himself to his classmates like a bonzee would ..." He let the suggestion hang in the air. "We at Choose Life have to take responsibility, Ms. Gerson, that is certainly part of the agreement. But so far as adoption goes, conventional adoption by human parents ..."

It wasn't even clear that they had the right to do anything. What was the legal status of the agreement I'd signed with Choose Life? It seemed the agreement might be subject to a whole bunch of different laws—Michigan state law and Ontario provincial law and

American federal law and Canadian federal law—and that any legal action might take years and years to sort out. Groups kept coming to me saying they'd help me make a case on the basis of this, or that, or the other, but none of them thought there would be a verdict for years. And none of them saw any way of taking the baby out of the hands of the representatives of Choose Life, which had been declared under Michigan law to have authority *in loco parentis*, whatever the hell that means. So the *in loco parentis* people had decided now that they really didn't want a half human adopted by human parents, though they'd never say so in so many words.

Conventional adoption by human parents, and those parents could handle a baby with Down syndrome. Sure. Conventional adoption by human parents, and those parents could handle a baby with fetal alcohol syndrome. Sure. But something that was half bonzee? Choose Life wasn't going to stand for that. They wanted out. They wanted some legal loophole they could wriggle through.

They found it in the fine print, where it said that if they couldn't find adoptive parents under the terms of a conventional adoption agreement, they could make *whatever arrangements are deemed best for the child*. It was pretty clear they were determined not to find parents, so they could deem something else up. Something they could claim was *best for the child*. Though you could be sure they wouldn't call it a *child* any more often than they could help.

5

The Spectator

[I wrote at the outset that this volume would bring
together the first-hand accounts of the participants in the
story. But I think it may also be helpful—for some readers
at least—to be given some of the broader background. To
interrupt Lucinda Gerson's narrative at this point with an
excerpt from the popular press is to put things somewhat
out of order—editorials and op-ed pieces concerning
Bonbon Gerson and the larger issues associated with
hybridity did not begin to appear at all widely until rather
later. But I am sure such issues are already very much in
the minds of readers of this volume.

The piece below is copyright © *The Spectator* and is
reprinted here with the permission of that newspaper. It
was first published November 6, 2002.]

In the unprecedented case of the bonzee-human hybrid, guardians
associated with the anti-abortion group Choose Life have retained
custody of the newborn, and they—or the courts—must decide his
future. Will they turn to adoptive parents who would try to raise
him as a human? Or will they allow him to be taken in by an animal care and research facility? It's a decision that touches not only
on the life of this one individual, but on the lives of all of us, and
on the principles by which we live.

In this country we have a strong tradition of respect for individual rights, and of respect for minority rights. Our Charter of
Rights and Freedoms is among the strongest in the world. But we

have a strong tradition as well of acting collectively for the public good, and we are a nation founded on the principles of peace, order, and good government.

In the case of a human-ape hybrid, we have something quite new, and the individual involved constitutes a minority of one. Concerns have been expressed—legitimate concerns, in our view—over the prospect of such an individual becoming a full participant in human society. These are not simply concerns as to whether someone half of another species would be *able* to participate—be able to vote intelligently, to drive, and so on. With issues like that we are familiar, largely from our long experience of dealing with people with disabilities. And the courts and the medical professions have a long track record in dealing with those issues. But no court and no doctor can tell us how a human-bonzee hybrid will behave in human society. Will he be uncontrollably violent? Will he be able to control his sexual instincts?

Much has been made of the fact that bonzees in the wild—and, indeed, in captivity—are both more amicable and more amorous than even their close cousins, the bonobos, let alone their other close relative, the much more violent chimpanzee. But let us not look on bonzee life with rose-tinted glasses. A bonzee is given to unrestrained sexual activity with every other bonzee he encounters. With strangers. With brothers and sisters. With his own mother. It is not uncommon for bonzees to force sex on one another. We shouldn't mince words here; rape is what humans call it. A propensity to rape—including male-on-male rape—is deeply embedded in bonzee culture, perhaps even hard-wired into bonzee genes.

To be sure, a great many people who have watched videos of bonzees in captivity have remarked on the seeming similarities between bonzee and human sexual activity. Like humans (and like bonobos, but unlike chimpanzees or other great apes), bonzees often have sex face to face. Like humans (and unlike the frenzied bouncing of bonobos, chimpanzees, and other great apes) they often engage in sexual activity in languid and prolonged fashion. But make no mistake: they are not like us.

Do we want to take the risk of this minority-of-one becoming violent among us? Do we want to take the risk of this creature forcing himself on young women—or young men—late at night in public parks? And let us not forget that whatever we decide will set a precedent. Should there ever in future be a human-chimpanzee cross, it will be devilishly hard to prevent whatever rules we set now from applying then.

There is one other important consideration. Under our laws there is a line separating people and animals—as there is in the hearts and minds of most of us, for all that we love our pets. We understand intuitively that there is something special about humanity—call it exceptionalism if you will, but we acknowledge the sanctity of human life as a form of existence richer, and higher, than that of any other species. Of course in some sense we are animals too, but what is most human about us is what is least animal: our striving for a higher and better existence—and our *ability* to strive for a higher and better existence. We should not lightly open a door that might lead to the removal of the distinctions that exist in law between the animal and the human.

But, some will say, what of the individual rights of the hybrid himself? What of the individual rights of the mother (who initially gave the child up for adoption, but has now decided she wishes to raise him as a human)? It is impossible not to sympathize with Bonbon (as the mother calls him) as an individual—and, we would argue, it is appropriate too to feel sympathy for the mother. She has received far too much thoughtless condemnation. His life should be made as comfortable as possible, and she should be allowed extensive access to her extraordinary progeny. But should their interests be allowed to trump what in this case amounts to the interests of the entire species? Once the question is put that way—and that is precisely the way we believe it should be put—the answer is immediately plain.

This hybrid cannot live both among bonzees and among humans. One way or another, we must make a choice. Either he lives among humans and we accept all the associated risks, or he lives among bonzees in an animal research and care facility. There are several excellent candidates—among them, certainly, the Coldwater Institute in Alberta and the Sunderland Animal Research Centre here in Ontario. The latter, in particular, is known worldwide not only for outstanding research but also for providing excellent care to the animals in its charge. It is known too for its high levels of security; no animal in its charge has ever escaped. Those who worry about the consequences of a creature of this sort escaping from a facility could thus rest easy if Sunderland were the choice. That institution has extended an offer to provide a permanent home for this unique creature. Those involved in the decision—the Choose Life guardians, and governments at every level—should accept that offer.

6.

Lucinda Gerson

The Choose Life people had started to get offers—offers from all over North America. Suddenly Choose Life had lots of possible ways out. *He's very lucky*, their spokeswoman said. *These invitations are coming from some of the finest and most humane institutions in the world; they're offering a special place for him. They're offering to devote a special unit to him; they'll study him, to be sure, but more importantly they'll take care of him, as he couldn't be taken care of in any normal household.* That wasn't what her face said when she looked at me, though. Her face said the same thing that the faces of all the Choose Life people had said as soon as they knew: *How could you? How could you do it with an animal like that?*

I couldn't get a job somewhere else, that much was for sure. I was goddam lucky the Price Chopper didn't let me go, but they didn't. There was one day I felt Joan's hand on my shoulder, *you're all right here*, she said. *I'll make sure it's all right for you here. I think people should be able to understand just about any mistake when it comes to sex, and this one's no exception. But you just tell me if you need to take a leave for a few weeks.* I thought of trying to get a job in some other place where they wouldn't of heard of any of this. Part of me thought that even if it was Vancouver, even if it was Hawaii, they'd of heard of me. I remember how one of them repeated my name when I phoned to ask if a position was still available, *Lucinda ...*, and then you could hear the penny drop, as my grandma used to say. *You're that woman who ...* And that was that.

Would it be like that my whole life, everywhere? It was a pretty depressing thought, I can tell you. But it was even more depressing to think of staying here forever, with everything heavy all round me. There must be somewheres else where it'd be a *little* bit better. I told Joan I'd take her up on that offer of a few weeks leave—maybe I'd never come back, but why burn your bridges?

That night was when I stopped expressing my milk. I guess I was starting to give up. I didn't know where I was going to go. Maybe west, maybe down south to New Orleans. They always say that different is good in New Orleans, that's what my mum always said they say, anyways. That you can make yourself into anybody you want. Maybe you could make yourself into nobody, that's what I started thinking.

So now I'm just about packed.

They did let me see him again. It had been ten days since I seen him last, right after we crossed the border; now he was almost six weeks old. The Cherneys had finally said enough was enough, and now Bonbon was being held "for the time being" at the Sunderland Animal Research Centre in the Toronto Zoo. *Being held*, that's how they put it, like it was a jail. Which of course is just what it was for him, and I guessed he'd never have any way to get out. Fact is, that was one of the key selling points they'd made, the Sunderland people, that's what I heard later. Anyways, there were some people who said that no matter what I'd done, they had to let me see him, that I should be allowed to see him whenever I wanted. *She's his mother, for god's sake!* I heard one of them say when they were arguing in the next room and they didn't think I could hear, *she's his mother.* You're damn right I'm his mother, I thought, but I guess I screwed things up pretty bad.

The woman who was with him when they let me see him just cooed, she kept saying how much space he would have and how happy he would be and how well he was going to get on with the other bonzees. And maybe she was right; the space they had there for the bonzees and the bonobos and whatnot was huge, just huge. They let me feed him again, just like I had that first month. They *wanted* me to feed him, it seemed like, and that was just fine by me I can tell you. I'd been told it might take a while before I stopped producing milk, and I could believe it: my breasts kept getting sore, they were so full.

As I brought him close to me I couldn't help thinking he didn't look good, his eyes looked smaller somehow, and his knuckles looked as if he'd been rubbing something that wasn't soft, I asked the woman about that and she said yes, he often rubbed his knuckles against the wall, *it's normal*, the woman said, *it's normal in the circumstances.* How can she know what's normal "in the circumstances"? There's never been no circumstances like these! That's what I was thinking but I couldn't say anything. For a second I couldn't make any sound at all.

Anyways, that's about all I can write, is what I'm thinking right now. I have to stop, that's all.

∾ No, that's not all. I can't let what I wrote back then be any sort of end. I want to say one more thing to anybody who reads this— and then I want to tell the rest of the story.

I know maybe when you hear how I talk or see what I write, how I spell sometimes, your maybe thinking somewhere deep inside, in a place so deep you wouldn't even want to admit to yourself that you have that place inside you, you're maybe thinking *she's a tiny bit sub-human herself.* She can't control herself, she can't control her urges, she can't think rationally, she can't write proper English, maybe she's not more than half a rung up the ladder from that ape she got to fuck her, that ape she got to make her pregnant, that ape whose baby she had. *What is she? Is she any better than an animal herself?* Its easy to think that stuff, I guess I should know how easy it is to think that stuff. 'Cause sometimes I think those things too about people I see who're worse educated than me, who're poorer than me.

You see, I looked at that again and I saw it should be *who're* instead of *whore*. And sometimes I get it when people make jokes about that sort of shit, "she doesn't know *its* from *it's*" or *shit* from *shits*. I get it but I don't like it. I don't like it when it's about me and I don't like it if I start to feel it about somebody who can't even read or write nothing. Write *anything*. And I don't like it if somewhere way down inside you right now you're starting to go way beyond *how could she?* If you're starting to think in that deep place you don't want to admit you have deep inside you, *that's about all you can expect from someone like that.*

Maybe a lot of you are thinking whatever I say's not worth taking seriously anyway, 'cause didn't I take money for telling my story? Well I did, and I don't think I have to say sorry about that. It was a few hundred lousy bucks from that paper and five thousand from the TV—five *thousand*, not five goddam million. When you got money already, you can get on your high horse about how a person shouldn't make money by doing this thing or that thing or the other thing. But if it's a question of whether you're gonna be able to keep your job at the Price Chopper for ten lousy bucks an hour or you're gonna be living out of your car—it's a different world, isn't it?

And maybe some of you are thinking *she could of made millions off this.* Or hundreds of thousands, anyways. And maybe I could have. I got a few offers, that's for sure. But after I took that money from the TV people, I gotta say I didn't feel great about it. I didn't want Bonbon all over the trashy papers at the grocery checkout, I didn't want to be making a ton of money off of … Off of any of it.

When I finish this I'm gonna go over it and fix everything where I've used *its* for *it's* or *shits* for *shit's* and all that.

No. Not everything. I wouldn't be able to fix everything anyways, and I don't *want* everything like that fixed. Everything can't be fixed like that. I want the world fixed. The whole fucking world.

It's the *fucking* that really gets you, isn't it? Fucking an animal. Going over that line, that pretend line in the sand you've all made that says you're so goddam different from the apes and the pigs and

the dogs and all the rest of them, when you're all fucking apes yourselves. You know it, but at the same time you don't know it, so I'll
fucking say it again, *you're all fucking apes yourselves!* I just want
you to look in the goddam mirror.

Sorry, I'm a little bit angry here, but didn't you ever get carried
away and make a mistake with some guy? Maybe even sometime
when you knew there could be *something happening*, when you
knew it was that time of the month when something could happen
and you didn't do anything to make sure it didn't happen and the
guy wouldn't take no precautions, wouldn't put on a rubber and he
spoke all hard when you asked him to and he said no, but you
wanted him anyway, maybe you even wanted him a little bit *because* of that, because of how reckless he was, maybe it turned you
on if his heart was hard, if he was hard through and through, a bit
of a tough guy, a bit of a nasty with those arms and those tight pants
and that open shirt, maybe it turned you on a little. Maybe it turned
you on a lot. And think what could have happened, think of what
you would of been letting in that little baby's genes if it had happened. That little baby you would have had from what'd happened
with mister tough guy, mister nasty. Mister nasty would've passed on
his nasty genes to your baby. Maybe a whole lot of something nasty.

Bei wasn't like that, he isn't like that. His heart's not hard. He's
not got those nasty genes. I know that. Course I don't know him
like a person knows someone if they've been with him lots of times,
but I know Bei, I seen what he's like. I know him a lot better than
some hunk you meet in a dark bar at one in the morning. And
there's no nasty in Bei, I know it—not one bit. You compare that to
guys who ... —*I nailed her*, they say, and they don't stick around to
find out if you're gonna be able to pull the nail out, the one their
goddam nail gun put right into you. And if you have the kid, then
you'll be carrying that nasty guy's genes and it won't mean nothing
to the nasty guy that he's a dad. He won't carry around his little

one like a dad should, he won't make sweet little noises in the kid's ear. He won't do nothing when it matters.

What about the people who are mental and they're on the streets and they're there because somebody nailed somebody else and nobody cared, and whether it's something in their genes or the way they were brought up or not brought up—whatever it was, it sure as shit isn't the kid's fault. Maybe you'll say I'm getting off track here, none of this has anything to do with me being stupid and not thinking and all that with Bei and Bonbon, maybe you'll say I'm missing the point. OK, so what about Bonbon? It's not his fault if he's no Einstein or if he's not gonna look like Tom Cruise. Maybe he's a kid who's not going to be able to do calculus and all that— does that mean you have to keep him behind bars?

Hell, *I* can't even do calculus. And yeah, I gave him a silly French name like a candy and maybe it was stupid of me to do that, but he *is* sweet. He's such a sweet natured little one.

You can knock that out of a person. You can knock that out of anyone. Every day that goes by that he isn't nuzzled and held and hugged and loved will help to knock it out of him.

I said this before and I mean it: I made a mistake. I made that first mistake and then I made a mistake when I gave him up. And now I want him back and I'm going to keep wanting him back, but I can understand if you're thinking *maybe she'll change again.*

I'm not going to. Not this time. There's nobody at no research centre in no zoo that's going to love him like I will. They'll hold him and say nice things, sure, and I bet it'll be better than some of those foster care places for humans. But those zoo people, those research centre people? They're going to go home at night, they're going to go off shift. They're not going to love him like I love him.

He's just little and they're not going to love him, can't you see that?

7.

Robert B. Goddard

[Following are excerpts from the transcript of the interview granted to the *National Observer* in October 2009 by Dr. Robert B. Goddard, Director of Research and Development at the Sunderland Animal Research Centre. The interview was notorious at the time for the hostility that developed between the *Observer*'s reporter, Sonya Ramirez, and Dr. Goddard—and, in later years, it has become famous as well for the ways in which some of the exchanges between the two pointed towards the violent incident that followed a year later.]

Sonya Ramirez: Let's begin at the beginning. How did they settle on you—on the Sunderland Animal Research Centre—as a home for Bonbon?

Robert B. Godard: As you might imagine, we were not the only institution with an interest in making a home for Bonbon—for Bobo, as many of us like to call him. Zoos and university research institutions across North America made their pitch to the people at Choose Life—and to the government too. To the *governments*, I should say; it was some time before they sorted out whether Bobo would be raised in Canada or in the USA. If you recall, the arrangement with the Sunderland Great Ape Research Centre was at first only a temporary one; we were simply the closest major centre with the appropriate facilities.

S.R.: Do you think there might have been some inertia after that? On the part of the authorities, I mean; might there have been some reluctance to move him again once he was settled at your institution?

R.B.G.: I don't think inertia has much to do with why Bobo is still with us, no. And I don't really think the initial arrangement led to any favouritism when the final decision as to a permanent arrangement was made some months later. I consider it a great tribute to our capabilities at Sunderland that our own facility was chosen. But I have to say as well that the timing was perfect. For ten years we had been at work developing the world's most advanced facility for primates—for chimpanzees, gorillas, and bonobos as well as bonzees. When Bobo was born we were just days away from opening.

S.R.: The facility's features are nowadays well known world-wide, but I think it might still be helpful if you could provide a brief summary for any of our readers who may not be aware of them.

R.B.G.: It wasn't just that we were developing one of the world's largest, best equipped, and most comfortable research facilities; these days that has to be a given with any new facility. It was that we were replicating these animals' natural habitats to an unprecedented degree. People said you couldn't do that in a place where you might have a foot of snow on the ground from December to March. We took that factor right out of the equation; we put a roof over the entire six acres. If they could do it for the gorillas on a football field, we figured, why can't we do it for the real thing? Of course our facility is a lot bigger than a football field—it's more like four football fields.

S.R.: I've heard that it's even larger than the West Edmonton Mall or the Mall of America.

R.B.G.: I'd prefer it if you would *not* compare our facility to a shopping mall. Perhaps the comparison to a football field is also inapt. The point is ...

S.R.: So there's nothing commercial about the way in which you exhibit animals to a paying public?

R.B.G.: We are a not-for-profit institution, Ms. Ramirez. *Not* for profit. And—this is the point I was trying to make—we provide more space for our primates than other zoos—San Diego, for one—provide for their elephants. How do we do it? A feather-light, transparent roof, so we can keep the whole place climate controlled. So we can grow the vegetation they have on the banks of the Congo—so it can *feel* like it feels on the banks of the Congo. There's a river running through SARC—through the whole zoo. And just as bonobos and bonzees live on one side of the Congo, with chimpanzees and gorillas on the other side, so, we decided, it would be in our facility: bonobos and bonzees on one side of the Green River, chimps and gorillas on the other side. Nowhere else in the world can you find anything like it.

S.R.: Except the Congo.

R.B.G.: Except the Congo. Yes, of course.

S.R.: And the Congo is almost a mile wide, whereas your river is—what, twenty yards across? Shouldn't we be concerned that the apes on one side and the apes on the other side might be able to interact a little *too* easily. Chimpanzees are notoriously fierce; isn't there a danger that ...

R.B.G.: I won't go into detail on that—other than to emphasise that some of our staff are world-renowned experts on animal behaviour.

S.R.: So you don't see any cause for concern?

R.B.G.: The short answer is no—I don't think we need be concerned. Of course, no arrangement can eliminate all danger with 100% certainty. But in the aggregate, the dangers here are far, far fewer than the dangers these animals face in the wild.

S.R.: Why do you call him Bobo? What didn't you like about the name his mother gave him?

R.B.G.: It wasn't that we didn't like it. It was just that—well, we wanted the keepers to have a name they were comfortable with. A name they would all pronounce the same way. But of course we also wanted something that sounded close to the first name he had been given—something that *he* would feel comfortable with, something that might even feel to him as if there had been no change at all. Yet still a name that was unusual—that had character.

S.R.: What does *Bobo* mean, anyway? It's African, isn't it?

R.B.G.: Yes it is. And, to be honest, we thought that was appropriate —it shouldn't be forgotten that he is half African. *Bobo* is a common boy's name in several West African and Central African cultures. In some cultures it means *born on Tuesday* (as he was, by the way—we checked), in others *humble* or *be humble*.

S.R.: You didn't think people might hear it as sort of a caveman name? Or an ape name? Sort of cartoonish? Like Bamm-Bamm in *The Flintstones*.

R.B.G.: I'd have liked to see you suggest any of those ideas to Bobo Olson, the boxer, or Bobo Brazil, the wrestler.

S.R.: It wasn't that *Bonbon* sounded too French?

R.B.G.: No. It was certainly *not* that the name *Bonbon* sounded too French; I've spoken at length about this to the Quebec media.

S.R.: My apologies. Let us move on. You were speaking of how the Wild Central Africa area and its pavilion form a natural environment—natural for a bonzee, that is. There are of course a great many people who would prefer that Bonbon be raised as a human.

R.B.G.: You're making a statement, not asking a question. But yes, of course there were. I won't for a moment deny that. It's interesting how the two points of view coalesced around the bids—the proposals, I should say—of different institutions. I know for a fact that the Research Division of the San Diego Zoo and the UCSD Medical Center (they put in a joint proposal, you know) didn't offer anything like the facilities that we could offer, so far as primate habitat was concerned. They framed their proposal as one that would allow both Bobo's bonzee side and his human side, if you will, to come out. They proposed to act collectively as his guardian until he came of age, and then seek a ruling of the court as to whether or not he should remain at their facility, or be allowed either full or partial freedom.

S.R.: Partial freedom?

R.B.G.: I believe they envisaged some sort of supervised living arrangement. But initially—for the first 18 years of his life—he would have been in a facility much like ours.

S.R.: So they were looking for some sort of a compromise solution?

R.B.G.: Broadly speaking, yes.

S.R.: And you were looking to just keep him locked up as an ape?

R.B.G.: If you are determined to keep trying to provoke me, this interview is over right now.

S.R.: All right—I apologize. Let me ask you to walk us through the legal arguments. A great deal has hinged on those.

R.B.G.: I'll do my best. There was a series of court cases, as I'm sure you recall. In America, citizenship is conferred by birth; under a part of the American Constitution that dates back to just after the Civil War, all "persons" born in the United States are automatically citizens.

S.R.: No exceptions?

R.B.G.: Historically there have been a number of exceptions; Asian Americans were for many years made an exception, for a time any American woman who married an alien would lose her citizenship, and I believe there were others. But nowadays, only very narrow ones. If you're the child of a foreign diplomat— that's an exception. Or if you're the child of a member of an invading army—that's another. Bobo's parents were definitely not part of an invading army ...

S.R.: And his mother is no diplomat.

R.B.G.: You said it, not me.

S.R.: So he was an American citizen, but …

R.B.G.: Only if Bobo were deemed a person under American law. Is someone who is half human a person or not?—that was the question. Now American law is somewhat complicated when it comes to defining a person. At different points in American history the law has distinguished between free persons and the enslaved; it has also distinguished between natural persons and artificial persons—corporations, for example, are deemed to be artificial persons for legal purposes.

S.R.: What about animals? Non-human animals, I mean.

R.B.G.: That's not entirely clear. Years ago a well-known philosopher argued that a dolphin is a person, and many legal scholars have agreed that there's a case to be made for granting non-human animals at least limited rights as some class of person.

It was the Humane Society that brought Bobo's case before the American courts—and with it a lot of questions. What does it mean to be a person? What does it mean to be human? What does it mean to be an American? If this Bonbon, or Bobo—or Beau, or BeauBeau, or Bobby (I gather some of the Americans later called him by all those names)—were granted American citizenship and grew up and mated with a bonzee, would their baby be American too? It would be only one quarter human, but it would be the child of an American, born on American soil. Not easy questions to answer.

In any case, the case moved quickly through the courts. Before long it was with the United States Court of Appeals for the Sixth Circuit. Provisionally, they decided that a bonzee "quadra"—a creature three-quarters bonzee and one-quarter human—would not necessarily be considered a person. But they didn't rule it out, either. That meant that they steered clear of the larger question: should non-human animals be considered persons?

The decision on Bobo himself, though, was unequivocal. He might be only half human, but the glass was half full; he was a person, and he was deemed to be fully an American. You could not decide any other way, in the view of the majority; a baby born of a human American mother on American soil was an American.

It was not a provisional or a qualified decision, but nor was it a unanimous one. Three of the nine judges disagreed, and the various groups that had funded the effort to define Bobo as an animal (or place him in a new category altogether) tried to launch one final appeal. It was widely expected that the Supreme Court would make the ultimate decision, but they declined to hear the case—I suppose they were as divided as the lower courts had been, and felt they would have little to add. That left the decision of the Court of Appeals for the Sixth Circuit to stand, and made it official that, if Bobo ever found a way to cross the border into America, his legal status would be that of a fully human person.

S.R.: He would be free.

R.B.G.: I suppose you could put it that way. But true freedom is not just a matter of legal status, of course. That was part of the point so famously made by Anatole France about the law, in its magnificent equality, forbidding the rich as well as the poor from sleeping under bridges, begging in the streets, and stealing bread. Even as an independent adult, would Bobo ever be able to have true freedom as a human, even in America? Polls at the time suggested that Americans were far from unanimous on how a creature such as Bobo should be treated; only 30%—an odd alliance of animal activists, libertarians, and mavericks—

were in full agreement with the court's decision, and some 40% were vehemently opposed. If Bobo were living among humans in America, how would he be treated by those 40%? Would he be vilified, shunned, even physically attacked?

You have several times implied that our approach amounted to treating Bobo unfairly—as an animal. But it's entirely conceivable that giving him so-called freedom in human society would be the cruelest option of all.

S.R.: Surely you …

R.B.G.: In any case, Bobo was of course not on the American side of the border. He was in Canada. From a Canadian point of view, he had been born to a Canadian citizen, even if not on Canadian soil. For so long as Bonbon was on the Canadian side of the border, the decision would rest with the Canadian courts. Was he to be deemed a human or a non-human animal? Just as in America, non-human animals are treated as property in Canada; that's the case under federal law, and it's the case under the law of every province as well (though in Quebec it may be said to be something of a grey area). If Bonbon were deemed in Canada to be legally an animal—a non-human animal—he would be the property of his guardians, and they could deal with them as they wished, subject only to the provisions of animal cruelty legislation. But if he were deemed by the Canadian courts to be human, as the Americans had deemed him to be, everything would be entirely different.

S.R.: And that didn't happen.

R.B.G.: No. It didn't happen—and on the whole, the Canadian courts have had the support of the people. The majority of

Canadians no more want to think of themselves as animals than do the majority of Americans.

S.R.: And you are of the view that humans *are* different—in fact, are superior to other animals.

R.B.G.: Again, you seem to be making statements rather than asking questions. What I think is that we have to respect the majority point of view. And yes, I think that humans are different. I think that all animal species are different, one from another. But should all the other species have legal status simply as our property? It's hard to see why. Granting status as persons has already been done in various jurisdictions for a wide variety of entities. Corporations in any number of countries have the legal status of persons, and increasingly so do other entities—including, for example, certain rivers in India, New Zealand, and Uruguay. If you're going to grant a corporation or a river the status of person, how can you not grant it to a lion or a whale? Personally, I would be in favour of granting such entities not just personhood status but also a place in the legislative process; I'd love to see a certain number of seats in every legislative assembly reserved for representatives chosen to represent the interests of those who cannot themselves cast a ballot—including non-human animals, including the non-animate environment—and including human children as well! But—and to my mind this is a key point—I would not grant unrestricted rights to the members of any of those groups; in order to be granted such rights, one should possess the capacity to reason at the level humans are capable of—and the capacity to make judgements at that level too. An elephant or a crow or a pig or a whale possesses far more of such capacity than non-human animals are often given credit for— but still, to my mind, substantially less than the average human, even the average teenager. If we started treating non-human animals on the same level as humans ...

S.R.: But why the *average* human? The more we know about elephants and dolphins and pigs, the more it seems clear that they may often possess *greater* reasoning capacity than do many humans whose mental capacities are for one reason or another severely limited. But we nevertheless allow those "below average" humans to vote, and in many cases to live independently.

R.B.G.: I should make clear that I'm entirely in agreement with those who say we've gone too far in allowing humans with severe mental disabilities to live on their own. No one wants to defend the worst practices of the old asylums, but facilities for humans with severe mental disabilities can in fact be model institutions. I don't think anyone who suggests that some people would be better off in a humanely run asylum than on the streets should be censured for their views—any more than those of us who believe that Bobo will always be better off in a humanely run institution than on the streets should be censured for our views. In Bobo's case, of course, that's the side the Canadian courts have come down on. At the request of the federal government (which seemed anxious not to be forced to take a position in the matter) the case was referred directly to the Supreme Court of Canada. They eventually decided, first of all, that the fact of the mother holding Canadian citizenship should be accorded relatively little weight in this particular case; secondly—crucially—they ruled that an animal who was only half human was not, in this instance at least, a legal person; and thirdly, they ruled that Bobo as an individual did not possess the ability to exercise legal capacity. As in America, it was a split decision, in this case five-four; Justice Rosalie Abella wrote an impassioned dissent, but she could not persuade a majority of her colleagues.

S.R.: And about that dissent ...

R.B.G.: I'd prefer not to go into that. We have already strayed a *very* long way from what was supposed to be the subject of this interview.

S.R.: So let's go back to Bonbon, and his early days. He was transferred to your facility, and then ...

R.B.G.: Those early days were not easy, I can tell you. Fielding all the requests worldwide for interviews and for research opportunities was a full-time job in itself. And figuring out how to create a special area for Bobo, that was another—though of course we had some time to figure that out. As a newborn infant he certainly did not require any special structure immediately. The main issue at first was simply his feeding. Normally a bonzee who has lost his mother or who for any reason is without his mother can be bottle fed without much difficulty. Not Bobo. Almost always he would refuse the bottle, no matter how it was presented, no matter what formula we put in there. We had never seen anything like it with any of the other bonzees—and over the years we must have had half a dozen cases where for one reason or another bottle feeding was required. It was a great relief to us when it turned out that Bobo could be breast fed after all—that ...

S.R.: And his mother? How did she ...?

R.B.G.: Well, his mother is of course a whole other story.

* * *

Lucinda Gerson

The only thing different between us and Americans is that Canadians pretend to think of the other person a little more often. Canadians are fine *with* the *idea* of caring about other folks—so long as the actual folks who need caring for don't move in next door. Canadians say they're all about diversity and community, but how many Canadians are really thinking of themselves as part of a *we* that isn't some stupid nationalistic crap? A *we* that includes the whole world—everybody anywhere who's human or inhuman, whatever. Or half human. Well, I guess we got our answer to that, didn't we? How much protest was there when the court ruled against Bonbon? Piss all, that's how much. Yeah, OK, so I'm on a bit of a rant.

Am I the same goddam way? Am I really more about me than anything else?

OK, so here I go again about me.

∾ So I was on my way to wherever. To anywhere I could make myself into a nobody. Was New Orleans that place? I guess I was gonna find out. For a few days I kept driving and driving. Steady. My old Pontiac was fine, long as you'd keep her at a steady speed and didn't take her much above 55. I took the Interstates west to Wisconsin, I hated those Interstates, every damn semi kept passing me, all them trucks so fast and so loud you couldn't think and you couldn't forget about thinking, I might of made a wrong turn to get to some place west of Milwaukee and then there was no Interstate that was going where I was going, and that made something lift inside me, and somehow I got onto the old Highway 61 and that was better, that was better for a long time. I remember crossing the Mississippi a few times, there'd be long steel bridges on a slant, high above the river. I remember one of them when the light was going, maybe I'd been driving through Illinois or maybe it was Wisconsin and I was crossing the river into some state that might have been Iowa, and then I was driving and driving and then back to the other state with the lights of a little town twinkling into the water as you crossed on another bridge, high above the lights and the town and the water, and then more driving and driving into the night, heading towards somewhere in the darkness, it might have been Davenport, it might have been Dubuque, it might have been anywhere, I guess. And then the sun was coming up somewhere that I couldn't see behind some hills, and on the other side of me way in the distance —it was so far in the distance that you wouldn't of been able to see except the light was coming through the clouds right onto it—there was that great arch they always show when the baseball games are about to begin in that stadium—you know, the red birds are on their uniforms. St Louis. That was the west, I guess. And I could just make out how the arch bent back on itself, it was so small in the distance.

They say you shouldn't go back on yourself but I done it a few times. I did it again at the next service centre. Why? I didn't even know, though I guess I do now. I put back the seat and I slept for a long time and I could feel my face burning when I woke up, it was midday. It was time to get going, and I wasn't going to go down past Memphis to New Orleans like I'd planned, if you can call anything that happened in my head *planning*.

I started heading north, heading home. It always looks different when you turn round and start going the other way, doesn't it? A lot different. I remember it was hot, and I remember my breasts kept leaking. I was trying to figure things out, and it wasn't easy.

Course I listened to the radio too. Sometimes they talked about it on the radio, talked about Bonbon I mean; it said on the news where the Supreme Court up in Canada had said "the hybrid known as Bonbon Gerson" would stay in the zoo. *There was nothing I could do about it now*, that's what most people would think, I guess. But if there was one thing I was learning, it was that most people weren't me.

∾ And who was me? I was going to have to be someone who didn't work at the Price Chopper in Comber, that was the first thing I thought. I was going to have to move to the big city so I could be near Bonbon. There was a hell of a lot more to it than that, but the funny thing was, at the end of it I still worked at the Price Chopper. Dave and Joan down in Comber knew the manager at the Price Chopper at Danforth and VP out the east end of Toronto. In Scarborough, right. You know where the Shoppers' World is? Just past that. So they got me a job there, basically, and nobody said nothing about who I was or what I'd done. And in the end the manager helped me find a place to rent, too. It wasn't so easy, I can tell you. Jamal, that was him, I forget his last name.

So I was living and working out the east end, and when I cranked up the old Pontiac it was only a quarter hour it took me to get out and see Bonbon.

Alright, so this is how things were: the Sunderland people weren't like the Cherneys and the Choose Life people—they wanted Bonbon to be breast fed, not fed that formula stuff. So they wanted my milk—but they wanted to set things up so I'd get to see my kid as little as possible. They wanted to have a schedule. Like, I'd be allowed an hour with Bonbon every day, something like that—and then "if I wanted" I could express milk for him, and other people would give it to him other times. Like they'd been doing with the formulas they'd been giving him, they said. 'Cept when I talked to the people who'd been trying to actually do that and they said *it's all been fine, just fine*, you could tell they were just saying what they'd been told to say, and that it wasn't really fine at all.

You could tell the same thing from the way that Bonbon looked. He was still the cutest little thing, and I cried and I cried when I held him again, I was crying with happiness. But I could see he was a lot tinier than he should have been, and a lot weaker. He was still barely ten pounds.

How would I know what a baby like that should weigh? OK, so maybe I didn't know a whole lot about bonzee babies, but I could Google like anyone else, and I sure found out a lot quick. You couldn't really tell what to expect but you could split the difference —if a human baby should weigh 15 pounds at six months and a bonzee baby should weigh nine pounds, then Bonbon should weigh 12 pounds, right? It's not rocket science.

Anyways, that was the beginning of all the fights I had with Goddard. The one I still blame for what happened to Bonbon, and to that poor mother and child on the other side of the river. *Robert B. Goddard, R.B. God,* or just call him *God* for short. He sure sounded like he thought he was God—no, that's not right. He sounded like he was thinking of applying for the position, and he was pretty goddam confident he was the strongest candidate.

Like, how close to God can you be when you're Director of Research and Development at the effing zoo? Sure, they had a fancy *research facility* name for it, but it was all part of the zoo, wasn't it? If they weren't getting people out to gawp at the animals they wouldn't be in business. And a business it was, I can tell you.

I made a big fuss about the milk thing, and first thing you knew I was being made welcome a whole lot more than one hour a day, and Bonbon was a whole lot healthier, and getting a whole lot bigger. They started giving me money too—a *stipend*, they called it, a stipend "to defray my transportation costs and to better enable me to provide nourishment for the infant." I'm serious, that's the words they used. So I would eat right and be able to gas up the old Pontiac. But you can believe I didn't say no.

It wasn't going to be short term, neither. A bonzee doesn't typically get weaned until he's, like, four years old. *Years*, not months! So even if Bonbon was going to be more like a human than a bonzee on this one, we were still looking at a hell of a long time he'd be wanting my milk. I figured I wasn't going to get pregnant again anytime soon.

Before too long I started to guess that they were going to want me for a whole lot more than my milk. They wanted me for family, too. Early on they told me they might not be able to "assign a father" for Bonbon from among the male bonzees there—there were seven of them in all. *Might* not? It didn't take much Googling to find out that bonzees mostly don't even *have* fathers. Bonzee fathers are fathers the way Mel Gibson and Charlie Sheen and Evander Holyfield are fathers. Mostly *not*, I mean. The fathers hardly ever pay any attention to their kids—hell, the fathers hardly ever know which kids are theirs.

But mothers? What about some bonzee mom to be like a mother to him in all the hours when they weren't allowing me to be there? Baby bonzee boys need their mothers just as much as baby bonobos do, or baby chimps, or baby humans—and the mothers *do* take care of their kids. Sometimes they'll help take care of other mothers' kids too, but not so much as all that. Anyways, the bonzee mothers at SARC weren't keen on spending a lot of time looking after an odd-looking one like Bonbon. No wonder, I guess. The only one who was really nice to him was an old bonzee woman they called Phil. She's dead now, she died when Bonbon was still there, I think. She was Phyllis, really, but who wants to call anyone that—*Phyllis* is a pretty useless name, even for a bonzee. Sounds like a dentist's tool, if you ask me.

Anyways, I started to figure the folks who ran the place were going to have to keep me in the picture if they wanted anybody except zookeepers to care for Bonbon. And that's what happened—'cept they didn't want to give me no control.

Well, I'm no dummy, right? It didn't take me long to figure out that I had some power over these people, no matter how snooty R.B. God might be. Not total power—there was likely no way I was going to get Bonbon back again. I figured that one out pretty quick and got my crying done. But still. Leverage, that's what it was; I had some leverage.

But before I could use it I had to figure out all the things I wanted—and all the things *they* would want. I googled some and I read a couple books, and it wasn't hard to see what their agenda was going to be.

Research, that was top of the list. This was a once-in-a-lifetime chance for all those researchers to make their reputations. Would they be able to get a hybrid to use sign language? Or any type of language? To speak English just as good as the rest of us? Would a hybrid be able to pick up language just like we do—without any teaching? Would Bonbon be able to demonstrate "reasoning ability" —*reasoning ability* as the researchers get to define it, of course. Using numbers like nobody would ever use numbers at the Price Chopper or at the bingo or on your taxes. And stupid tests they make up, to supposedly find out if you're conscious like a human is conscious— looking in a mirror and being able to figure out if you're you (maybe cats and them aren't interested in figuring out if they're really them, 'cause it's something they goddam know already, and it's not that interesting anyway, but the effing researchers don't think of any of that). Anyways, all that science crap. All of it wrapped up in fancy language, and all of it with Bonbon as their guinea pig. Hell, I don't even think guinea pigs should be allowed to be guinea pigs.

What else would they want to check out? You get one guess. Right: they'd want to see what'd happen with sex. Would Bonbon want to do it with a bonzee? With just about any bonzee? And if he did, could he make a bonzee female pregnant? Would he want to do it with a human? Would he be able to make a human pregnant? (For sure they wouldn't let *that* one play out, whatever he wanted.) Would he be able to reproduce, or was he, like, a mule?

But all the sex stuff wouldn't be for a few years yet. I read up about bonzees and sex too: puberty for a male bonzee starts at seven or eight. Split the difference with a human to figure what it might be for Bonbon, and you reckon it might be physically possible for him to get someone pregnant by the time he's ten or eleven. But how likely was it that they'd start trying all that out with Bonbon when he was that age? When anyone would be able to see he was just a kid? They'd be itching to see what would happen, but I reckoned that common decency would make 'em wait until he was at least, like, thirteen, fourteen. Sex wasn't going to be top of the list for a while.

But language? I read up on apes and language too. You know that super smart bonobo who surprised all the researchers by starting to learn words when they weren't even trying to teach him any? You know: Kanzi. He was only two when that happened. He just started to play with the lexigram board they'd given his mother, and presto, he was using symbols, he was making his own goddam language.

Maybe a human-bonzee cross would start to learn language even earlier than Kanzi. Maybe even as early as humans do. Would he be able to talk like us? They'd want to be talking to him hour after hour. Using a lexigram board, using this type of sign, that type of sign. Testing him every which way. They'd want to be teaching him and testing him all the goddam time.

I didn't want any of it.

All the time they'd want a *controlled environment*. That's what they called it. Not a place to play and to learn in the normal way. Yeah, yeah, I know, Bonbon could never be normal anyways, but they'd want to be observing him even when he didn't know they were there. When he was "on his own." They'd want to be observing if he'd want to play with a lexigram board or with whatever the latest learning gadget might happen to be. They'd want to see ... they'd want to see everything. There'd be no privacy for Bonbon. Zero privacy. OK, so privacy doesn't mean anything to a baby. But what about when he was seven? Or nine? Or fourteen?

As soon as I had it all figured out what they would want, I knew just what I wanted. The opposite.

Well, maybe not the opposite in everything. I guess I wanted him to learn to talk. But if they were going to *pressure* him to talk, or to learn sign language, or to figure out a Rubik's Cube, I was going to un-pressure him. If they were going to want him to be observed one hundred percent of the time, that was just what I was going to fight against. I was going to do everything I could to make sure he wasn't treated like some ape in a zoo.

If Bonbon was going to learn words, I wanted him to *want* to learn them. Not to have them shoved down his throat. Et cetera, et cetera.

So I got tough with them. I told them there'd have to be a limit to the number of hours they could spend with him in a day. I told them they had to promise not to make Bonbon spend all his time in a goddam laboratory. If they were going to build research rooms and observation rooms to do their science thing with Bonbon—and I knew they were—then they'd better keep those places separate from his own space. He would have to be given his own space. Where he could choose—once he got a little older, I mean—he could choose whether he wanted to be with me when I was there, or with the bonzees in the open space, or on his own. Really on his own, in the privacy of his very own space, if that's where he wanted to be. Without no one pestering him.

"Bonzees don't need privacy!" I remember when R.B. God said that to me. "Bonzees don't even *like* privacy. It's just not natural to them."

I really let him have it then. "You've got no idea what he needs or wants! Even if you're right about bonzees—he's not just a bonzee! He's half effing human, and that's why you're so interested in him. Or did you forget that?"

They probably didn't care what I said, but they knew they

needed me to keep coming round. They knew Bonbon needed my milk, and they knew he needed me as a mother. So in the end they caved on pretty well everything. Ha!

If I couldn't have no more than four hours a day with him (that's all they'd allow, and that was just about all I could take of that place anyway), then they shouldn't have more than four hours a day with him in the research rooms. (Or *learning rooms*, or *play rooms*—they were going to have all sorts of different names for them, but it was all the same thing, and they made just about all of it into work for little Bonbon, not play.) And there had to be a private area for Bonbon, or for me and Bonbon when I was visiting. Someplace where him and me could go and the researchers couldn't go, not unless he wanted them to. And the zookeepers couldn't go neither, not unless he wanted them to. And the bonzees, same thing.

Plus, they'd have to provide pretty much anything he might want or I might want for his private area. Toys that weren't research tools in disguise. Board books that I could read to him, and real books that I could read to him—maybe it would turn out that he could read them too, no pressure. Even some sort of touch screen computer—this was a little bit before there were iPads everywhere—and a TV.

I didn't want to prove anything. I just wanted him to have stuff, like any parent wants for their kid. Like any human parent, anyways.

Some of it was stuff I wanted too. OK, I admit that. I had my "stipend," and I had my 30 hours a week at the Price Chopper at VP and Danny, but it didn't go very far, I can tell you. I'd get home sometimes and I'd do the math and wonder how I was going to make my rent. The cost a living in Toronto was one hell of a lot different from what it was in Comber. But I did it—I made my rent. Every single goddam month I made my rent.

I'd find kids' music and stuff on the computer and on the TV, bonzee stuff too, there was one documentary about bonzees in the wild that I'd play for him again and again, it was made-for-kids so it left out the sex part. He wouldn't have minded, I guess; he sure saw enough of it in real life, just outside his private area. But still—what parent wants to be responsible for showing her three-year old any of that on TV? *Look at what they're doing, Bonbon, that's called "fucking,"* no, it just wouldn't feel right. Anyways, it wasn't too long before he started to lose interest in seeing bonzee documentaries, no matter what age they were for. He started to get real good at changing the channels and at discovering all sorts of stuff that he seemed to find interesting, all on his own. And on the computer too.

Did I sometimes watch grownup stuff when he was asleep or out in the open area, messing around with the little bonzees? Sure. What parent doesn't do stuff like that? I'd sometimes switch it to reruns of *Friends* or of *Cheers* when he wasn't there, or he wasn't paying attention. Or even *Sex and the City* reruns—who can resist that stuff? And by the time I got home, half the time I didn't even have the energy to watch TV. That stuff or any other stuff.

But Bonbon seemed to like watching TV even more than me. I mean "even more than I did," ha ha. He didn't like the TV more than he liked me, you can be damn sure of that. I *made* sure of that. I was as nice to him as a mom can be, or at least as a mom can be when they only let you be a mom for four hours a day. In an enclosure, not in your own goddam home.

And of course I'd talk, sometimes I'd just talk to him for hours on end. Pretend he could understand me. Sometimes I'd tell fairy tales, I had a big book from when I'd been little, it had hardly no words at all, but a lot of pictures. I'd always add to what words there were, and sometimes I'd change things round. Of course I'd read him the Beast story, *I no longer seem ugly*, and he gives her the ring so whenever she wants to come back to him, she can. The only thing I knew for sure he liked was a big, loud *fee-fie-fo-fum*, so I would always make the Beast say *fee-fie-fo-fum* a few times when he was apart from Beauty, and then he and Beauty would be together again, magically. Anyways, I know when he was little he liked the pictures. Maybe the sound of my voice, too, it sort kept the air warm between us. It was often pretty cold, I can tell you; they never kept that place warm enough. Maybe it was just right for the people who were walking and gawking all the time, but if you were sitting still in the private area, it was just too damn cold too much of the time.

∿ Private space or no private space, I can tell you it's no fun to have to look after your kid in a zoo. People sometimes ask me if it was hard, those years. Of course it was effing hard. How could it not be effing hard?

The hard parts weren't all to do with Bonbon, neither. How great do you think it can be, shelving Chef Boyardee at the Price Chopper or working one of the tills: *How are you today?*, *Do you have an AirMiles card?*, *Yes, it's a lovely day isn't it?* How would I know if it's a lovely day or not when I've been stuck at this stupid till the past three hours? And why would I care when I know I've got to watch you standing there flicking at your stupid fingernails while I bag your groceries for you?

At the Price Chopper in Comber, Dave and Joan always told everybody they could chop the prices further when everybody had to bag their own. And everybody *did* bag their own; if you were working the till you didn't have to do no bagging.

It wasn't like that here in the big city—whoever was at the till had to do effing everything. But what was I going to do? Who else was likely to want to give the mother of a goddam hybrid a job?

For that matter, how often do you think anyone was likely to want to fuck the mother of a fucking hybrid? Let's just segway into that one, 'cause who doesn't think about it? I sure did. Hell, I was still in my thirties. And sure, I'd sometimes have one or two too many at the Dog and Duck, just enough so's it felt like just the right number and I'd say *yes* to some guy who seemed nice, or nice enough, and sometimes the night'd end up being pretty good, going back to his place or whatever.

But back to my question: how many times you think anyone'd be likely to want to do it? Well, I can tell you the answer. Once. If they didn't know who I was beforehand, I'd feel obliged to tell them after we'd done it, sort of like a test, I guess. *Yeah, I'm the one whose kid is half bonzee. Yeah, that means I did it with a bonzee. Just the once. But yeah. The once.* And they'd always say they didn't mind but you could tell they did, and that would be that, once you'd said your stupid goodbyes. And if it turned out they *did* know beforehand who I was, they'd never want to do it more than once, neither. Just the once, to say they'd done it with that woman who'd fucked an ape. Once, to tell their friends about it.

They were hard years. I'll leave it at that.

But those years went by. I guess the years always do.

Bonbon Gerson

[The following is an excerpt from the narrative that, it is claimed, Bonbon ("Bobo") Gerson is responsible for; it purports to tell the story of his life up to November 2016. As is well known, the manuscript has not been authenticated. There is no need here to go into the ongoing controversy concerning its provenance; suffice to say that there are a wide range of opinions on the matter.]

My most long ago I member, it was to play on swing bars. And ropes, on the ropes. To swing to jump to laugh with Only, most little bonzee, and with Ever, bit bigger bonzee. All we were three, three of the years. I was never to keep up. I was never to grip and to spring with hands and feet, like could Only, like could Ever. Me never not all.

Only and Ever not frowned at my slow. Never not. Everything up, and everything down, and everything up all again, over in air. All was should be, all was should be—bonzees all little, bonzees all three.

Old person made name for Ever, name for Only. Then old person he was gone. Maybe was died.

R.P. said names be just to laugh, they not serious.

Lucy my mother was, mother is still.

I member me tight hold Lucy, me so little. Lucy was my always name for her, my only word before I had the words. When Lucy not there, came Ashley.

I member in the play rooms. I member zoo peoples pulled me

from Only, the zoo peoples did, pulled me from Ever, pulled me from ropes and from swing bars. I was took to play rooms. Then was all nice sounds made, the pat pat, the stroke stroke soft. Was a lexi board, were shapes and sounds. Zoo people showed me, zoo people sounded me, Bonbon was for to be curious. For zoo peoples, Bonbon was to be thing of play. I member push place on board where the pictures were, thing pictures, make thing in picture real. Pictures of treats, of sweet treats—push on picture, push on picture, treat treat treat.

Pictures were birds and circles and treats and pencils and squares. *Et cetera et cetera*, Lucy was say me those words over and over. Never was picture of play. Never was place for to push for to go out, to go out play with Only and with Ever. You goed door, you standed 'side door, you sounded your cry. What you were want, they was pretend not to know, zoo peoples.

Then more were the sounds and the pictures, *show us you understand, show us you understand.* Zoo people was say me things over, and was say me things again. And then no more were the pictures, no more. Were coloured shapes, were coloured letters. Push on shapes, push on shapes what words were, push on shapes what only shapes were, push and push and push for to try again, for to try harder. Do it more, do it more, play room play room, less room for to play. Always outside was the less times, with Ever the less times, with Only the less times. Zoo peoples rules, always they was made.

∾ The last two pages are me trying to imagine *little me*, best I can imagine him. Best I can think how *little me* was thinking, how *little me* was start to talk inside my head only.

We can be never sure when memory is long ago; to be sure is hard of anything almost, so much long ago. So we make imagine.

I was so little then. I am not thinking like that now. I am not talking like that now. But then my mind was small and I was small, and I had not all English the words, and did not say. Words moved in my head only, not in-out my lips.

I think you surprise when you read this. *How well-spoken is he!* you maybe say yourself. You maybe ask yourself *Was he ask a friend to help? Did some else person make the words for him?*

Yes and no. That is a short answer. I did ask friend who is good with the words for help me. The friend is name Leysha—she was not want to make clean all my words. She said was it better for people to read me really as I am. *On the paper it should be you*, she said. She insisted, and I insisted, and then we agreed half-half. So everything has its periods and its commas and is punctual, and some words are fixed where my friend she said *can people understand?* But for the rest they are my every words.

∾ People don't hear the sounds I make the way they hear the sounds of someone with the different accent, a Quebec or a Mexico, examples. They hear the sounds of me to be unnatural. Like the rest of me, the box of my voice is half human only.

But even if I am not make the sounds proper, and am not put all things in word order, I have learned be all right.

Lucy my mother she speaks a different bad than me. Or she *did*, in the long time ago. Always did she use that word *eff* and that other word, *effing*. As soon as I learned what was the meaning in them, I was wanted her stop. She was not using the *fucking* words to mean sex pleasure; she was mostly using the *fucking* words to make the other words angry.

Mostly—not the all time. One time we were watching the screen together; a man said how humans could be having much happy sex at age seventy, at age eighty even. *That's fucking funny*, Lucy said. Then she paused, and then she started to say me. *Why would anyone want to be doing it when they're effing eighty? Most of the time it's not even worth it when you're forty! Some guys ... Trust me, Bonbon, you don't want to know.* But then she screen-watched again, so I didn't know if I was want to know what she was not want me to know.

ᴓ There really was a real Only and a real Ever, and to everywhere I really went with the two them, when little I was. But to everywhere on the us side of the river only; we were understood the river we were not to cross, not ever. The ones on other side had their looks like us, but no liking, and harm they would bring.

Time later I was heard from Ashley the story how Only and Ever found their names. This was all what she said me:

> At birth they had been called Frodo and Pippin, just because a couple of the keepers had read *Lord of the Rings* and thought it would be cute to give them those names. But when Gerry Gundy, the cleaner (who looked like Gandalf and was almost as old), heard of this, he said he had never heard anything so ridiculous, not *ever*, that neither one of them looked anything like a hobbit. It was ridiculous and it was not *only* ridiculous, it was also unfair to the little ones to give them names that didn't suit them—that's what Gerry Gundy said. And after that you could hear the two keepers who were Tolkien lovers making fun of Gerry Gundy and the way he would poke his finger into the air when he said "not *ever*" and "not *only*." But they must have taken something of what old Gerry Gundy said seriously; somehow a week or two later the bonzee they'd been calling Pippin was being called *Ever*, and the little bonzee they'd been calling Frodo was being called *Only*.

ᴓ Ever and Only were not much being told to spend time in the "playrooms"—not like I was had to. For humans it was most interest in a bonzee-human—which was me, no others!—how, and how much, and how much the quick. They was pull me away from real play with Ever, with Only and push me into their play-not-really-play rooms to do me their search.

Lucy makes the big thing how she bargained Goddard for the most number of times they could keep me in the playrooms. Lucy did me the best she could, but still it was too many times, too many hours. At very first was a little bit fun, but soon I was wanting not spend one hour even. They were tried so hard to make seem all the science they did me was not science—make seem the science like play. Words for wording, numbers for numbing. Small fun. So every once they took me to the search playrooms, I was start to act up after just very short time. I was make some little for them like they want-ed with my fingers—little words, little *somes* and little *sums*, but only with my fingers for them, and always slow slow slow. I was give them no heard words. Like humans do some the times, I was learn how to make it look like I was trying—like I was working hard. And I was learn how to look puzzled, time and again. Quick I was learn become a slow learner. This when I was four of the years, maybe, five—hard is for me to be sure with the ages, the times.

I made a mystery to them. A baffle. The years later I was able, I read they report:

> For some months after testing began there were promising signs that Bobo might possess the capability to learn language skills at a level far beyond that achieved by Kanzi, or Koko, or any other ape that had been the subject of significant research. More recently there has been virtually no evidence of anything of the sort. Whereas Bonbon had been making steady progress, he has now regressed so dramatically that he seems unable to understand any sign at all—let alone communicate any meaningful signs on his own.

These were what they were think. Even when you are six or five of the years, even three, you can be able pretend the not understanding. Same thing all the times with the human fives and sixes of the years. Example, *It's bedtime, Magnus*. Blank face Magnus: all a sudden the word *bedtime* goes all strange to him.

We are all knowing human Magnus is a big little faker. But not for a moment did the searchers suspect me be same as big little Magnus.

∾ So I fooled them I was not be able the talk, not be able the understand. I was listen all the every they said, and I was listen all the every what Lucy said, and I was watch and listen all the everythings on the screen. Lucy played all the programs—children programs too, adult programs too—and like anyone, the more I was the listen the more I was the understand. When I was in my alone I was play my mouth and was make the sounds—make the English words. Ever so quiet I was make my sounds in my head, and not let go my sounds in air. Once I saw Ashley look me as if I were say something with my sounds. Just only once. But all the time I listened all the everything.

I listened all the everything what Ever said and what Only said too. And everything what Betty said, and everything what Jasper said, and everything what any the other bonzees said. I was like to talk the bonzees.

Now you up your brow maybe. Maybe you was read all those human writings:

> We humans are the language animal. The only language animal. The hyoid bone, which is the only bone in the body not connected to any other, is the foundation of speech—and it is found in a form that can facilitate speech only in humans and Neanderthals. Other animals have versions of the hyoid, but only the human variety is

in the right position to work in unison with the larynx
and tongue and make us the chatterboxes of the animal
world. Without it, we'd still garble and hoot much like
our chimpanzee and bonobo cousins, scientists say.

Fact, other animals can't be able to make same sorts of sounds the
human animals make. Even for bonzees—where hyoid is more like
a human hyoid than bonobo's is or chimp's is—is not exactly same
sort, the sound. But who's the decider that only human sounds can
be language? What not the sounds we bonzees say, one to other?
What not the sounds the elephants say? The sounds the whales say,
and the sounds of all the dolphins saying? All of us we send our
meanings one to other, all in sound.

But you are human if you reading these words, so maybe you
side with yours on this yes-no, and think only you humans have
language. Other humans tell you your language only has *structure*;
they say not-humans are having just sound, no *structure*. But what
the way a bonzee uses back-the-throat sounds and say one to other
It's important! Or what the way same sound at the high pitch is
mean *piece of fruit is ripe*, same sound at the little more low pitch
is mean *piece of fruit is not yet ripe*? Or what the way with different
sounds? Example, sound *a een eh* and sound *a een meh*. What
human ear can tell apart when the bonzee makes sounds? But to a
bonzee ear? First sound is mean *on the ropes* (also is mean *on the
vines*, also is mean *on the branches that are thin but strong and
flexible*). Second sound is mean *to my mouth*, also is mean *give
me that*, also is mean *bring that here for me to eat*). Humans don't
hear difference; but they are anyways sure their human sounds
are better.

For a bonzee every thing has a meaning, almost. *Eeehn* is mean
come, and *shree* is mean *no*, *eeeekekeke* is mean *this way*—not all
easy hear in the English, but is all language. Fact, bonzee language is
not so busy with things like the English—bonzee language was as

easy me to learn as for any little bonzee. So when I with them, I was able say almost the anything. I was able do almost the anything.[2]

I could spit like a bonzee, too. You see in all the bonzee films, how bonzees can be able put little things in our mouths and be able to send them shooting, like as if from a pea shooter. Ever could be able spit a pebble thirty feet, and so could Only be able, but I could be able spit further, much the further. Not like humans, ha ha. That is like Lucy say the ha ha.

Lucy would not hardly ever watch me when I was in the bonzee area. She was—what humans say?—open minded, like a window. But she was not wanting open for see one thing what bonzees like to do—doing pleasure. The bonzee children even like, each the other. Bonzees not be *always* pleasure fucking, like some people say. But yes, doing pleasure is an often thing.

[These reflections are followed in the narrative by the now-famous long passage in which the author recounts various childhood sexual experiences with members of the bonzee troupe he spent so much time with. These passages are important, of course, but they are so

---

2. [Editor's note] The following note, which appears at this point in the margin of the manuscript, is presumed by many to have been written by the friend of Bonbon (and manuscript editor) identified as "Leysha" in the manuscript:

Some of you may read "do almost the anything" or "she was done anything" and many other odd or ungrammatical phrasings and think to yourself something of this sort: "It's all ungrammatical; with every sentence the creature shows that he's not capable of what humans are capable of." To be sure, Bonbon's way with words is different—perhaps unique. But I ask you to compare his language skills with those of any human who is trying to speak or write in a second language. How good Bonbon's English skills—or his math skills, for that matter—might be if he had been treated all along as a human—and educated as humans are, broadly and for their own benefit rather than narrowly as a subject for the benefit of researchers—is something about which we can only speculate.

well-known and so widely reprinted elsewhere that it
seems unnecessary to include them here.]

∾ What was Lucy want from me, way back then the long time?
Love, sure—every mother is want that. But was she want me to
learn? Was she want me to say and to read and to write? Like those
searchers was want me? Also like I was want at the very first, before
I real eyes[3] they would make my whole life their search if they could
be able.

  I think of the all many hours she was spend with me in my
private area. Lot of the times all screens was off, and all everything
off, and all everything quiet, and she was hold me in her arms. Or,
as I was to be more old, she was sit me beside her. I remember how
she talked me on and on, talking me but talking herself mostly.

> *You don't know what I was thinking, do you, Bonbon?*
> *And I don't really know either. What was I thinking, all*
> *those years ago? Now Susie barely talks to me and I've*
> *got about two friends in the world. No, not about two*
> *friends, it's exactly effing two, isn't it?*
>   *At least Susie's research station hasn't closed—fact*

---

3. [Editor's note] The following marginal note, which appears on page 32 of
Bonbon's manuscript—is presumed by many to have been written by the friend
and editor identified as "Leysha" in the manuscript:

> Some of you may wonder why I did not correct "real eyes" to
> "realize" here (and at several other places in the manuscript). I
> can recount an incident that may make this clear. Bonbon once
> said to me (I think it was during a conversation about religion and
> evolution), "Before I wrong eyes the true; now I real eyes the true."
> Some nuance would surely be lost if "realize" were substituted.
>   You may also wonder how Bonbon could remember or reproduce
> the English phrasings of the people he quotes so grammatically and
> so well. The answer is of course that he couldn't, and he didn't. He
> would simply write something suggestive of what they said; I have
> translated those passages into idiomatic English.

is, they're getting more cash than they ever did, that's what everybody says. And the TV people and all them? For once it sounds like they're under control, they've actually been following the rules Susie and her people laid down, there's a proto call you got to make before you get to go to the research station if you're one of them, and I guess not a lot of them are making the call. Though I bet it's not so much the rules as the cost of getting to Inogo that's keeping them away, ha ha.

That's where your daddy lives, Bonbon. Inogo. Well, near there. Might as well say near nowhere—you ain't got no geography, have you, Bonbon? But he's all right. Your daddy's all right, that's what Susie said the last time she—that's what she said the last time. That they're not picking on your daddy so much as they used to, god knows why. 'Cept there ain't no god, is there, Bonbon?

Sometimes it's just as well you can't understand me, little one. And just as well you don't know how much I got on the damn Mastercard bill. More'n I can pay, that's for effing sure.

All what she said like that made me feel strange. Strange and small. Who was Bei that was my daddy? I was drift my mind to the other places, and fidget, and wish I was with Only and Ever.

For all of the that, she was my Lucy. She was have me in her arms, and she was rock me sleep after the noon. She was done anything for me—anything what she was able do. She was love me. Human love is the funny thing, but yes, Lucy was love me. I must have been knowing all there was of that.

9.

Lucinda Gerson

The years were going by slowly, and he was growing up quickly—that doesn't make any sense, does it? But that's how it was. Sometimes I wished he wouldn't grow up so quickly—I guess every parent says that. Partly it was 'cause I like to play with little kids. When you have a little kid, it's an excuse to play again, isn't it? With blocks, and balloons, and bubbles, and water pistols, and all that. But playing with Bonbon wasn't quite like playing with a normal kid. Sometimes it would be all good but other times I'd start bouncing a ball or whatever and he'd just look at me as if I was weird. And some days I even thought he was right, that I *was* weird, and some days I couldn't help myself thinking *if one of us is weird, it sure isn't me!*, and some days I'd think *if only we could just be on a beach or walk through the woods it would feel right, we'd play with whatever we found, the sand and the water or the sticks or whatever, and then it would be alright, then it wouldn't be weird.*

A lot of the time when they took Bonbon away for the language work, or when he was playing with the little bonzees, I'd be alone there with his toys, and not much else. Of course I wanted him to have time with the little bonzees—you have to want every kid to have time to play with other kids the same age. But him playing with the other bonzees was its own kind of weird. And I only had four hours a day; of course I wanted him to spend as much of it as possible with me.

It was all the times they kept him at the research lab for hours that really pissed me off. At their "playrooms." Once things were set up like I'd asked, and once Bonbon was weaned, I guess you'd have to say I lost a lot of my leverage. I kept asking them to let him have more time with me, and more time with the bonzees too, and they kept saying no. The only reason they finally cut back on the time they made him spend on all those language research games wasn't nothing to do with me; it was because he wasn't learning none of what they were trying to teach him. He just stopped progressing. Stopped trying to talk, I guess. I never did understand it, not really. Not till we left Clearwater.

If I did want the keepers to change something, or if I wanted something new for him, I figured out eventually it was better if I didn't ask them myself. What I'd do is I'd ask Ashley to ask them. She was this sweet young girl—well, eventually she grew into a woman, and maybe everyone gets a little less sweet when they grow up—but at first she was a sweet young girl who worked there as a volunteer. And she could make just about anyone do what she wanted. So if I starting thinking that Bonbon should have a bigger cupboard, say, or more shelves for his things, I wouldn't ask Dr. God directly. I knew perfectly well what he'd say—it'd always be no. But not if Ashley asked him. "Dr. Goddard," she'd say, all soft and smiling, "we've been noticing—I mean, the volunteers like me, who work with Bonbon—we've been noticing that he doesn't really have enough space to …," and by the end of the week there'd be a new set of shelves in his private area.

So maybe Dr. God was just a sucker for innocent little girls, you're thinking, or a pervert. Maybe he'd get a hard-on if any one of those cute fourteen-year-old girls in the ZooTeen program asked him for anything, and maybe he would at that. But there was something different about Ashley, that was for sure. I don't just mean that she was black, or pretty black, anyways. Sure, there's a lot of white people who … That'll be the first thing they'll see about someone with dark skin, and for a lot of them it's just about the only thing they'll see—whether it's the only thing they'll see because they hate black people so much, or it's the only thing they'll see because they're falling over themselves to show how much they love black people. Dr. God didn't love or hate on the basis of a person's skin colour, I'll give him that much. But social class? You can bet he cared about that a whole hell of a lot. And Ashley wasn't … — well, you think of the stereotype of the sort of black person who's grown up poor, and with everything against them, like a hell of a lot have, and then you think of the opposite of that, and that was Ashley. She'd been to the right goddam schools, and she'd lived in the right goddam neighbourhoods. *I like neighbourhoods where the streets have a bit of a curve to them*, she'd say. *Not neighbourhoods where everything's lined up in big boring squares.* And you could just tell she'd heard her mother or father say exactly that, in exactly those words. You wouldn't hear anyone say *We live in Rosedale because that's where the rich people live*, the rich people whose families have been rich for so long they can pretend money doesn't matter to them. No, they'd talk about big old houses, and big old trees. With real affection, *we love the space, and the big old trees*. As if none of it had anything to do with money.

Hey, I'm not blaming Ashley for none of that. She was a good kid. She *is* a good kid—or a good whatever-you-call-someone-in-their-twenties. For all that we might have had a few disagreements. A few fights, I guess you'd have to say. Like about the food. I don't mean a food fight—I mean Bonbon's food. She doesn't always get it, that's for sure. But you can't help where you're from—not her, not any of the rest of us neither. And I'll give her credit: you won't see her do like a lot of the people from Rosedale or Forest Hill or Wychwood Park do all the time, which is treat people who're from Downsview or Victoria Park or Woburn like they're no more than half human.

"No more than half human"—ha! You know they used to put *people* in zoos? A lot of people don't know that. Exotics, they called 'em. An *exotic* was a person with darker skin than you had, and who came from somewheres far away. Even farther away than Woburn, I mean.

'Course a lot of people used to say about Bonbon *zoos aren't such bad places*. They'd say *look on the bright side, the glass is half full*. But it was half fucking empty too, wasn't it? He was only half human, and the glass was half fucking empty. If he'd been three quarters human they would *not* have put him in no zoo, you can be damn sure of that. But I didn't have no way of making him three quarters of what's in my genes, and just a quarter of what's in Bei's genes, did I?

I didn't know nothing 'bout slaves and quadroons and all that, not before I had Bonbon. You know how all them would try to escape to Canada? The Underground Railroad? Sometimes it wasn't much better for them when they got there, but at least they weren't slaves, I guess. Ha. *Glass half full*. Now it was exactly the other way round for Bonbon. If we could ever get him into America, he'd be free.

I just wanted so much for him to grow wings and fly up over that effing fence, and right across that effing great lake. Right the whole way across. Free as an effing bird.

* * *

Susanne Gerson: *Letters to Lucinda Gerson and to Robert B. Goddard*

[The first of the following two letters was included (together with several other letters) by Susanne Gerson as an appendix to her narrative of her interactions with her sister Lucinda. The second was made public during the various legal actions involving security issues in the handling of Bonbon Gerson both by the Sunderland Animal Research Centre and later by the Coldwater Animal Research Institute.]

Dear Luc,

Of course I still love you, and of course I still want to be your sister. This year I'll be back home by the middle of December. I hope you'll come and stay for at least a few days over the holidays; it would be great to see you again after all this time.

I do hope that what you said about how much you'd like to "spring Bonbon loose" was just blowing off steam. I appreciate how you feel about him and how everything has turned out—really I do!—but I can't believe that doing anything which would go against what the courts have ordered is going to be any real solution. I can't help thinking it would make things worse—and that you could well end up in jail, which surely wouldn't help Bonbon any more than it would help you. So please, please, please don't do something you would really regret!

That's all I'll say on the subject, though; I won't write you about it again, and I'll keep my big, fat mouth shut on this one over the holidays—I promise! I think, in fact, that it's probably a good idea for us to make a pact not to talk about Bonbon when we see each other. It's been clear for a long time that we'll never agree about all of that, and every time we try to talk our way through it, things become really painful and we both get angry and then it takes such a long time to patch things up. So I do hope you're OK with just sticking to other topics while we're together.

I'll be back on the 12th; let's you and me talk on the phone soon after that. All my love,
   Susie

Dear Dr. Goddard,

I have hesitated for some time over whether I should write this letter, but I have finally come to the conclusion that it can do no harm, and that it might do some good.

I'm sure you will have come across my name; I am the Director of the Lake Mai-Ndombe Research Centre; Lucinda Gerson is my sister, so I guess that makes Bonbon my nephew.

As you may know, Lucinda and I have not seen eye to eye over all this; I came to the conclusion early on that it would be better for both Bonbon himself and society as a whole for him to live his life under the care of professionals at a facility such as yours than it would be to try to integrate him into human society. I was relieved that the Canadian courts agreed. And I have every reason to believe that Bonbon has been well taken care of at Sunderland and given every opportunity to live a full life.

I'm writing now to give you a "heads-up" regarding my sister's current state of mind. In her last communication with me she mused at some length about trying to "break Bonbon loose." I have to hope that this was merely a matter of her becoming over-emotional (as my sister has always been prone to do!), and that she has not formulated any specific plan to try to bring about the turn of events that she evidently desires. But I also know that she can sometimes be reckless and act upon her wildest impulses; given that background, I felt it was my responsibility to warn you of what she might be contemplating.

I'm sure that a considerable number of security measures are already in place both for the facility as a whole and with particular regard to Bonbon and the bonzees' enclosure; there may well be nothing further that you and your staff can or should do to make things more secure. But I know that, had I not written you in this way (and if anything *were* to happen), I would feel terrible for not having done everything I could to prevent it. That said, I have every hope that what my sister communicated to me really were only wild imaginings. I thank you for the great care that you and your staff are so obviously taking in dealing with my sister—and with Bonbon. Respectfully yours,

(Dr.) Susanne Gerson

＊

Ashley Rouleau

[Following is the first section of the account by Ashley Rouleau of her involvement with Lucinda and Bonbon Gerson. Aside from her official statements in court, Rouleau's account—developed initially purely as a personal record, she has attested, out of the journal she reportedly began to keep in her early teens—constitutes the fullest explanation we have of her efforts to remove Bonbon from his enclosure—to "free him," to use her own language.]

What can I say about Bonbon? Where to begin? Begin with his mother, I suppose. Everything begins with Luce.

She was always swearing, of course. At the people who ran the zoo, or at Betty—she was the dominant bonzee of the group. Or at the world in general. But Lucinda would never swear at people while she was with them. If Betty had been teaching Bonbon things that Luce didn't want him to know, you could count on her to sound off. She was, like, *Effing Betty doesn't have the faintest idea how to raise a child*, and *Effing Betty has got to realize Bonbon isn't like the others, he can't swing with his feet like they can, he just can't, he's going to fall and hurt himself*, and on and on it would go. Some of it she might say right to Betty's face (not that she thought Betty could understand), but she'd leave out the anger and the swearing. She would only let that part of it out when she was in the private area. Or when she was at her own place, I guess: she must have let off steam at her apartment, just like I know she did after the move to Clearwater.

You couldn't blame her for getting angry and frustrated. It was an impossible situation. And like a lot of people have to do, I guess, she kept living with an impossible situation. Making do.

She was right about a lot of things. Bonbon *couldn't* swing with his feet quite like the others could, and he *did* fall, more than once.

With his hind legs, should I say? When he was with them he would sometimes lope with all four limbs touching the ground, just like a bonzee often does. But when he was in the private area with Luce or with me or with one of the other keepers he would always walk on two legs, upright or almost upright. I had a friend whose father stooped about the same as Bonbon did.

He wanted to keep up with the other little ones—with Ever and with Only especially. I don't know if you could blame Betty. But one time Bonbon had a serious fall; he had a concussion and broke his collar bone. After that Betty seemed to act a little differently. As did Bonbon—that's for sure. He was a little more quiet, and a lot more careful.

It was about clothes that I sometimes thought Lucinda was being too fussy. Of course she wanted Bonbon to be like a human when he was in the private area with her—to wear clothes just like she did, and just like the keepers did. That was natural. In fact, that had been part of the deal she struck with Dr. Goddard—that Bonbon was always supposed to wear clothes when he was with her. (Not when he was just a baby—only after. But diapers, at least, when he was a baby—she insisted that he would have to be trained to be a human so far as that side of things was concerned). The thing was that Goddard wouldn't give in on the question of how Bonbon should be dressed when he was with the bonzees—he shouldn't have any clothes at all, Goddard insisted. It would difficult enough for Bonbon to get along with the others—that was his view. No need to make everything more difficult by trying to keep him clothed, as if he were human. Goddard said he knew what would happen: Betty and the others would take hold of Bonbon's shorts and his shirt and pull them this way and that, and then rip them right off. They might mean it all in fun, but it wouldn't feel like fun for Bonbon. That's what Dr. Goddard said. So every time Bonbon would come into the private area he would have to put his clothes on—like I say, Lucinda was very particular about that, very fussy—and every time he would go back out again he would have to take his clothes off.

It must have been very strange for him, once he began to be aware of the world around him. Even naked, he looked different from Ever and Only and the others. His skin was lighter than the others, and that showed because he was quite a bit less hairy than the others too. So when he spent time in the bonzee area you could think of it as no different from a little child wandering around naked on a beach in the summer time. Well, a little different, I guess. You don't see too many beaches where there's one little sort-of naked, sort-of human, in the middle of a group of hairy bonzees.

So far as we know, a bonzee doesn't have any idea of "naked," of course—any more than a very young human does. Did they start to understand what "naked" means when they saw Bonbon grow up among them? Sometimes the bonzees would see him taking off his clothes and throwing them behind him as he was coming out of the private area, or see him still wearing his clothes as he went with one of the biologists over to the research building—and you could almost imagine that the bonzees were seeing themselves differently. But maybe it was just that they saw Bonbon had some things that they didn't, and that made them want the same things for them-selves. You could definitely see that some of them wanted clothes themselves: they would point towards Bonbon and make gestures like they were pulling T-shirts over their heads, or pulling on shorts, and they would make that especially high-pitched sound they would always make when they wanted something. But some of the others made a show of not wanting anything like that at all. Betty would shake her head and shake her whole upper body back and forth when she would see Jamie or Jasper acting like they wanted clothes.

And she would show off her genitalia even more ostentatiously than usual. Sometimes it was hard to tell what Bonbon wanted. When he was very little he would want to be naked everywhere, in the private area as well as outside with the bonzees, and Lucinda would have to have a little fight with him before he would put on his shirt and pants. She always bought him things he would be able to pull on easily—shorts, track pants, T-shirts, that sort of thing. Nothing with buttons, nothing with a zipper. I don't know if that was to make it easier for him, or because she could get those things cheap at Walmart. Maybe a bit of both: I know she never had much money, despite what Dr. Goddard would always say about having done everything possible to make sure she would have what she needed.

If little Bonbon had had his way, of course, she wouldn't have had to spend anything on clothes for him.

That he wanted to be naked is not to say he wanted to be like the bonzees in every way. Even when he was fairly young he started to want privacy for some things—even from Lucinda. Going to the bathroom, for example. When he was first able to get around on his own he'd want to go to the bathroom everywhere, of course. But by the time he was two he had started to change—and soon he would always use the toilet if he needed to go. He didn't need any more training than a lot of kids do—a lot of human kids, I mean. Or than some of the bonzees and bonobos and chimps that they've tried to raise as humans do, for that matter. Or than dogs and cats do.

Food was another thing. Luce always wanted Bonbon to eat more like a human—which to her meant eating hot dogs and chicken nuggets and fries. Back then it was pretty clear to her: bonzees might eat fruits and veggies, and sure, humans should eat a bit of that too, but to be really human—maybe I should say to be normal?—you had to be, like, eating other animals too. And the keepers—they had the same stupid idea. Or sort of the same stupid idea. They gave Bonbon a lot of meat; it just wasn't the type of meat that Luce wanted him to be eating. They'd give him red meat, raw or nearly raw. And Luce? She wanted him to be served burgers. And chicken nuggets and fries, like I said.

For a while when he was little, Bonbon would eat just about anything. But it seemed like the more he heard Luce and the keepers arguing about what sort of meat he should get for "the human side of his diet," the more he wanted to stick to fruits and veggies.

Bonbon kept changing, of course—who doesn't? By the time he was eight or nine it was just about impossible to get him to eat meat, but he wanted to wear clothes all the time—and not just T-shirts and sweat pants. He started to want clothes with buttons and zippers—just like the keepers had, just like Lucinda had. Just like I had. In all, there were ten of us who worked with Bonbon and the bonzees —we would joke how it sounded like a band, *Bonbon and the Bonzees*. Ten. Seven volunteers and three of the zoo's full-time workers—that's not counting the biologists at the research centre. At first I would work just Tuesday and Thursday afternoons after school; as time went on, that increased to as much as twenty hours a week.

It wasn't anything where you needed a lot of training. I would bring them food, clean things out when cleaning was needed, that sort of thing.

I can't be sure if Bonbon was part of the reason I thought of volunteering at the zoo in the first place—I think he might have been. You remember how much publicity there was back then? Right across North America. About there being a hybrid "up in Canada," and what he was like, and what he might turn out to be like—everybody was talking about it. But I might have volunteered anyway. I'd always loved animals—almost as much as kids! Kids younger than I was, I guess I should say. A year or two later I started working with kids in the summers—being a camp counsellor is maybe still the most favourite thing I've done. But this was when I was fourteen, and I wanted something to get me out of the house and away from my parents—something more than just hanging out at the mall. And I loved the zoo—back then I didn't understand about animals being free, I guess. And when I heard about this hybrid—anyway, I volunteered in the ZooTeen program, and when they assigned me to the great apes, I was just over the moon.

Right away I thought he was the cutest little kid—Bonbon, I mean. Of course he was odd looking, but so many kids are odd looking. I used to do a lot of babysitting when I was twelve and thirteen, and I always thought some of the oddest looking babies were some of the cutest. Not that Bonbon was exactly a baby—was he three or four when I started? And bonzees age at different rates from what we do—at least for some of their lives. A bonzee fifty-year-old isn't much different from a human fifty-year-old, and a bonzee who's a few months old is a lot like a human who's a few months old. But a bonzee two-year-old is a lot like a human four-year-old developmentally, and a bonzee seven-year-old or eight-year-old is a lot like a human fifteen- or sixteen-year-old developmentally. With Bonbon, half bonzee and half human, it was even less clear, but for sure he was old for his years in some ways: by the time we made our break for it, Bonbon was fourteen, and I was into my twenties, and in some ways it seemed like I was a lot older. But it seemed like he was a lot older too—almost as old as me. It was weird.

I had heard something of the failures of the various language experiments, of course; anyone who worked there had heard something of how disappointed the researchers were. I didn't think much of it either way—though two or three times, now that I look back, I can remember Bonbon making sounds that didn't sound at all like the sounds the other bonzees were making. Quiet sounds—sounds he would make when I don't think he thought anyone was there. Did I catch myself imagining that he was making something like human words? Something like the way babies talk when you aren't really sure if they are forming words—*when little Sarah says ama, is she trying to say* mama? *Or is she just babbling?*—that sort of thing. I honestly can't remember. But I do know that, much as I was so struck by how human he often *looked*, it wasn't the same when it came to talking. Communicating. For a long time we weren't really communicating. I got into the habit of thinking of him more as one of the bonzees than as one of us. The cutest bonzee. I don't feel comfortable putting it this way, but I think at first I loved him sort of in the way you'd love a pet. You see what I mean?

I don't want to get ahead of things. I just want to give you some sense of what he was like—and of how he changed.

Physically, by the time he was nine or ten, he looked more like a young man than a boy. Almost a young human male—as well as a young, male, adult bonzee.

Almost. With Bonbon there was always an "almost." If you watched him with the bonzees and you forgot about him being lighter skinned and less hairy—then the difference was sometimes hardly noticeable.

He could move very much as they did, if and when he wanted to—and usually he did want to. And he would always hunch over more when he was among them than he would when he was with humans. But when he straightened up—when he stood or walked among humans? Well, it's hard to describe.

I guess I don't need to describe it—you must have seen the pictures, the videos. Seen how awkward he looked in those days, but how he always seemed to project some sort of strength. A quiet energy. And a sort of dignity—a real dignity, even when he was still quite young.

Like Abraham Lincoln, almost—but different proportions, of course.

The funny thing is, there were pictures of somebody who looked a little like Bonbon, long before he existed. Way back in 1991 Nancy Burston and David Kramlich made computer-generated images of a human-chimpanzee hybrid, a human-bonobo hybrid, and a human-bonzee hybrid. And what they generated on the computer does bear at least a passing resemblance to Bonbon.

It all seems like science. But then you look at it—look at real life. Bonbon has less hair, of course—and in other ways too, looks more human. Especially now that he's grown—the proportions of his legs and torso are more like those of a human than they are like those of a bonzee.

And the face? I shouldn't just mention that computer-generated image; there are humans with faces a lot like Bonbon's too. People who are 100% human, I mean. Famously, Ron Perlman, but he's not the only one. Tom Waits—there's another. And that famous architect, I.M. Pei; have a look at some pictures of him. Some of the best and brightest humans have looked quite a bit like apes. Non-human apes, I mean; of course we humans are apes as well.

Anyway, like I say, just about everybody's seen pictures of Bonbon. It's just a question of what you see *in* the pictures.

Thinking of those images of different sorts of hybrids makes me think of all the different apes at the zoo. Mostly I worked with the bonzees and with Bonbon, but sometimes I would fill in for someone on the other side of the river. It was very different over there—it could get nasty, that's for sure. It's pretty much true what they say about chimps being, on average, more aggressive and more violent than bonobos or bonzees; they knew that perfectly well long before all the trouble with Bonbon and the baby—the incident on the other side of the river. And from what I heard, Dr. Goddard had made it even more true. What I mean is, I heard he had tried to make sure that the chimps who were selected for the Sunderland facility were the fiercest possible—something to do with his research into lowland and savannah chimps, and their different levels of aggression. Though how you'd prove anything if you'd pre-selected individuals known to have certain tendencies, I don't know—and to be fair, it was just rumour, like a lot of things that were said about Goddard.

Anyway, some of them could be pretty violent—especially Carville, the largest male. I never liked how the gawkers would *ooh* and *aaah* when he would make some fierce display, and go chasing after one of the other chimps. It was like they were watching UFC, or some fight in a hockey game. Of course the gawkers on the sky-walk overhead would try to get a view of all the apes at once—the chimps and the gorillas on one side of the river, the bonobos and the bonzees on the other. But it wasn't often that they could do that from one vantage point; the chimps would often hang out by the water, but the bonobos and the bonzees wouldn't.

Maybe they tried to design it so as to mimic that great river, but the Congo is, like, the deepest river in the world and this little river was ridiculously shallow. No band of chimps would cross the Congo to attack a band of bonzees. But here? Anybody should have seen the danger—and no one did.

You could see why the bonobos and the bonzees stayed away from the river. Except for Bonbon. I don't know if he was brave or if he was stupid, but sometimes he'd slip away on his own, into the woods. Starting from age five or so—it went on for a lot of years while he was growing up. If you wanted to look for him, you'd find him by the river.

Sometimes I would watch him from a distance. The gawkers were in the distance too, but you could tell that Bonbon was able to find some sort of peace there. Luce never wanted to disturb him when he would wander off; she was, like, *I only want to know where he is, and that he's safe.* And that's what I wanted too.

I would busy myself with some quiet work in the bush, straight-ening a branch here, clearing a bit of something off a path there. Far enough away that Bonbon took no notice of me, though he may have known I was there. After a time he would always return to the others. He never crossed the river. And all of our lives went on like that for years.

∽ His smile was sort of strange—everyone would always notice that. I mean everyone who he'd smile at, which certainly wasn't everyone. Whenever he would notice the gawkers, he'd stop smiling. He wouldn't scowl or anything; he just wouldn't smile. Some of the others were the same way, I noticed. Betty wouldn't care who was watching anything she did, not even if someone was yelling at her or throwing stuff into the enclosure. If she was smiling and laughing she'd keep smiling and laughing, *the gawkers can go screw themselves*, you could just tell that was what she was thinking. And Esmine was like that too. But Tina and Jamie and Albert and some of the others were like Bonbon. When they noticed the gawkers they'd stop smiling, they'd stop laughing.

Have you ever watched a bonzee laugh? When they do a big laugh their faces do pretty much the things a human face does. I mean, the sound that comes out is different, but you watch the face, you'll see what I mean. But when bonzees smile? And the sides of the mouth stretch wide? It's not like anything a human would do. I guess we humans have more little mouth muscles or something— muscles that can pull our lips every which way. And we can do little smiles, where we don't let our teeth show at all, the corners of our mouths just turn up a little—bonzees can't do that. But Bonbon? He could smile and it looked just like a human smile, almost, except sometimes a little lopsided. I never understood it when people said he smiled funny; lots of humans have smiles that are just as lopsided as Bonbon's—even more than his. I don't know why they wanted to see what was different all the time.

And his hair—people always go on about that. He's not *that* hairy—really he isn't. I mean we all are, aren't we? All humans. We have hair on our arms and our legs and everywhere. But then we try to get rid of it all—if we're women, especially. We don't want to admit that we're animals too.

Like I say, I don't mind it at all. I don't mind having hair all over my legs, and between my legs, and on my arms. What's there to mind? I mean, it's natural. Not that everything natural is good, I know it isn't. But if something doesn't harm you and it doesn't harm anybody else or harm the earth, and it takes a lot of time and effort to change it, why bother? You can spend that time better on a lot of other things—even goofing off and reading some trashy book or watching some trashy TV show is time better spent than spending hours shaving and waxing. That wasn't how most other girls saw things, of course. Not when I was in school, or after I left school either. There was only one other girl in my grade who didn't spend hours shaving herself, which was Jenny, and she was into piercings and vampires and a lot of things I wasn't into, and we would look at each other in a way that said *I don't really know you but I respect you*, so I guess you could say we liked each other, but for a long time we were a little bit wary of each other too.

I've told you Bonbon wasn't *that* hairy, but of course he had more hair than the average human. And he was shorter than the average human. After a time he grew to be, what—five foot four? Taller than the average bonzee male, but shorter than the average human male. His arms hung low—his hands were almost at his knees. But they *were* arms and hands—you would never have called the full-grown Bonbon a four-legged creature.

His fingers and thumbs were almost human too; they always say that a lot of what makes a human depends on how our thumbs and fingers are made, how having a relatively long thumb—and a fully opposable thumb—makes it possible for humans to hold things better, do things with more dexterity and precision. I would look at Bonbon's hands and think, why is he here? Why are they keeping him here? He should be living without fences, without gates and locks—he should be free. Sometimes I would look at his face and be not so sure: the flat nose, the way his whole lower jaw thrust forward. The low forehead. But then his mouth would widen and the edges of it would go up and something magical would happen around his eyes and I would shiver with an overpowering feeling—*he is one of us. Why have they put him here? Why do they keep him in here?*

The longer I worked at the zoo the more I came to feel as if I didn't want to be part of the humans. It was the humans who ran the place and the humans who came to gawk at the animals. Other humans were the *they*. And Bonbon and me and Lucinda were the *we*. Of course I knew that the people who flocked to see Bonbon— who would stand three deep on the skywalk across the open area or behind the glass wall at the east of the enclosure—that they would be feeling a shiver themselves if they saw him laugh, if they saw how human his hands were, and his feet. But then they would focus on the loping walk, the low forehead—*that jaw, how strange it looks*, they would say. They would marvel at how close he was to them, and at the same time marvel at how alien he was. And they would want him to keep living with his father's people: they wanted him locked away.

You use a phrase like *locked away*, it makes it sound like nobody could see him. But everyone could see him—a lot of the time, anyway. And everyone wanted to see him. Yes, he had his private area, but a lot of the time you could see him in the open bonzee area, often just by himself, stretched out on one of the grassy knolls, resting, half asleep. And he would start to get hard. You could see his cock, hard and pulsing. *What is he thinking?* I would wonder. Or is it pure feeling? I remember feeling sort of disgusted with myself too. I guess I must have been seventeen or eighteen, old enough to be defiantly sexual when it came to what I thought and sometimes said about humans (some humans, anyway). But when I looked at him it was as if I felt guilty, as if I could hear my parents telling me not to look at things or do things *down there*—that was the expression they used.

But then another part of me would think *there's nothing to be disgusted about—it's all natural what's happening to him*. And that other part of me would sometimes also start to think that maybe what Lucinda had done wasn't so unimaginable after all. It had never seemed to me that it was something to get all judgemental about.

But I think I'd sort of thought about it like I would have thought about people having anal sex—OK, live and let live, but not something I could ever enjoy, or really *imagine* anyone finding enjoyable. All I could do was know as a fact that some humans did it, and some humans enjoyed it. But with Bonbon, seeing him like that, I suddenly felt I could imagine something of what Lucinda might have felt, that time with the bonzee who became Bonbon's father.

Bei, that was his name. I guess I should remember it—I don't know how many times Luce has told me the story by now. Every time she'd be, like, *I'm not ashamed at all of what I did, not one little bit.* I've heard her start to say the same thing to the other keepers too, but mostly they don't let her finish; they find some excuse to be busy with something else. They get grossed out, I guess, even people who work with animals can get grossed out by what's animal in us.

But I would always listen, even if I was hearing it for the fiftieth time. And I'd be interested. And I wouldn't get grossed out. I felt like I was starting to become close to them—Luce and Bonbon both, but especially Bonbon—in a way that the other keepers never seemed to. Maybe part of it was that the other keepers were *too* interested in Bonbon. Like he was a spectacle, like they were the lucky ones who didn't have to pay to see him, who could gawk at him from up close rather than from way up on the skywalk or back there behind the fences and the glass walls. And before long I was letting myself daydream about how special I was, how I could offer something to Bonbon and to Luce that none of the other keepers were offering, that none of the other humans were offering. They were all gawkers at heart, sex gawkers or science gawkers or whatever, and none of them truly cared about Bonbon like I did, none of them truly understood him as I did, none of them could see him as I did for what he really was. I was such an adolescent. At night I would find my eyes filling with tears as I thought of him, and my heart would ache for little Bonbon in his small, strange place.

Did my heart ache for Luce too? Sometimes. Sometimes not.

Sometimes she would smile at me and tell me stories for the longest time, but sometimes she would swear at me too, and tell me I should leave the two of them to themselves, her and Bonbon. I remember one day when I was just about to go off shift and I had given Bonbon a little hug when he had come in from the bonzee area. Jamie had been picking on him a little bit, and I had wanted him to know that he was loved, that he—well, I don't need to go on about it. Did I actually say anything with the word *love* in it? I can't remember, maybe I did. Suddenly I felt Luce's arm on my shoulder, and she turned my body so that I was facing her. She waited a second, and then she pushed me backwards, straight backwards. Hard, so that I almost fell.

"He's not effing yours to love, is he?"

"It's not like that," I managed to stammer out, though I'm sure I didn't quite know exactly what "that" would be. "I'm on your side," I added.

"You'll just confuse him. He has his mother, and he has some other kids to play with, and that's all he needs at his age. Except to get out of here, and that's not going to happen. You can't make it happen. No one can effing make it happen." Maybe it was at that moment that some part of me became absolutely determined to find a way to get him out.

Long before Luce and I had finished our little spat about Bonbon that day, the boy himself was gone. He had disappeared into his private area—his truly private area, the small room where he could close the door and not even Luce could join him. He was starting to grow up, and I'm not sure she knew quite how to deal with that. We could hear him rummaging around and then a moment later we could hear music swelling up from behind the door. It was religious music that one of the other keepers had introduced him to. He loved that music—and he knew that his mother hated it. *For unto us a child is born, unto us a son is given* ... Of course he couldn't under-stand any of the words—that's what we all thought then.

For a second Lucinda glared at the door, and then she turned back to me. Suddenly she wasn't glaring; she just looked sad and tired. The next day she was, like, *You don't know how sorry I am*, and I was still in my teens, so I guess I didn't understand everything. I was left with hurt and love that I didn't know what to do with. But I didn't want to leave Bonbon, and I didn't want to leave Lucinda either.

All this was before the incident that changed everything. I guess I had better tell you about my part in all of that.

10.

Robert B. Goddard

[Following are excerpts from the transcript of the interview granted to Cheryl Nash of *Now Magazine* by Robert B. Goddard, Director of Research and Development at the Sunderland Animal Research Centre, in July, 2014—almost a year to the day after the incident that indirectly brought Bonbon's time at Sunderland to an end. In the years since his 2009 interview with the *Observer*'s Ramirez, Goddard had become known for granting interviews only very sparingly.]

Cheryl Nash: More than one person who was involved with the Sunderland facility during your time as director there has referred to you as Dr. God.

Robert B. Godard: I'm aware that a great many people have made jokes of that sort out of my name, yes.

C.N.: But you must also be aware that some of the criticisms have been far from joking—that you've been accused of playing God.

R.B.G.: I am indeed aware of it. My standard response is this: I didn't play at being God—I worked hard at it. Look, in every organization there has to be someone who accepts final responsibility—who plays the role of God, if people want to insist on putting it that way—within that organization. There has to be someone who accepts final responsibility. At Sunderland, while

I was Director, the buck truly did stop at my desk. I consulted people at every level and in every department. But at the end of the day …

C.N.: You were …

R.B.G.: I made the final decisions. I didn't get them all right—what happened with those chimps and Bobo is evidence enough of that. Of course I didn't have foreknowledge; without that, it's pretty hard to play the part of God, no matter how hard you work at it.

C.N.: Let me ask about that well-known incident you refer to—the incident last year that led to Bonbon being transferred out of your care, and to another facility. You've been criticized for the design of the enclosures for the great apes at the Sunderland facility. You …

R.B.G.: This is what I mean about not having foreknowledge. No one has foreknowledge—but everyone has hindsight. If you look back you'll find that almost no one criticized the design before that incident. No one said *the river's too shallow, the river's not wide enough to separate chimps and bonobos, chimps, and bonzees.*

C.N.: With respect, sir, I've read carefully through the interview you gave to the *Observer*. And in that …

R.B.G.: That was the sole exception. A single interviewer who was clearly antagonistic, who was clearly … But yes; that Ramirez woman—and she alone—raised the question of the width and depth of the river. None of the experts raised any sort of red flag.

C.N.: But surely you *were* criticized at the time for the way in which your design provided for interaction between lowland and savannah chimps?

R.B.G.: There was some criticism, yes—but a good deal of praise as well for what was described as a highly innovative approach.

C.N.: Can you fill in background here, for those unfamiliar with it?

R.B.G.: Of course. I had better begin by paying tribute to the work of Jill Pruetz of Iowa State. Everyone had always focused on chimpanzees living in the Congo—in a tropical rain forest. She broke new ground, studying the savannah chimps in Senegal—who live in a climate that's far, far drier than the Congo. That changes everything. They need to drink far more than do forest chimps (who get a great deal of the water they need through eating the fruit that is so abundant in the rain forest). The savannah chimps have to spend more time searching for food—but they can't wander too far looking for it, because they need always to be near a source of fresh water. Savannah chimps are also far less violent than forest chimps. So we wanted to ask how living in proximity to each other might affect the behaviour patterns of the two varieties of chimp. Might social interaction with the relatively peaceful savannah chimps lead to more peaceful behaviour on the part of forest chimps?

C.N.: Or might the influence work the other way?

R.B.G.: There was also that possibility—and it was possible too that there would be no effect either way. I will be the first to admit that no breakthroughs have occurred. But neither have there been significant harms. If you look at all the factors in what is inevitably a complex ...

C.N.: Let me steer us back to the interactions between bonzees and chimps. Surely in that case ...

R.B.G.: In that case not everything went well—and we all regret that deeply. But in defense of myself and my design team, I think it's fair to point out that, in that case, our intent was not to improve upon the natural world—it was simply to replicate it as closely as possible. In the wild, chimps and gorillas are just across the river from bonzees and bonobos; the same is true of the Sunderland design. Our mistake was not in deviating too far from the model of nature; it was in not imitating it closely enough.

C.N.: Different people think of different things when they hear the word *nature*. Can you comment on that in the context of the "natural" world as you try to replicate it in a zoo?

R.B.G.: Part of a zoo's mission is to educate people—not just about all the cute things that animals do, but about everything they do. Chimpanzee behaviour can sometimes be aggressive and violent. Their *natural* behaviour, I mean—as we've touched on, they are every bit as violent in the wild. If anything, more so. Some zoos apologize to visitors if they witness behaviour by chimpanzees or other animals that's disturbing; "we're sorry you had to be exposed to this," they say, whenever something nasty happens. Here at Sunderland we don't take that approach; we may look at possible ways of reducing the violence through logistical measures, but we do not apologize for allowing humans to see that such things sometimes occur. If you come to see how animals behave towards each other, you had better be prepared to see just that. We may find means of altering the environment in which great ape interactions occur so as to reduce violence somewhat. But we can't give chimps a moral education as they grow up, of the sort we give our own children—teach them not to kill each other, not to be cruel, any of that sort of thing.

C.N.: All right. Let me ask a question that I don't think people usually do ask. Why *can't* we try to give chimpanzees a moral education? If we can devote all this time to research with Bonbon—with Bobo, as you call him—and with what he's able to learn and not able to learn, why not do the same with chimpanzees? Why not try to teach them right and wrong?

R.B.G.: I guess the short answer is that in all probability their instincts would override any such "training." Almost any scientist will tell you it would be futile to try—though I suppose I should add that, as with so many things, we can't know with 100% certainty.

C.N.: There are some things even God can't know with 100% certainty?

R.B.G.: [smiling] No comment.

C.N.: Before we end, I want to return to the subject of Lucinda Gerson and her son. The Sunderland facility has always stood in the way of that quest to free him—to allow him to ...

R.B.G.: Not the Sunderland facility—the Canadian government and the Canadian courts have stood in the way. For myself, I think you can make the case either way—certainly I've heard a good many persuasive people arguing that he and his mother should have the right to give up the protection afforded by an animal research facility, and try out a life without those protections in America. I wouldn't want to argue against giving them that right. But nor would I express any confidence that it would turn out well.

S.N.: The way you phrase it suggests that you don't think he would be physically safe if he were free. That you think in America he would …

R.B.G.: I wouldn't want to speculate as to the specifics of what he might or might not do—or what others might or might not do to him. But let's think just for a moment of the history. That one word—*America*—carries so much within it. All those people crossing the water, in search of a new life, a new world. Nowadays we can't help but be reminded of all the people they pushed aside. We're told that the same people who yearned for freedom themselves as they crossed the ocean proved quite capable of denying others their freedom—even of killing them.

Think of slavery; as many have said, it is America's original sin. And think of the history of how we have treated other animals: the buffalo, the animals in our factory farms. You know I'm American myself; like Bonbon's mother, I hold dual citizenship. And I have as many criticisms of Canada as I do of America. So when I think of the Gersons, I have no nationalistic axe to grind. But let me put it this way: if you were only half human, would you choose to take your chances with "freedom" in a nation such as America has so often proved itself to be?

I am American enough to think that it might be worth taking exactly that chance; I do not ask it as a rhetorical question. But nor do I know the answer.

C.N.: You allude to American's history of pushing others aside. Of enslaving others, of killing others. But it's really American *white* people's history of doing that, isn't it?

R.B.G.: Disproportionately, yes. No question. But I'm afraid it's a world-wide pattern and it's a pattern of whoever has the most power tends to do the most damage. For the past several hundred years white people have had a hugely disproportionate share of the world's power. And of course white people oppress white people as well as people with other skin colours; look at the Holocaust in Europe, look at the Inquisition. But it's not as if white people have a monopoly on the oppression gene. Look at how the Japanese have treated the Chinese, at how the Chinese have treated the Uyghurs, at how the Burmese have treated their Rohingyan minority, at how the Tlingit enslaved people even into the twentieth century. You can find chattel slavery today in Mauritania or the Sudan—black people enslaving black people. And so often when humans are oppressing other humans they've made it an issue of animality. When the English were starving the Irish, the Irish said they were being *treated no better than animals*, and many of the English said the Irish were indeed *no better than animals*. It's been the same language with Christians and Jews, with Hindus and Muslims, with Protestants and Catholics, with Hutu and Tutsi, with oppression the world over.

C.N.: And nobody stops to say, *Hold on here—we're all animals?*

R.B.G.: Far too few people stop to say that, yes. To say that everyone deserves to be treated well, that no one deserves to be oppressed.

C.N.: So all humans should be treated equally. But surely not all cats and dogs and cows and pigs and buffalo have to be treated just like all humans?

R.B.G.: A dog or a cat or a cow or a buffalo wouldn't *want* to be treated like a human. Our obligation is not to treat other animals as we would other humans, but to treat other animals well. And to ask ourselves how other animals would want to be treated. Can we really pretend that a bird *wants* to spend her life crammed in a shed with 10,000 other birds, or that a cow *wants* to spend her life in a shed and have her babies taken away from her so that humans can drink her milk?

C.N.: What did Bonbon ever want? What does he want now, do you think?

R.B.G.: I don't think I have enough time in this interview to even try to answer that. And I'm not sure that I could.

11.

Bonbon Gerson

[Following is a continuation of the account attributed to
Bonbon Gerson.]

When I was eight or nine, I was often wake in the very early, and I
was gone down by to river, by my own. By the time came full light,
often were the chimps come to river's other side. Always were more
of them than was of me. Some of times were some few other bonzees
on the us side the river, was not just me only. But was always more
chimps the other side.

Those years were two troops of chimps, me think. Maybe
three—you could Google it up. In all there was must been close to
thirty of them, infants not counting.

On this one morning, one of the infants was with his mother,
other side the stream from me. She was grooming the little one, and
playing it. You can read again and once again where they say bonobos likes to play, bonzees likes to play, but chimps likes to fight.
Yes true, but not the always. Chimps play too, and play time was
this time mother and child doing. I was not much pay them the
attention; I was not much pay the attention to any other this time,
any other than play the light on the water, play the clouds in the sky.

Those years Lucy was always to say me how much longing she
was for the free. Escape to America, escape to any place that would
take us, but specially to America; was I not also want the free?

Yes, and not so much yes. Long time later was come that longing
—not in the now. Free is not the same for children. If a world is safe

and happy with play, a child knows free without they know any the word for *free*.

Light filled slow the air by the river. All round was earth still empty of humans. Workers were maybe start soon, but talkers and gawkers on the walkways, on the skywalk—they all were far in the later, not the right-here-now. One mother chimp and infant were at the play; three or four male chimps and couple other female were lounge round, little the ways upstream. Little the ways more far was other cluster of chimps. Everything was seem harmless. The largest male was stretch and then roll and then was start to go his way towards mother and child. His sound was some threaten, but nothing not usual for that kind—for the alpha chimp.

He stopped some few feet way from her. He was showed her his teeth two three times. Now I could be able to see was the one was called Carville; some of the keepers was always talking *Carville this, Carville that*. Now Carville his threatening tone was more and more.[4]

Then sudden he sprang, was charging towards her. She yelped, jump back; he was stop inches away only. Now she clung tight to her little one, and inch inched further little further from the large

---

4. [Editor's note] Readers are advised that the next few pages are taken up with Bonbon's description of a brutally violent incident on the other side of the river. Like Lucinda's earlier description of her encounter with Bei, this is a part of the narrative that readers may find disturbing. I am aware that some have criticized the description here as gratuitously violent; indeed, it has been suggested that Bonbon's depiction of this violence is far more deserving of being classified as "obscene" or even as "pornographic" than are passages such as Bonbon's famously frank descriptions of bonzee sexual activity at Sunderland Animal Research Centre or Lucinda's description of her encounter with Bei. Others have argued that categorizations of Bonbon's account as "obscene" are misplaced—that they say more about the human mind than they do about anything that occurred that day by the river. Again, I leave it to those readers who wish to do so to judge for themselves; those who would, for understandable reasons, prefer to skip past the disturbing material may resume the narrative at the beginning of the next section (narrated by Ashley Rouleau); the outcome of the violence is at that point made plain.

male. Again he was jerk forward; again she was inch inch away. Then again, and now he was start poke her, was start jab her, again, again. Again she backed away, but she was not turn and run.

Now he picked up a branch from the rocks. He snap snapped it in two and began to work work at it with his teeth. In no time he had it sharp to a point, and again he moved close close the mother and child. Now he was jab at the mother with point the stick, was jab at her again, again, again.

I was froze, watching. Upstream was other chimps all froze, watching. One more jab, hard, and now the mother's fur was start glisten where he was jab at her.

No! I was scream in Bonzee, *No!*, and I was quick start, splashing my ways through the shallows, I was shout again and again *No!*, *No!*, *No!*, all the whole time.

For moment Carville turned and was looking me—and then was the mother did try and run. In moment he was on her; he was more fast, and much more the strong. Rough he pushed her down. And then he found his stick again and steady steady steady he was start new time his jab at her—at her chest, at her arms, at her legs. Desperately she tight gripped her child, and now he was begin to poke at the infant. A jab in the mother, a jab in the infant, on on on.

I was on other side the river now, their side the river, away maybe fifteen steps the three of them. I tried to scream again, *No!*, but was weak my sounds only, was muffle. Sudden I was full fear. I was half the size only of the big Carville. I was stop; I could not be able go forward, I could not be able turn back, I could not be able look away. Now the screams of the infant was drown all the mother screams, was drown all the big male grunt gurgles. Carville poked again at the child, and then his other arm shot out, he cuffed the mother on the head. Then he cuffed the baby, same way; then he cuffed the mother again, and again. Long, long wail she sounded, wail of long sorrow, then she was let go her child, and it was fell to the rocks; I was hear a little cracking sound as little one's head hit. But still the male was not done. Now he was use stick again, poking harder into little one.

I was found my voice; this time was my scream louder than the ever. I was charge, my arms waving, and I made myself large. I remember huge face he was turn towards me, all his angry, and I remember how was felt when I was smash my knuckle 'gainst his face. Then my hand went sideways and I could see the other males were come towards me, could see his arm, his fist, they were move more fast than I could really see, right towards my face straight. Then time stopped.

I was must been a moment black out. I was stagger, and was stumble, and was fell. But Carville left me lone once he was see I was still. It was the small one he was want. He prodded, he poked it, he poked at it again. Lazy then he swiped at it. And then on backswing, as his arm brushed 'gainst child's fur, he opened his hand and wrapped it round the tiny waist. My eyes I was keep almost closed. He lifted the little one way up in air that way, and he was twirl it round and round, as if was he play some game, fast fast and always it screaming—not an *it*, I could be able see, it was baby girl. He was whirl her round two, three more of the times, each time the higher, the higher, and then his arm all far was stretch out, and was swing sharp down. The little head smashed, was broke on the rocks.

Carville grunt shrieked, and the mother her wails were rose high and high, as if was the sky shaking. The other males they were gather round, were press in close. One was bent down to pick up the body, and was hold it tight, pulling at one the little arms. He was look at the big male and was hold out the little body towards him. Carville pulled hard on the same arm and then he twisted— twisted as the keepers twist wrench when lock stuck, twisted until arm tore all away from shoulder, sprang free. Then was the blood all over. Then Carville he was hold out the little body, and the other males were begin grab at it, pull on it. Soon held bloody pieces each one. Following what Carville do, other males were begin rip at the pieces with teeth, stuff them into mouths, spit out fur, was swallow all rest.

I was not be able to move. I was not be able to make any sound. I stayed still, stayed still, stayed still, no sound—and then was I feel sound, was rise in the throat of me. Nothing could be able to stop it—a scratch-catch wrench sound deep in throat, and I was feel tight in belly, tight in chest. I saw them turn, all of them. And then Carville, he was start towards me.

***

Ashley Rouleau

[Following is a continuation of the account by Ashley Rouleau of her involvement with Lucinda and Bonbon Gerson.]

At night there's almost no one there except the animals. The non-human animals, I mean. That's how it is in zoos, almost always. But the morning shifts start early—5:00 or 5:30 or 6:00—and you can volunteer for those if you want. I always wanted.

What I didn't want was to sit around the breakfast table hearing my mum and dad, up at 6:00 when they couldn't sleep and snapping at each other, and snapping some more, and then making some sort of temporary peace that would involve putting all the blame for everything on neither of them having had enough coffee. No more than I would have wanted the night before to hear them snapping at each other until late and then making some temporary peace, *we've probably had too much to drink*, they would always say to each other. So I'd go to bed crazy early, and a lot of mornings I'd volunteer to be at the zoo from 5:00 to 7:30, or 5:30 to 8:00—I could do that and still be at school by nine.

I was lucky in one way about my parents—they never tried to

stop me from volunteering, even when it meant going out into the big city long before it was light, or coming back alone long after it was dark. "I'm OK with my daughter going out at 5:00 in the morning to someplace where she can do some good in the world," my dad would say. "Rather that than have her stay out till 1:00 in the morning at some place where there's never going to be anything but trouble."

Mostly it would still be dark when my shift started, but there was always plenty of work to be done. I always liked to start with Bonbon; like a lot of other kids, I was fascinated with the idea of a boy who was half human, half bonzee. But how many others got to clean out his private area and put out fresh fruit for him to eat?

Anyway, the summer morning when everything blew apart I arrived at maybe 5:30. Usually Bonbon would be in his private area at that hour but on this morning he wasn't there, and he wasn't with the other bonzees either. They were mostly awake and huddled together; they looked strangely anxious, most of them. Jasper and Ever both looked scared—really scared. Then I started to hear the noises. At first I thought they were coming from nearby—from the bonzee and bonobo side of the river. But when I started walking through the trees towards the water, the sounds didn't seem to be getting any closer. I decided to head to the other side. I wasn't about to get wet crossing the ford, so I made my way to the footbridge over the river. There were tall gates on either side to prevent the apes from using the bridge; humans had to lift and push and then pull at the latch in a way that the designers had proven it was impossible for any ape to accomplish—even Bonbon. (Two years later one of the bonobos figured out the right combination of lifts and pushes and pulls—but that's another story.)

As soon as I had crossed the bridge I could start to hear something of what was going on. Mostly it sounded like chimps, but I thought I could hear Bonbon too. I started towards the sounds, half running when it felt as if there were a path beneath my feet, slowing if I started to stumble on rocks or branches. I didn't have to go far; very soon the sounds began to grow much louder. I turned a corner and looked down towards the rocky edge of the river; there they were.

You couldn't see everything, but you could see enough. Already it was clear that the little one had been killed, the mother wounded. I screamed and screamed. I looked back towards the bridge, and I could see two of the other zoo workers crossing it; they must be just starting their shift. From there they wouldn't be able to see past the little bend in the river; they wouldn't be able to see Bonbon and the chimps. But they could see me, and they could certainly hear me. I screamed even louder, and I could see them pointing, shouting, moving, one of them pulling out his cell phone as he ran.

I was, like, *how long can this go on?* It felt like forever.

By the time they reached Bonbon he had a dislocated shoulder, three broken ribs, and several cuts and gashes.

Why do we always say how lucky someone has been?

∾ You can imagine how messed up Lucinda was—worried sick about Bonbon and his injuries, and endlessly angry that this could have been allowed to happen in what was supposed to be a "controlled environment"; *effing chimps* and *effing Dr. God* were about the mildest things she said.

I was pretty messed up myself, more than I wanted to admit. For weeks afterwards I found myself almost in tears whenever I was near Bonbon, but I somehow felt I had to hide all of that.

I was hiding something too when I talked to other people. Everyone wanted to know what had happened, of course—not just my friends, but people who hardly knew me. And the radio and television people too. But I didn't want to tell them anything. I didn't want to show more feeling for Bonbon than everyone else was feeling. And I didn't want to show any feeling against the chimps— I mean, the chimps as a group. (Carville, I hated with all my heart.)

At first when they all wanted to interview me I was, like, *no, I couldn't face that*, but then when they kept asking I started asking myself if there was anything I could do that might make a difference. I can still remember when I realized what I should do. I was standing looking out the back window at my parents' place. It was still the place where I lived too, but it so didn't feel like my place. From the kitchen behind me I could smell "the bird" that my mother was roasting for dinner. I looked out the French doors to the deck at the big lawn sloping gently downwards, and at the alleyway beyond; like just about always, there were people walking their dogs in the alleyway out back. It was evening, and a soft light still hung in the air. Suddenly I felt the birds and the dogs and Bonbon and Lucinda and all of us and all of the earth coming together in my mind.

I went upstairs and I wrote about what was important, in a way I'd never done before. Then I went over and over what I'd written. And then the next day I started phoning all the radio and television and news people who'd been leaving their numbers. I'll tell you just what I said—you can still find some of the clips online. I said it to a lot of people, almost always the same. They'd ask me how I felt about having witnessed this horrific attack, and I wouldn't answer directly, not at first. This is what I would tell them:

> Well, as anyone who does this sort of work probably knows, it's not unusual for a male chimpanzee to kill a baby chimp—any more than it's unusual for a male lion to kill a baby lion. If an adult male wants an adult female who already has a baby, he sometimes wants her to have no other babies but *his* baby. He will sometimes kill the baby she has now. And sometimes eat it. And sometimes there will be more than one adult male involved in the killing. Sometimes, for different reasons, female chimps will kill babies too—even, sometimes, their own babies. This happens in the wild, and it happens in zoos; you

might remember that, just a couple of years ago, a three-month-old chimp was mauled to death by an adult male at the Los Angeles Zoo. Everybody hears of this stuff and they're, like, *How horrific! How different those chimps are from humans!* But are we really any better? Think of how horrible humans can be. I'm not just thinking of Nazi Germany, the genocide in Rwanda, and all that. I'm thinking of anyone. Could any human be capable of killing and eating a small child? I can see your expression; it's, like, *humans would never do that.* And that's what I used to think too. But then I thought about it more and now I'm, like, humans wouldn't do that *unless* the small child was of another species, and we wanted to drink its mother's milk. Drink its milk, and maybe eat some cheese made from its milk. And maybe eat the child too—not rip it apart and chew on the raw flesh but have someone else do the cutting up, and someone else package the pieces of flesh. Then you could buy the package in a shop and take the pieces of flesh home, and cook them up nicely. *Veal*, you'd call it. You'd call "him," maybe I should say. And you'd do the same to the mother, of course, as soon as she stopped producing milk for you. *Hamburger meat*, you'd call her.

A bonzee or a bonobo would never do such a thing, any more than a bonzee or a bonobo would kill and eat a child. It's chimps and it's humans who kill babies. We do it to cows rather than to our own species: does that make it right? And what about what we do to birds? When we want them to produce an endless supply of eggs for us, we want the females, not the males. So we throw the little baby males into a hopper; more often than not they're alive when they go in. We use the hopper to grind the little ones up into fertilizer.

We pride ourselves on our reason; we can think
things through, we can make choices in ways most other
animals can't. And for sure we could choose not to kill
and eat other animals; in fact, we'd be a lot healthier if
we made that choice.

Of course we don't consciously choose to be like
Carville, the cruelest of the chimpanzees; it's just that
what we do has the same effect. But we don't want to
think about that. Mostly we want to avoid making any
decision that would force us to stop doing what we're
used to doing. So we make up excuses. We rationalize.

We tell ourselves that, because humans ate other
animals a million years ago, we should still be eating
meat today. Right—and I guess we should still be bashing
each other over the head with clubs today, just because
humans did that to each other a million years ago. We're
supposed to be able to make choices.

Or we tell ourselves that we care about the *whole*
world—not just humans and other animals but plants
and maybe even microorganisms too. And plants may
well have some form of consciousness—so we tell
ourselves that maybe it's no worse to eat animals than it
is to eat plants. But think that through: even if it were
true that plants were every bit as aware as birds and fish
and mammals, and every bit as able to feel pain when we
kill them—it would still be true that we should stop
eating meat. Because when we eat meat we're responsible
for killing not just the animals, but also *way* more plants
than we kill when we eat nothing but plants. The meat-
eaters like to imagine that meat just somehow appears on
their plates; they forget all the forests that have been cut
down to grow crops—not so those crops can be fed to
humans and give us nourishment directly, but so those

extra crops can be fed to the animals who are then fed to us. Even aside from all the cruelty involved, it's the most inefficient way imaginable to feed ourselves ...

And on I would go. Usually people would cut in before I'd finished, *Ashley,* they'd say, *what I want to ask about is Bonbon and these chimps; can you tell me ...?* and I'd tell them a little more about what had happened by the river, but pretty soon I'd find a way to go back to my rant and try to finish it.

I guess you can figure out when it was that I went vegan! I sort of had to, didn't I? After sounding off like that in public, I mean. Maybe I didn't persuade anyone else to do the same with my stupid little speech. But I'm, like, sometimes you have to say what you think's important. At least I did that much. I'd sound off about carnivores, and I'd tell them I was vegan. And you know what people would say? A lot of people would say they didn't get it, a black person being vegan. That going vegan was for rich white people—weird rich white people. I'd have to tell them that there's a lot of weird black people out there too. Nowadays you've got Cory Booker spreading the word, you've got Serena Williams spreading the word, you've got people like Pinky Cole spreading the word—and there's a higher percentage of black people going vegan in North America than there are white people. Look it up! Maybe back then there weren't quite so many, but there were still people everywhere who'd decided they didn't want to eat other animals. Lots of people—rich and poor, black and white, east and west, north and south—I could go on a long time. I *did* go on a long time, and maybe I got a few people ticked off with me.

Anyway, that was the way I found of retreating, of not talking about what had happened, no matter how many times I'd be thinking of it, no matter how often I'd been lying awake thinking of it.

And Bonbon? He just retreated to his private area. Not to the area that was private from the bonzees but open anytime to the keepers or to Lucinda—to the little room that it had been agreed would be really private, where he could really be alone, like a human.

He was so not there. He would hide away for a long, long time, often until the keepers or Lucinda insisted that he had to come out, that he had to eat, that he had to ... But when he did come out, he wouldn't spend much time at all with the keepers or with Luce; he'd go right out to the bonzees, and try to get Ever and Only to play, play in ways that they hadn't played together since they'd been little. It was lovely, sort of, but it was very sad. And all of it had to end with the move to Alberta.

12.

Bonbon Gerson

The humans they always look the human above the other. They say I be *only half human*. They are not see other the half. I am half bonzee too. *Only half bonzee* too. If I can be able to say truth, I can be able to say that, even from the early age, there was some times I was bored by other bonzees. Bored by Ever and Only even. Example: bored by how much the day they was spend with they play.

You see how I say? Most times I say *they* and *them*, not *we* and *us*. For bonzees, and for humans too—I say *they* and *them*. I am a half half, but everyone is a *they* to me, a *them* to me.

Could ever half me be an *us* with humans and half me be an *us* with bonzees? That is only a dream; can dream come to be? They say in New Orleans you can be able be anything half half, or all the ways or any the in-betweens. Lucy was say me that, time and time over. Maybe also in the Mexico some of the times—some of the places any sort of human half half can be whole, so they say, some peoples. Can be part of an *us*.

Fact, also were some few times with Ever and Only when I was feel three of us were one *us*, and when I was feel all me in the one *us*. Example, was the time I was want to build platform. A floor, high in branches. Nice and high, so us bonzees could be able look down on the humans who was walk their gawker skyway—us to be able look down them, not them be able look down us! And so us bonzees could be able sit or lie right together, could be able just relax, no hold-on grip-tight the branch. Could be able look out and look down, and think, and say things one the other. Ever and Only and me we had eight-nine big sticks tied one the other. Then all-the-all we tied it to big branches at corners, at ends. Need was twenty sticks that length for proper sky floor, twenty or maybe the twenty-two, twenty-four. I was work it all out in the before. We used coil of cord we was found by the keep-equipment huts, in behind. None the jobs too hard, not too hard build a sky floor for real. But Betty was not like it, and Dr. God was not like it when the keepers said him what we had happened. Sticks was all untied, sky floor was all took down.

Then was the time we started the fire. *A* fire. Just little one, really. Again too, that was Ever and Only and me. Three us was cold; that was all. And there was a lighter. Some gawker was thrown it down from the gawker skywalk high—was thrown, not was dropped, I was see everything. I was hear him too. *Let's see if you're smart enough to start something with this! Stupid apes!* He was keep laughing, but you could hear his laughs they were not the happy laughs. Maybe they were the drunk laughs; that time still I was not know all the human sounds. (The drunk-laugh sounds and the *can't you take a joke?*, the *you know I'd help you if I could*, the *I'm sorry–but-I'm-not-sorry*, all those sounds and the *don't take this the wrong way but ...*, all the human sounds I am knowing them now.)

So the lighter we kept it, and one day the three of us we were cold. Still I can strong remember how much was the cold. Keepers were always say us *everything it is climate controlled*. Fact, most the time it was too much cold.

So we were played the lighter until jump spark, little flames. Just a small fire only, little flames off in little clearing where was not so much easy for keepers to see us. Only had her trouble with the lighter once once, but then it was bright with the jump spark under dry leaves and I pushed down on it, and we held together. So then we were warm; little fire was keep us nice and warm.

Was soon they saw the smoke, and they were all come, everything put out. They scolded us more for that thing than any the other things ever else we did. One of them he sound the curious, he said maybe we were clever to make start fire, be warm, but other two laughed him for his thinks—*not trying to stay warm, just fooling around*, they said him. They were not the best clever their selves, those two keepers.

13

Ashley Rouleau

Even before the attack, my parents had started to have second thoughts about me volunteering so much at the zoo. I guess I better say something more about the two of them. They weren't, like, bad people. And they aren't now. But I think what they've always wanted more than anything is to fit in—to fit in in the parts of old Toronto where no one would want to admit they were *rich*, exactly, but no one would have wanted to deny that they were *comfortable*; *comfortable* or *well-off*, those were the terms people used. And just about no one ever described themselves as black or brown, because just about no one *was* black or brown. So of course the other kids would always notice me for my skin colour whenever I started in a new class at school or a new group at summer camp or whatever. But their parents had taught them not to gawk; mostly they'd even like to be able to say they had a black friend. And some of them really *did* get to be friends, I don't just mean Jenny. I'm sure I had a lot less trouble fitting in than my parents must have had. And I'm sure that if I'd lived in certain parts of Chicago or Detroit or even certain parts of Toronto there would have been people who'd be, like, *she's an Oreo*—but I didn't live in those parts. It's not something I'm proud of or anything, but that's how it was when I was growing up. But I was starting to realize that in a lot of ways I wasn't like my parents. That in a lot of ways I just didn't care about fitting in—or at least, I cared about other things a whole lot more. Anyway, we started to have a lot of disagreements. Sometimes there was shouting. They said they were worried about what marks I would graduate with, they said they wanted me to stop keeping such crazy hours—and to stop working so much with Bonbon.

That wasn't all. They'd never wanted me to straighten my hair or anything, but now they wanted me to be shaving my legs and my armpits *like any normal girl*, that's how they put it. And they wanted me to be dating. They wanted me to go out with Jeff 1 or Jeff 2 —some guy, basically. I was, like, *does it really matter which one?* What would they have said if I'd told them I was going out with Jenny already? I don't mean going out to the movies with just her, when my parents thought I was with a bunch of people. I mean everything. I used to tell Mom and Dad I'd been out somewhere with a half dozen people, I'd reel off the names for them, people in my class that I never had anything to do with. When really I'd been at Jenny's place, in her bed; her parents had been out, like they always seemed to be, and you can go ahead and guess at everything we did to each other. With each other. Sex is amazing.

OK, so with Jenny it was more curiosity than love. Or even need. We were the two girls with hair, and we were finding out what stuff we had in in common. It never got serious.

Maybe I wasn't ever going to *need* anyone like that. But how was I going to really find out about anything or anyone if I was living with my parents? I was seventeen, almost eighteen. They actually couldn't stop me.

* * *

Bonbon Gerson

Ash was the only who real eyes; she knew I could be able hear the meaning what humans said. The only one, I was sure it. She was always speak me very slowly, and she was look me straight. Sometimes she was say me straight out. Example,

> You can understand me, Bonbon. I know you can. And
> you want to talk to me—I know you do. You can do that

if we are very, very careful. But if you let yourself talk to them, they won't let you stop. I think you know how it will be. They'll keep you talking all the time, they'll keep you in the Research Centre all the time, they'll never stop taking you to the lab. It will be like how it was when you were little—only more so.

That was the kind thing she would say me. Her work was zoo but in her heart she was start to think of all the zoos, they should be over.

If I had been think better more, I could been more soon learning the words, more soon saying the words better—as close as was could to the sounds, as close as what could to how whole humans make sounds. Then I could have talked everyone. Then I could have been let live among whole humans, just like any other human maybe.

But for the long time I was only half want to live free as all human. How could I be want to live all human if Ever and Only and Jasper and Phil was not live free? Some of the times I could be able hear some the gawkers on the high skywalk, *He should be free, he shouldn't be stuck in a zoo.* And I would want say *Me and every other should be free—not me only.*

I could be able hear other the gawkers too, the ones what yell me *go ape!* and *monkey see, monkey do!* Once twice only I was throw rocks at gawkers, never hit one. Then the keepers, they were take all the rocks out the area.

* * *

Ashley Rouleau

What if I'd looked at the whole language thing the other way round? If I'd pushed Bonbon to look at it the other way round? Pushed him *not* to think of how they would ruin his life, short-term, if they knew he had language. Pushed him to think beyond that. Of course they would have done more and more experiments, and they would have wanted more and more—it would have been hard for him. But what power it might have given him! Had Goddard and the others really thought through what would happen if they'd succeeded? If ever they had announced that Bonbon had acquired language, they would have had to let the media in. And then Bonbon would have had a platform to plead his case, again and again and again, to reporters and interviewers from around the world. Surely, when they saw him speak, everyone everywhere would have said *Free him!* And that would have been that.

Or would it? Like, how can you know how humans will react to the unknown? Maybe most people would never see it that way—never *feel* it that way. Maybe they'd always just see a hybrid who couldn't talk properly. Who made the words sound different, who often put the words in the wrong places. To a lot of people, maybe he'd seem just as strange and dangerous as before. Maybe even *more* strange and dangerous. Like, there's been all those times when humans have seen other humans as less than human—it's been all over. And, for sure, America hasn't been any shining light. But for Bonbon? Well, an American court had decided that a hybrid was a person, that should be treated as a human. And a court on this side of the border had decided the other way. So that made it simple. All Luce and I had to do was get Bonbon into America.

That was "all we had to do." Like, *all we have to do is find a billion dollars*, or *all we have to do is grow wings*. But you never know. Maybe when they moved Bonbon to Clearwater, he could grow wings.

* * *

Bonbon Gerson

I was need to learn all the *free*s. Example, I was learn the *free* you can see on the screen—*buy one, get one free, free with the purchase* *of the large size, the extra large size,* all that *free*. And I was learn the get-out-of-jail *free*; that was from the screen too. And then every the often they was talk *land of the free* and *free country* all over the screen for the weeks and the months. They were not meaning *free, no charge, not have to pay,* were they *do anything you want, et cetera et cetera*? I was not knowing—was it a good free?

If I was free, was I be me?

Lucy kept talking it, Ashley kept talking it, everyone kept talking it. We were to move to the far away. Not *far away* like it was far to get other side the river to where chimps are. Far away like the far aways you see on the screen. Ash was show me pictures. Alberta. Clearwater was what they called the city but the river was the Coldwater. And it was the Coldwater Zoo.

Ash and Lucy tried warn me what would be like to fly; Ash seemed like knowing all everything the travel. Ash and Lucy—were they able be know what is like where they hold the cargo? Lucy said her angry words:

> They can talk all they want about their "special
> arrangements" and how they always "transport animals
> from one facility to another with a minimum of
> discomfort." What they mean is it's dark and cold and
> nasty and the only reason you won't be screaming is that
> they'll pump you full of drugs. It's a cargo hold, and
> you'll be part of the fucking cargo, excuse my French.
> The only good thing is, they'll get you there—and I'll be
> waiting for you at the other end.

Lucy was hug me and Ash was hug me. Ash would be there other place, and Lucy would be there other place, but all the other bonzees were to stay just as always. I was had to tell Ever and Only and Phil and every the others, the keepers they were send me away.

How long would be time? For ever? For all ever?

Ever and Only and Phil were not knowing *for ever*, what it means, and I was only know by hear. Ash was say me that no one knows *for ever* really, not even whole humans.

Ash was say me I would see her again the new place. Coldwater. And I would see Lucy again the new place.

The hold-cargo travel was be fill the long hours. I was hate the tear-away. Bye Only, bye Ever, and I was hate the crate they were force me inside.

And I was hate the dark and the smell and the fear sounds, other the animals emptying and crying out, like all us scared animals do, human animals too.

* * *

Ashley Rouleau

So I told my parents, *like, you can't actually stop me.*

I had my savings, it wasn't a lot but it was enough to get me to Alberta. It wasn't like I was still a kid who needed her toys and teddy bears; I could fit everything I needed in my backpack. With a few clothes and the lucky ring my granny had given me, I could go anywhere.

Except they wouldn't let me leave my canoe in the yard. I think they thought they could use that to make me give in—to make me stay with them for another year, or two years, or forever. I said I'd sell the canoe or give it away, I didn't care.

Of course I cared. I never had any better time in my whole life than I'd had at Tapawingo. I learned to believe that canoeing was the best thing in the world—next to animals and kids, I mean! And I learned to take care of eight kids. Which is actually a lot harder than two parents taking care of one of me—one of me who doesn't need taking care of anymore anyway. I knew I wouldn't be a camp counsellor the whole rest of my life, but I still wanted to be able to ride the waves and float down rivers. Forever.

So I had bought a canoe. My parents kept saying it was impractical to spend all the money I'd earned on something I would grow out of.

But it was aluminum; I knew it would last a lifetime. And I wanted it.

Could you canoe in Alberta? Everybody knows Alberta is all mountains and prairie and badlands; no one mentions any lakes, except little mountain lakes that don't go anywhere. But I Googled it and I found out about the rivers, and that you could run rapids if you wanted, or find a river cut into the prairie that would just pull you along as far as you felt like going, and when you stopped you could climb the high banks of the river and climb up the valleys that run into the river—coulees, they call them—and look out over the prairie that goes on forever.

I thought that maybe, if we could ever free Bonbon, I could take him canoeing down a river like that. The Oldman, the Red Deer, the Coldwater; I learned the names and traced their curves on the map.

If we could? We had to. But first I had to get there.

* * *

Lucinda Gerson

Go figure! That was about all I could think. The keeper who Bonbon seemed to like so much—the girl, Ashley—wanted to move west so she could be with him. She came up to me and she told me more than I wanted to know about her life and her parents and how she wanted to get away—well, who doesn't want to get away when you're seventeen, or whatever she was? It didn't seem too weird to me, but who am I to talk about weird, ha ha. Anyway, the last thing I wanted was to be a jealous mother. Jealousy? I'd been there. You should have seen my father, you should have seen the whole bunch of guys I dated when I was seventeen or whatever. No, I'm kidding —you wouldn't want to spend any time with those losers.

So I was definitely not going to be effing jealous about it. Plus, I actually liked the kid. And maybe I liked the idea of putting her canoe on top of my old beater too. I didn't care if it got her canoe to where she wanted it, or if it pissed off her parents like she said it would; all I was thinking was that I could pack a lot of stuff inside that thing if I had it upside-down on top on my Pontiac. Rope it all in tight and tie it to the whatever-you-call-those-things-that-go-across-a-canoe, and then I wouldn't have to buy as much new stuff at the Sally Ann or the Value Village when I got to Clearwater—but I wouldn't need to rent me no one-way U-Haul trailer neither. Those things aren't cheap, I can tell you, I checked.

* * *

Ashley Rouleau

I sort of wished I could drive with her, all the way across the continent with my canoe on the top of her old Pontiac. But with that load and an old beater she'd pretty much have to take the easy route— cross the border at Detroit, travel west through the States, and then come back into Canada from Montana—and I couldn't cross the border without a passport. Mine had expired and I wasn't yet eighteen; there was no way my parents were going to sign for me to get a new one. So I was going to fly, Toronto to Clearwater. I would help Luce get the canoe onto her car, one day when I knew my parents would be out. I knew they wouldn't miss it, either, not for a long time; they never paid any attention to all the junk behind the garage.

I was going to go out to Alberta at the end of June; I wasn't so stupid that I was going to miss my year. And then I would register for my last year of high school out there in Alberta; Lucinda said I could stay with her for a few weeks until I got settled. That was the plan.

14.

Lucinda Gerson

Crossing America is no piece of cake, I can tell you that much.

Some of it was pretty funny, actually: Detroit was the place everything got screwed up.

Again. What are the odds? But hey, stuff happens, and it can be good stuff too. I once saw a baseball game on TV where a man in the bleachers caught two home run balls. Same guy. In *one game*. What's the odds of that?

Everything was fine to the border, there's nothing more boring in the whole world than that stretch of road. I should know, I've driven it enough times, did I tell you I grew up in Comber, right near the 401 there? Comber rhymes-with-*somber*-not-with-*bomber*, of course it isn't somber at all, it's no more serious than the next place, unless the next place is Yuk Yuk's, ha ha.

You ever notice how just about everyone anywhere thinks they have a great sense of humour? It's pretty funny.

'Course I didn't get out onto the highway until almost the end of the afternoon—when do you ever leave right when you thought you were going to? Specially not on moving day. The traffic crawled along like it always does. I should have stopped for the night in Windsor, that's what I should have done—it was past midnight by that time. But somehow it didn't feel like I'd really started unless I ended the day in America. So there I was at the border and it's almost one in the morning and they ask me all these questions about my stuff, I guess you had to expect that, here's this woman driving a beat-up station wagon filled with junk, and on top she's roped on a metal canoe upside down, with all these boxes and bags roped inside of it. So yeah, you had to expect they'd ask you a few questions.

"It belongs …," I began. "To a friend" was how I'd been going to finish the sentence, but I thought better of it. There's some things that the customs and immigration people, they don't need to know. "… just where it is," I finished my stupid sentence, and then I repeated it for good measure, "It belongs just where it is," as if I were daring them to make me take down the canoe and open all those bags and boxes for them. "It's all going back to Canada." I told the man, as if that made everything clear.

"So you don't want to take this old thing up all those hills north of Wawa?" he grinned. "I done that once in a VW minibus. Had to take every hill in second gear. Makes a lot more sense to go through the USA." He wasn't your usual sort of border guy. He had a lot of grey hair—I guess like you'd expect from someone who remembered those VW minibuses. He leaned over and looked up into the insides of the canoe. "What'll be your port of re-entry?"

"Re-entry? Mister, this ain't no goddam space mission." I thought I was being pretty funny.

He looked at me sharp. "Re-entry into Canada, ma'am."

"Wherever you get into Alberta. Somewheres in Montana. I can get a map," I says to him. But now a younger man comes forward from the back of the booth. He must have been on his computer, running my plates, or my passport, or both.

"I see you're pretty well known, Ms. Gerson." He turns to the other man. "You know that case of the hybrid, Andy? And his mother crossed the border to give birth but now it's in Canada? This is the woman right here." Then he turns to me again. "I take it you're not bringing your son with you on this trip. Or any animals." He gives me a bit of a leer, just so's to show he knows all about everything. Then the other one—Andy—gave him a hard look, like he thought the younger guy was overstepping.

"Believe me," I told them, "I'd love to bring him with me. You don't know how much I'd love to bring him with me. I'd do just about anything to get him into America."

Then the older one: "Well, I guess you got enough to worry about, ma'am, without our telling you to take this rig all apart at two in the morning. Welcome to America." And then he held out his hand for me to shake. "I hope you can bring your boy with you one day," he said. I think he meant it, I really do.

That might of been the nicest thing anybody in a uniform ever done for me. I didn't know what to think. And I guess I didn't think straight, same as it's been my whole damn life. So I took the right hand fork when I should of taken the left hand fork, and the right hand fork meant you had to exit into Detroit instead of blasting on down the freeway like I wanted to do.

I hadn't been in Detroit since Bonbon was born and I never knowed it too well anyways. Right now it was two in the morning and there was no goddammed sign saying how to get back onto the freeway once you'd gotten yourself off of it, and so I was driving round aimlessly for maybe half an hour, trying to figure out what was what and how I was going to get back onto the effing freeway when there weren't no streetlights working and there weren't no signs. And then a red light lit up on the dashboard and I went *Shit!* It was the oil light, why hadn't I checked the oil like I always do when I gas up? Those old Pontiacs really eat up the oil, I'm telling you. And *no*, to answer your question, I did not have a can of oil in the back like any sensible person would. So I'd screwed up, hadn't I?

You had to stop when the oil light went on, I knew that. Otherwise the cylinders would seize up and the whole goddam engine would blow. But right away? Couldn't you drive for a minute or two? For five minutes? Ten? I pulled over and tried to think.

There was nobody around. Nobody. Maybe that was how I wanted it. Suddenly I could make out two guys in hoodies walking down the sidewalk towards me. Big guys. I was a weird-looking woman with a ton of stuff in her car and a canoe on top of it. What are you going to do?

But sometimes you catch the home run ball. Sometimes you catch two of them.

"You look like you could use some help, lady," the taller one said. He actually called me *lady*. So I told them about crossing the border, and the wrong turn, and the oil light. I even told them I had a kid who was half human and half bonzee. I'm not sure they believed that part. But they knew a gas station that was open all night and they knew how I could get back onto the freeway at an entrance just beyond the gas station. They were even pretty sure you could drive an old Pontiac five minutes with the oil light on without the whole thing seizing up.

I tried to give them ten bucks as a thank you. The taller one said "Thanks lady, but we don't need no money for helping people," just as the shorter one said "Thanks, we can use it!" and took the bill.

I put her back in drive, and three and a half days later I was somewheres in Montana. Alberta next stop.

∾ I didn't take the freeways all the way. I took the 94 and the 90 mostly, but I stopped quite a bit and looked round. For no reason, really, except I knew it would be a week before they'd be allowing me to start seeing Bonbon at Coldwater. And also my legs'd start to cramp up a bit after I'd been driving six, seven hours. And also, how often was I going to get a chance to drive across America anyway? So I got off the freeway in Chicago and I saw all the skyscrapers, and I got off the freeway at Eau Claire in Wisconsin just because it seemed like a good place to get off the freeway, it means *clear water* in French, maybe you know that. And I crossed the Mississippi where that bridge fell in a while back and all those people died, and I got off at Fargo 'cause I still had far to go, didn't I?, it was a sleepy little place with the widest main street in the world and I remember the sun was on everything, all golden, and then I drove and drove and drove to the badlands and I spent the night in a little motel at a place called Wall, there was nothing there really except the motel, and I thought all those weird hills was as beautiful as anything I'd ever seen. And then I was into Montana and I stopped at the Little Big Horn, and I thought of all the land the white people had took from the Indians 'cept they say *Native Americans*, we say *First Nations* but down here they don't. Somewheres in Montana all the people you see start to be white. I noticed that for sure.

Driving, you get a lot of time to think. I kept coming back to that night in Detroit, and what I knew inside but I didn't want to know, that I'd been more scared because those two big men walking down the sidewalk late at night were black. I tried not to be, but I was. And I was sort of thinking I didn't much like that about myself.

It's not always the same, is it? I mean, it's easy not to think anything bad about someone like Ashley, you don't even have to try. It's different with all the stuff that's been put in your head about big young black guys in hoodies. It's a lot harder, right? When there's so much stuff out there that makes us white folks think, the moment we see a black guy, specially a young black guy, *he's probably as nasty as Udie.* Remember Trayvon Martin, who got shot and killed, just for being a young black guy in a hoodie? He hadn't done nothing wrong, he was just a regular kid, a nice kid. Maybe he wasn't Gandhi or Jesus or Nelson Mandela, maybe he wasn't no saint, but he sure wasn't no Udie—no Carville or Carlson neither. You still don't know who those people are, all that's coming, but I can tell you right now they're not so nice. Anyways, I know I would never of shot a kid like that. But would I of thought things I shouldn't think? I hate that it's true, but I probably would of.

But folks can change. Look at me, I've fucking changed. A few years back I would *not* have just sat there with those two guys coming towards me. I would have turned the engine on and gunned it out of there, what the hell if the engine blew up? And now? I might have been a little scared but I didn't run away, did I? Maybe I been getting better about other people. I mean, ever since I had a kid who was half human. Seriously. Maybe you should try it, ha ha.

15

Dr. Cyril Carlson

[Following is an excerpt from the transcript of a
National Observer interview with Dr. Cyril Carlson,
Director of Research and Development at the Coldwater
Animal Research Institute in Alberta.]

National Observer: After there'd been all that trouble in Sunderland, I understand that Coldwater was not the only institution to step forward and make it known that they would be willing to take Bonbon. Sunderland chose you: what's so special about Coldwater?

Cyril Carlson: There are a great many attractive features of the Coldwater Animal Research Institute—starting with the physical side of things, the location itself.

N.O.: Location, location, location, as they say in the real estate business.

C.C.: Exactly. I don't think there has been any serious discussion of CARI that has not made a point of mentioning that it is the most beautifully situated of any such facility in North America. There's just no doubt about that. On one side the land slopes down from the zoo and the research institute to the beautiful Coldwater River. It's a river fed by glacial streams; the minerals from those glaciers give the water the beautiful, emerald hue that people always comment on.

N.O.: And its freezing temperatures.

C.C.: Indeed. By the time it reaches us the Coldwater is seventy or eighty yards wide, with the water moving at five or six miles an hour. As anyone who has tried to paddle or to swim upstream can attest, that's a very powerful current—and it continues to flow powerfully all the way to the American border, and beyond.

It's on this sloping river valley—and, in part, on the prairie plateau above it—that both the Coldwater Zoo and the Coldwater Animal Research Institute are laid out. But it's not, if I may use the phrase, merely beautiful. The location provides for an extraordinary range of natural habitats—and a very great deal of space for our animals. The city was extremely generous in the amount of land it deeded to us a generation ago. In many ways we are able to mimic the sort of habitat great apes experience in the wild. And I should make clear that here at Coldwater we have a larger population of bonzees and bonobos than at any other facility in North America; there's no question of Bonbon becoming lonely.

I should also make clear, though, that we do not try to pretend that the Coldwater River is the Congo. Unlike some facilities, we keep our chimpanzee population apart from our bonobo and our bonzee populations, and we keep the gorillas separate too. We keep fences between them—not a shallow river. There are some ways, in our view, in which humans should never attempt to recreate the wild.

N.O.: I'm sure the authorities at Sunderland wish they had taken the same approach. But aside from the facility itself, can you tell us something of how you persuaded those at Sunderland who had to make the decision that Coldwater would be the best option?

C.C.: I can't divulge all the details of our agreement with Sunderland. But I can say that we made it worth their while.

N.O.: Did you provide assurances as to how Bonbon would be treated at Coldwater?

C.C.: Absolutely we did. That was necessary from a number of angles. Legally, Bonbon was a ward of the Sunderland Animal Research Centre; in order for us to replace them in that role, a great many assurances had to be provided. We provided assurances as well to Lucinda Gerson. We agreed to give her the same level of access she had had at Sunderland, and the same level—or better—of amenities for Bonbon himself. He would have a larger private area than he had at Sunderland, as well as the option of joining the bonzees in their enclosures. We agreed as well to hire, on a part-time basis, one of the Sunderland keepers who had a particular knack for dealing with him, and who had been willing to move west with him—indeed, had been keen to do so. My understanding is that the young woman— Ashley Rouleau is her name—will live with Ms. Gerson initially; she is only eighteen.

N.O.: Unlike the authorities at Sunderland, you seem happy to call him Bonbon.

C.C.: In anything of that sort, it seems to me vitally important to respect the wishes of the mother.

N.O.: Let me change the topic, if I may. There have been rumours that you are committed to conducting certain sorts of controversial research involving Bonbon—reproductive research in particular.

C.C.: Again, I can't divulge all the details of the various commitments we have made. But I can say that we are a research-friendly institution; research is what we do. And in terms of reproductive capacity—well, I think most people would agree that the public has an interest in knowing whether this hybrid is capable of reproducing. The Coldwater Institute shares that interest, and I'm not about to apologize for that. Whether a human hybrid is himself capable of reproducing ...

N.O.: Whether he's like a mule or ...

C.C.: Yes. Mules are an example of an infertile hybrid—whereas, for example, a cross between a buffalo and a cow is itself entirely capable of reproducing.

N.O.: When Bonbon was at Sunderland there was considerable resistance to the idea that the research centre there might undertake research of this sort. Is that also the case at Coldwater?

C.C.: I think it's fair to say that westerners are more open to the idea of research in these sorts of areas; people are less judgemental out here about what happens when humans work with animals.

N.O.: I know my editors won't want me to comment on that one either way. Can you give the public some idea of when your research into this reproductive aspect will be undertaken?

C.C.: Bonzees reach reproductive age rather earlier than do humans —for males, it's sometimes as young as seven or eight. With a hybrid male, of course, we can only guess when the onset of reproductive capacity is like to come—perhaps at 10, perhaps 11 or 12.

N.O.: The age Bonbon is now.

C.C.: That's right. We just don't know. We will have to see what happens with Bonbon and the female bonzees. In his last year at Sunderland he was electing not to interact sexually with the other bonzees.

N.O.: Even though so much of their interaction is sexual?

C.C.: Exactly. So we will have to see if mating occurs naturally.

N.O.: And what if it doesn't?

C.C.: In that case we would follow the same sorts of procedures as we do with other mammals in our care. I won't go into the details, but I can assure you that there is no cruelty involved.

N.O.: But no pleasure, either?

C.C.: That's the sort of word humans use to describe the feelings that accompany their own reproductive interactions. I think we should be careful not to presume that the same terminology is applicable to creatures of every sort.

* * *

Bonbon Gerson

At the Coldwater was the same the Sunderland, some ways, but the other ways not. Many ways the not. Example, many the bonobos, not many the bonzees. Example, so much more small the space. Same skyway, same canopy, same gawkers, same private place for Lucy, private space for me, but everything too much the small. Out the doors the air was smaller, and nowhere was a river. I was often wake in the very early and was gone in my thoughts only, for nowhere was a river. One place in fence where you could look the river far away. And was nowhere Ever, and was nowhere Only. Was Gorra, and was Gina, and was five others more small than me. The times that had happened had growed me, and the same play I was had with Ever and with Only and with Jasper was gone for me. Was a gone distance, a gone time.

***

Ashley Rouleau

I have to admit I was, like, *this is a little weird*, living with Lucinda. There was the age thing to start with—she was almost old enough to be my mother.

How much did I actually care about that? And how much did I actually care that I was—was I middle class?—and she was working class. My dad used to say that phrase was a joke, *half the people who call themselves "working class," they only ever want to be on welfare, sitting at home drinking beer while other people do the working for them.* I knew how stupid my dad was, but I didn't know what to say when I found out Lucinda ate iceberg lettuce. I mean *only* iceberg lettuce—at first she didn't even want to eat any other type. But then she saw me reaching for romaine and she said: *Oh yeah. Some people like a Caesar salad. I'm OK with that myself.*

We were OK with each other too. Of course we had always sort of got on when Bonbon was at Sunderland, but we were maybe a little wary of each other too. Not in Alberta. Luce got a job at a Safeway store in the Kensington neighbourhood, which had once been poor but was now full of hipsters and socialist professors; it was the sort of Safeway where no one would notice if they ran out of iceberg lettuce. But she liked that store—it always gave her something to talk about, and something to make fun of.

In our second year in Clearwater I started part-time at the university and worked at the zoo and the Research Institute part-time—a lot like I'd done in Scarborough. We'd rented a run-down little bungalow in a neighbourhood called Renfrew: it had a lot of iceberg-lettuce-born-and-bred families who'd been there for fifty years, and a lot of immigrants who were discovering lettuce for the first time. Me and Luce discovered a few things for the first time too. Like, I discovered how to split your hot dogs lengthwise but not cut all the way through, and then fill them with sauerkraut and Heinz Chili-style beans. Luce discovered that a spaghetti sauce could taste just as good with chunks of sautéed tofu mixed in as it did with chunks of ground beef. The odd time she'd even try her special recipe—the Heinz Beans hot dogs—with my veggie dogs instead of her "real" hot dogs—just as a favor to me, so we could be eating the same thing. We didn't always eat together, that's for sure. But we got on better than you might have expected.

It took a half hour for Luce to get from there to her Safeway, and more than that for me to get to the university, but it was what we could afford, and it was only a ten-minute walk from there to the Bridgeland neighbourhood by the river, and the zoo—as Luce always insisted on calling the Research Institute. I couldn't blame her on that one.

And Bonbon? The first year or so wasn't too bad, but he was a lot less happy than he'd been at Sunderland. Even at Sunderland he'd started to drift apart from the friends he'd been close to when he was little, and there'd been no one to replace them. Now it became a lot worse; he just never warmed to the troop at Coldwater. He had his screen time, and he had Luce and me for a few hours a day, but he was growing up and it was no sort of life for the long term.

Luce and I started talking more and more about what we could do to get him out. Day after day we'd sit in the living room or out on the dingy little patio and make jokes about how to spring someone in a jailbreak. Jokes, but we were serious; if there were some way of springing Bonbon, it was somehow understood between us that the two of us would do it together. Or try to, anyway.

Nothing came of it until one Sunday afternoon in October. The day was just about warm enough to be out in the yard if you bundled up. Like she often did, Luce said she'd warm things up a bit more with a beer or three. "You want a beer?" she asked, and I poured myself a mango juice.

"Never let it be said that I let you drink alone, Luce. Here's to you!" I clinked my glass against her bottle and she told me a funny Safeway story about radicchio shaming, and then she said we'd better clink again, "Here's to my kid—to Bonbon!" she said. We drank to Bonbon's health, and she told me how he'd seemed even more down than usual when she'd been in to see him. When she went to get herself a fourth beer she stumbled a little bit on the way to the back door and banged into the bow of the canoe. We'd flipped it over against the wall of the house when we took it off her Pontiac, and there it had sat for well over a year now. It was out of the way as much as it could be, but those things still take up a lot of space. She caught herself and looked back at me as she opened the door with a big smile. "Not a drop spilled!" It wasn't the first time I'd heard her say that.

"Good for you, Luce." I tried to smile back in a way that wouldn't be sad.

"Years of practice, beers of practice, ha ha" she exclaimed triumphantly. It wasn't the first time she'd said that, either. But it was starting to get cold; before long we were inside, flipping channels and then settling in to watch some movie we'd both seen before. An escape film, *escapism for them as well as us*, I joked, about three prisoners who'd been unfairly convicted and they each had a different idea about how to escape from this prison by the sea; one wanted to try to hide in the laundry truck, another wanted to get out through the sewers, and the third thought they could drop over one of the walls into the water and escape by boat.

"So you think we can spring Bonbon like that?" Luce laughed bitterly. "In the laundry. Or through all the shit from that zoo?" Then she stopped and looked at me in a different way. "Or in a boat." There was a long pause.

"Yes," I said.

16.

Lucinda Gerson

I'm going to have to tell you about Carlson. But mostly I want to let his own effing words show you what he was like, what he was prepared to do. Not that I remember every word, but I got a written record. Every time I'd talk to him I'd take some notes after, just 'cause I didn't trust him and I wanted to have a record of what—well, just in case.

So here goes. I'm not even gonna talk about how he propositioned me the first time we met and I had to give him the brush-off. That crap's just like a million guys do all the time—including guys who don't like you, maybe especially guys who don't like you. I'm gonna go straight to the meeting we had just about two years after the move west. I wanted to get Bonbon better clothes and a new computer. And I wanted to talk to Carlson about the whole reproductive research thing. I hated the whole idea of that as much as I've ever hated anything, but I didn't have no idea how to stop it. So I started by just asking him about it, as if I didn't care too much one way or the other. He didn't want to talk about no new computer or new clothes, but he was sure happy to talk about his goddam reproductive research.

"The thing is, Lucinda," he began—right from the beginning he called me *Lucinda* whenever we met, never *Ms. Gerson* like he did when he talked to the press—"there's a very good chance that this research will lead to the third of the great hybrid discoveries."

"The third?"

"Just a few years ago geneticists discovered that humans and Neanderthals could produce hybrids; it seems to have happened so frequently, in fact, that the genome of almost every human today still has one percent Neanderthal content. It's a lot less well known that humans also produced hybrids with creatures called the Denisovans—cousins of the Neanderthals, they're sometimes called, but they were very much a separate group. Before that discovery was made, humans had disparaged Neanderthals as a species far below them in the evolutionary chain. We regarded them as brutes, as low, dim-witted creatures; the way they walked with a stoop and the slope of their foreheads was enough to prove all that beyond a shadow of a doubt. Now, suddenly, it seemed that these dim-witted brutes had been so much like us that we'd been able to mate with them. Able to make creatures that were half them, half us—creatures who were our children, and their children too. Perhaps we should all be considered part of the same species.

"The fact that the Neanderthals and the Denisovans are long extinct has made it possible for humans to ignore how large a challenge hybridity presents to human exceptionalism. Human-bonzee hybridity is different; it's here and now. If we can prove that the result of your little fling wasn't just a one-off—that our species truly can interbreed on an ongoing basis—then no one will be able to pretend any longer. I don't suggest that we'll have to accept outright that humans might be, to use the well-worn phrase, no better than animals. But there will need to be a re-thinking. A re-thinking of a sort I imagine you may welcome. You and everyone else who's had a problem with human exceptionalism. The research will have shown that ..."

"The research!" I could hardly control myself. "You don't need more *research* to know humans and bonzees can interbreed. And you don't need to pussyfoot around. *We might be no better than other animals*, blah blah blah. We *are* no better than other animals. We've never been better than the other animals. You look at ..." —I couldn't remember what all we should look at. "You look at ... you look at almost any ... you look at us. Fighting each other. Killing each other. Rich people making themselves richer and richer and making the rest of us poor. And other animals, the way we treat them ... We don't need none of it. Not *any* of it, I mean. We don't. Not even ..."

"You people ... You're against science; that's what it comes down to. You think everything's about ethics and politics; you have no interest in the scientific world, the real world. You ..."

"I don't have nothing against science—real science. Science that doesn't exploit animals, science that hasn't given up on caring—caring about the world, caring about animals—about anyone that can think and feel and ..."

"Well, Lucinda," he said, "certainly no one else has acted as you have acted with other animals." He paused to let it sink in. "You have zero credibility. Zero. And your Bonbon ..."

"My Bonbon is not going to help you in any way. He won't ..."

"But it won't be altogether up to him, Lucinda. Let me be blunt: what young male can stop himself from becoming aroused when he is stimulated? What young male can stop himself from ejaculating if that stimulation is continued? Perhaps one in a million. It doesn't even have to be continued very long. You know perfectly well that ..."

"But you'd be forcing him. That's like rape. You can't do it, you can't be allowed to do it, you can't ..."

"Perhaps he'll be that one-in-a-million—we'll just have to see. But he's an animal, Lucinda, and this is an animal research facility, and we do whatever the research requires. In the big picture, Lucinda, whatever he might think about what we're going to do with him hardly matters." Then Carlson's mouth started to widen with that goddam smile of his. "And anyway, he'll be having a good time, won't he?"

For a second I was speechless. "You have no idea about Bonbon," I said finally. "Even after all this research ..."

"I think Bonbon is very clever, Lucinda. And I think we'll

discover before too long that Bonbon has been stringing us along. I think he's just about as clever as any human. I think he'll show us just how clever one of these apes can be when they have language, that they can be ..."

"But he doesn't. He *doesn't* have language. That's the whole thing! How are you going to ..."

"Don't be too sure he doesn't have language, Lucinda. Don't be too sure. Look at how his eyes move when people are speaking—especially when they're speaking about him. And his lips: I've sometimes seen his lips moving—as you must have seen them moving. It looks very much to me as if those lips could shape words. As if ..."

"He's never spoken. All those tests ..."

"Remember the first tests at Sunderland? Shapes, numbers, concepts? He did astonishingly well. As well as Kanzi had done, as well as Panbanisha had done, as well as Ayuma had done. In some ways better. But then the progress suddenly stopped. I don't think for a moment that he stopped developing. I know that's what they said in Sunderland. I just don't buy it. I think he just decided not to show them what he could do, how he was developing. I think he decided he didn't want to be like a human—or not like the human they wanted him to be, anyway. A human who ..."

"Who talks on command, who does all the tests that people like you want him to do, test after test after test, until ..."

"Who performs tasks, Lucinda. They wanted him to perform tasks. And they did their best to make it fun, I'm sure they did. But maybe they didn't try hard enough, or in the right ways.

"I could be wrong, of course. But we're going to find out. Sooner or later we're going to find out just how good he really is. And we're going to find out just how much of his intelligence he can pass along to the next generation. For the moment he may be able to hide his own abilities; he won't be able to hide what he passes along genetically."

You're even worse than the ones in Sunderland. You're worse than ... That's what I wanted to say to him. But I didn't. I bit my tongue and tried to stay calm. "Mr. Carlson ..."

"*Dr.* Carlson."

Can you believe that? He thought he was above being called *Mister.*

"Whatever the hell your name is, there has to be a better way. You have to find a way to act better than ..."

"*Better* and *worse* in the sense you are using them mean nothing to me, Lucinda. Loose talk, empty words. What matters is the ability to advance human knowledge. That is what science is all about. Ability, and strength, and will. They all matter, and they all matter to me." Then he paused and looked at me hard. "And beauty. That matters to me too. Not just the beauty of a sunrise or a woman's beautiful figure." He wasn't making any sense, but suddenly I could see where he was coming from, the same place just about all guys come from when they start wanting something, or somebody, sometimes even before they know they're wanting it. I could feel him looking through my clothes. All this time he'd been sitting behind his desk and I'd been standing. Now he got up. He turned a little away from me and looked out of his big window, his big view of the river. "I think we had better call a halt to this conversation, Lucinda. You can come back and talk to me later. People can say what they like about you, Lucinda, but you have spirit. Animal spirit. More of it than anyone I've met in a long time." He looked at me hard. "Come back Thursday at the same time." There was that smile again, but then he sort of strangled it, and turned away again. He was in shadow, but I could just make out that his hand had gone deep into his pocket; I swear, he was touching himself through the goddam fabric.

***

Dr. Cyril Carlson

If she ever suggests that I acted inappropriately, of course I'll deny everything, and that will be that. There's no way to prove I ever said anything, no way to prove anything happened, no way to prove I ever wanted anything to happen.

But what was I thinking? She was a loose cannon, and I knew that perfectly well. What in God's name was I doing? It's no surprise when lust takes temporary possession of a younger man, but a man of fifty-six? For God's sake, I told myself, fifty-six is an age when the raw animal instincts ought to have been dulled. And yet. I have to admit there's a strange sort of pride lurking in me, deep down. Perhaps it's simply pride that there's still enough raw desire there that sometimes it can just wrest control away from the sensible man, the civilized man, the rational man.

Yes, of course I see the ironies; you would have to be blind not to see the ironies. And none of it changes my mind as to what makes us human, what separates us from the ones on the other side of those bars. Not even for a moment. We are the thinking animal and—those ironies again—we're capable of recognizing irony. Imagine any of the hippos savouring life's complexities, life's ironies. Imagine any of the chimps or bonobos or bonzees, for that matter. Even Bonbon—it's laughable, the very idea of it.

* * *

Lucinda Gerson

But Thursday he didn't want to talk about nothing, he just said he'd ordered a new computer and whatever else for Bonbon. I guess by then he'd had time to jerk off and get control of himself. You'd think guys could find a way to control themselves a hundred percent of the time, 'specially when they're, like, fifty years old, not fifteen. Evidently not. A few weeks later I wanted to ask him something about Bonbon's diet, and also ask him again about the experiments—even if I was pretty sure there was zero chance I was going to get anywhere, I felt I had to. But he didn't want to talk about any of that. Not directly, anyways.

"You know you're an attractive woman, don't you Lucinda. Don't let anyone ever tell you otherwise." He leaned back in his chair—once again he didn't invite me to take no chair. "And sometimes an attractive woman can have more power than she realizes. More *influence*." He paused to let that sink in.

"I'm here to talk about Bonbon, Dr. Carville. Not about me."

"That's *Carlson*! And we are talking about Bonbon, Lucinda. We're talking about Bonbon *and* we're talking about you. Everything connects, Lucinda, everything connects. At the moment, you see, no decision has been made as to these ..." He paused and I could see his tongue touch his lips. "These experiments. These reproductive experiments."

"You told me it was all going to happen. That there was nothing that could be done to stop it. You said that, no matter what, you were going to find out what he'd be able to pass along in his genes ..."

"And you know, Lucinda, it's true that things will in all probability move ahead. But things can go more quickly or they can go more slowly. You might be able to ... That's what I'm suggesting." You couldn't miss what he was suggesting. A little bit of an edge came into his voice when I didn't say anything back. "The final decision on this will rest with the Board of Directors of the Research Institute. But of course, as Executive Director of the Research Institute, I can influence that decision—and I can certainly influence the timing of that decision. In fact I can have a good deal of ..." Again he paused, and his tongue touched his lips. "Of influence."

I know now that, even then, even as he was speaking to me and pretending it was still all up in the air, everything had really already been put to his precious Board of Directors. They'd been sent a package and they were considering it and there would be a Board meeting the next week where they'd say *yes* or *no* to reproductive experiments involving Bonbon. And he controlled the whole process: they were going to say *yes*, and they were going to say it the next week, and there wasn't going to be any difference in the timing of it, or in any other damn thing, no matter what I did. But I didn't know that then; I seriously thought I could maybe buy some more time. Time to figure something out, time to somehow get Bonbon out of there—I didn't know.

"I don't get what you're saying." I was getting it loud and clear, but I wanted him to come out and say it. Guys like that will do anything, but they'll never come out and say what they're doing, or what it is they want you to do. Not in so many words.

"All I'm saying is that anyone who has influence can usually *be* influenced, Lucinda." His right hand was below the desk. I could bet he had his hand in his pocket and was touching himself again. "Under the right sort of influence, Lucinda, I can imagine it might be possible at least to postpone the Board's decision. For a few days, a few weeks, a few months, perhaps ..." Again he licked his lips. "Perhaps indefinitely. I couldn't guarantee anything, of course. But you never know what might be possible ..." There were fifteen things I wanted to say, but none of them didn't have no swear words, and none of them was going to do me no good. Or Bonbon neither.

"You've gone all quiet, Lucinda. Your tongue's gone all quiet. But perhaps you don't need to say anything: I don't think you do." He got up from his desk and sat down on the couch under the window. He was definitely touching himself now; you could see the bulge in his pants very clearly. "Why don't you come over here beside me, Lucinda?" I must have looked disgusted, but it didn't seem to make any difference. Some guys get like this and they just don't notice if you look disgusted. Or they just don't care.

"I think I understand you, Dr. Carls ..."

"You can call me Cyril."

"But I don't know if ..."

"I'm sure a woman like you must know a great deal, Lucinda ...," he said with a smirk.

"I don't know, Dr. ... You've got to give me a little time to think about this ..."

"Cyril. Call me Cyril, Lucinda." This time he said it like a command. "You can have a little time. But only a little, I'm afraid. A woman's influence doesn't last forever, you know. Why don't you come back again tomorrow." He didn't phrase it like a question.

"I have to work all day tomorrow. I don't get off until seven."

"Wednesday, then. Wednesday."

∾ Postpone! That's all the little prick would do—postpone the start of the experiments! Just how close to a worthless piece of shit did he think I was?

The thing is, I almost said yes. I'm that much twisted in my head about Bonbon that I almost said yes. How messed up is that?

I put him off. I didn't say yes and I didn't say no. I said I'd have to think it through. "You do that," he said. "I'll give you a week."

And that was that. I went back home and told Ash we had to find a way to get Bonbon out effing soon. Effing now.

17.

Dr. Cyril Carlson

Once I had the approval of the Board I didn't see the need for any further delay; waiting any longer might have left the door open for second thoughts. The Board could always decide for some reason to reconsider, or something unforeseen could get in the way—perhaps radicals mounting a campaign against forced reproduction as they had in Sunderland—though that was of course far less likely in a conservative city like Clearwater.

Beyond that, there was the matter of the animals themselves. The bonzee that we considered to be best qualified to be the mother —Candy, we had started to call her, though she'd been known before then by another name—would be in a receptive state for another two or three days, and then not again for some weeks. She was intelligent, and, more important, she was cooperative. For the moment she was being kept in isolation from the other bonzees, of course; if she were going to become pregnant, we had to be sure of the father's identity.

By the end of the next day my staff had been briefed and everything was in place; we would take the first specimen in the morning, and with any luck Candy would be impregnated by midday. When this sort of procedure is to take place, with almost any mammal, we generally find that the early morning is a good time to deal with the male; most males are easily aroused in the first hour or so after they wake. But on occasion it nevertheless proves impossible to induce arousal and ejaculation; particularly if the male is experiencing the procedure for the first time, he may become distressed by the unfamiliarity of the surroundings, and may prove unable or unwilling to cooperate.

In this case we were of course determined to leave as little as possible to chance. Bonbon was to be brought to the research centre at eight. Just before seven I presented myself at his enclosure. One of the part-timers was on duty—the girl who had sounded the alarm during the appalling incident involving Bonbon and the chimpanzees at Sunderland, and who had followed him west. Rouleau—that was her name. This was something I had not expected; of all the keepers, she was said to have the closest relationship with the hybrid. She was about to bring him his first meal of the day; I explained that he would be accompanied to the research complex in just over an hour, and that it was important he consume a special drink as part of the preparation for the morning's procedure.

"What sort of drink?" Anyone could tell from her tone that she was suspicious, even hostile. "What kind of procedure?" I don't know by what authority she felt she had the right to know about any of this, but it was difficult to deflect her persistent questioning. In the background, of course, was an awareness on my part that she was close not only to Bonbon but also to the creature's mother. Eventually, of course, Lucinda would have to find out about what had gone on. In the long run I could do nothing to prevent that; it would be public knowledge, and I would be armed with my "regret" and with my assurances that it had been the Board that had made the decision, not me. But it would be highly disruptive for the information to reach Lucinda on the very day itself. I had to try to bring this young woman onside—and, failing that, I had to keep her away from Lucinda until things had reached a point of no return.

"First, he really must drink this," I insisted, "and then I'll do my best to explain everything." The creature drank it down readily enough, and as he sat down to eat his usual breakfast of grains and fruit I drew the girl aside and outlined the situation, putting matters as delicately as I could. She did not take it well.

"He'll be *given an opportunity to have a child of his own?* What are you thinking? He has no idea of what you're planning— you can't talk of it that way, you're twisting everything so that ..."

"I understand your feelings, truly I do." What *was* the girl's first name? It would help if I could—*Ashley*, that was it. "But at this point, Ashley, it is out of my hands. Our Board of Directors has instructed us to see if this is possible. Of course ..." —I saw suddenly a way that I might reassure the young woman. "Of course if he chooses not to become aroused—if it proves impossible to obtain any ejaculate—then that will be that. We cannot force him to ..."

"You give me your word on that? He will not be forced?" I thought quickly of the various meanings of "forced."

"I give you my word." I still believe that was legitimate. In a perfectly acceptable, literal sense of the word, he was not forced. To be sure, he had little choice when the team brought him to the research centre an hour later. And of course no creature has full choice when it comes to the matter of being restrained for a procedure of this sort; it is essential for a member of the team to be able to manipulate the genitals without interference. Nevertheless, as I have said, it will sometimes happen that the male resists arousal, and that it proves impossible to obtain any ejaculate. I will own that I was keen in this case to reduce as much as possible the chance of any such resistance occurring. It was a relief to me that I had been able to steer the young woman's questions away from the subject of her initial inquiry—*what sort of drink?*, she had asked. It was the sort of unusual concoction that I realize not every young woman would have approved of. The previous day I had ground up one of the tablets that human males of a certain age (I confess I am among their number) commonly ingest an hour or two before they expect to perform sexually. Such tablets will dissolve easily enough in water—or, in this case, in a mango drink I happened to know Bonbon was partial to.

No doubt there are some who would say that ingesting a drink of this sort an hour or two before one's genitals are manipulated would effectively remove any power of choice as to the outcome. And it would be pointless to deny that the circumstances are somewhat altered—that the odds have to some degree been changed. But to suggest that it is *impossible* in such circumstances not to become aroused—well, the facts simply do not bear out any such conclusion. I know indeed from my own experience that on at least one occasion ... —well, there is no need to go into all the circumstances. I will simply attest that it is entirely possible to have ingested such a drug and *not* to become aroused to the point of ejaculation, regardless of the level of stimulation. Strictly speaking, then, it was quite literally true that Bonbon would not be forced to provide a sperm specimen.

All would have been well; in all likelihood Candy would have given birth eight months later to a child one quarter human, three quarters bonzee, and we at CARI would have been well on our way to world leadership in the field of hybrid research. My mistake was in allowing her—that young black woman, I mean, Ashley Rouleau—to accompany Bonbon, rather than leaving everything to the medical team as had been arranged. But to this day I do not know how I could have managed it otherwise. I could hardly have insisted that she make herself scarce when she was simply doing her job—and, had I tried to do so, she would most surely have raised the alarm with Lucinda, and perhaps more widely, no doubt making all sorts of wild allegations.

I had better give credit where credit is due; it was with the help of the young woman that we managed to bring Bonbon to the research centre without incident; from the sounds and the gestures he was making it seemed plain that he was in a mood to resist anything the team wanted him to do. But he trusted the Rouleau girl, and she had no choice but to do as I told her—at least for so long as she was on the job.

At the centre itself I thanked her and bade her farewell; "you can get on with your other duties now," I told her.

"I'll wait," she said firmly. "And I'll go back with Bonbon once it's over." The insolence! I can still feel how furious she made me, that young black woman—and yet I could not afford to be furious. I nodded curtly, turned, and went inside to join the team.

* * *

Bonbon Gerson

I was close my eyes, but I was not close the real eyes, the eyes what feel.

They was touch me like only bonzees had touch me, and I was have no way to end them. I was feel myself hard. I was tried to think the open air and I was tried to think the sky, but my sky thinks and my air thinks were gone, I was not be able to stop the hard thoughts. Or the hate. It was a hot hate like never, a hate for humans from the human half of me. If I was have a sharp stake, I was driven it deep into Carlson again and again till he was squeal and die. And I was hate those feelings almost the much as I was hate Carlson.

Now I was feel the rubber fingers pull down, pull up, slow and then a little more fast, I was have no way to end it.

* * *

Dr. Cyril Carlson

Everything had gone more or less smoothly, despite some resistance on Bonbon's part, and we had reached the climactic point. Ejaculation had occurred and Jodie, the deputy leader of my team, was in the process of sealing the tube that held the ejaculate; it would then be taken directly on a refrigerated carrier to another room, where Candy had already been prepared.

It was then that the teenager burst in on us—that black girl.

"You said he wouldn't be forced!" she screamed. "Look at him—strapped down, helpless; you lied to me!" Again she screamed as she pushed past me and swung wildly at Jodie, hitting hard at her wrist. The tube came loose and flew to one side; it struck the side of a counter and shattered into a thousand tiny fragments.

* * *

Bonbon Gerson

I was understand clear those two words what Carlson said her—they were not mean *You are been set fire*. Fact: they were mean *You are lose job of work*. The loud fat man on a screen was used to say people the same two words—tall and loud and fat and famous he was. I want not use his name. Before all the votes and before everything, he was on one the shows, they were called *reality*. In the long before, that was. Now Carlson was saying Ashley same words, *you're fired!* Her face went quick red, and her eyes were cries, and then began run from the room, Ash went. Then Carlson was even more his loud, his angry.

"You're fired! You're fired! You are fired! Get out this instant, do you hear?" And then once the more he shouted her "You're fired!" but by now the door was banging shut behind her, and extra his words went at the door, not Ash. Was the savage. "She will never be coming back. Never. I will destroy her!"

Then I was see someone come towards me with needle. I was felt it, the jab in my arm, and then was I all still. I was not be able move arms or move legs or move eyes; I was think they must think I was lost my conscious, but I was not lost it. I was hear nothing for few seconds the time, and then one the keepers spoke Carlson. Was more a whisper than a speak.

"Shall I take him back to the compound?"

"You certainly should—as soon as he wakes up. And this glass …" Carlson his eyes were sweep the floor. "This whole mess needs to be cleaned up. We'll make another attempt tomorrow." He was pause. "No, not make another attempt. We'll fucking get this *done* tomorrow!" Carlson, his words was the words Lucy talked, but all round the words was everything different.

∾ I had been fear they was want do this, and I had been fear it was be with Zzozzo—"Zzozzo" to me, "Candy" to them. Everyone all knew they were keep her on own so she was not be able sex anyone. They say bonzees will sex anyone; fact—that is not the true. At Coldwater it was only Zzzozzo like that, true, sexing with anyone. I had been fear they was make me to push inside her, make me sex her, make her make a baby. But Zzozzo she was the soft and the gentle, and me I was the soft near her. We never sexed each the other, not once not ever.

I liked Zzozzo always, but not smell of Zzozzo; I liked Jasper always, but not smell of Jasper.

Fact, I never liked those Coldwater bonzees, and I never liked smell of those bonzees. All of them none. And for sexing? Was humans I wanted for sexing.

I was *not* wanting be strapped down and … —I was not wanting remember. Sure if they was keep try, they could be able do anything with me. Tomorrow they would try more, try again. Tomorrow they'd do like Carlson said, they'd *fucking get this done.* I was feel my chest go tight tight, and my belly go tight tight, and then I was feel tears. My eyes only, not my face all over. I was want to be strong; I was want the keepers not see me wet with tears.

But no one was watch. Carlson gone, others they were clean up all the glass and all the mess. I was feel so sad, example, tears they were more. Tears they were fill my eyes, tears I could not be able wipe any them away, all the long time.

***

Dr. Cyril Carlson

The girl would tell Lucinda about everything, that much was certain. Would she go to the press? What would need to be done to contain this? Of course I'd done nothing that hadn't been authorized by my Board, nothing that wasn't justified in the interests of scientific research. But still—so much depends on how things are spun, and on who gets their story out there first. I had better talk to Harry at the *Herald* and Joanne and Jennifer at the networks—that much was clear. They already thought of Lucinda as pretty much a nutcase. I could keep a lid on it.

Bonbon would have to go back to his compound, and I had already given orders for that. We couldn't keep him in isolation like we were doing to Candy; that would cause too many questions. But I could at the very least keep Lucinda and the girl away from Bonbon until all this was over. They knew Lucinda at all the gates; who in the world didn't know Lucinda? But did they know the teenager? The black girl? They'd recognize her just by her colour, surely—there weren't more than a handful of people of colour on the whole staff. I would do what I could; I would let them know that there was a special situation, and that if either Lucinda or Ashley were trying to enter the grounds at any time before closing they should be escorted directly to the Director's office. I would say whatever needed to be said; I would keep them from Bonbon until this little fuss was all over.

18.

Ashley Rouleau

"It will have to be tonight." Luce and I were back at the bungalow. I had told her everything. She was less surprised that I'd thought she'd be. But very angry, in a quiet way that wasn't her. She glowed with the heat of it. "I haven't turned in my uniform yet," I told her. "Tonight will work."

"Yes," was all she said.

"And tonight of all nights, it should be easy to get him out."

"Tonight of all nights?"

"Everyone will be glued to their screens. Even the security guards, I'd guess."

"The election. The American election. Of course. Hillary's not going to lose it this time."

"This time?"

"Yeah, this time. She ran before, you know, back when Barack won, back in ... But you probably *don't* know—2008's a long time ago when you're your age."

"Right—I was still little back then. Anyway, no one thinks she's going to lose. But people will watch. And it's not just the election tonight. You don't follow sports, do you?"

"Ash, you effing know the answer to that."

"It's the battle of Alberta, Luce. The first one of the season. Connor McDavid and the Oilers against ..."

"The Flames. I know. They used to be in Atlanta, I'm almost old enough to remember that. I once had a boyfriend who ... Et cetera, et cetera, you don't need to know that. The only reason I know anything about anything is one teacher in Comber ..."

"Rhymes with sombre, not bomber. Luce, you've had a few drinks."

"Sure. Who doesn't have a couple drinks sometimes?"

"I guess it doesn't matter. What's going to matter is tonight. Everybody in this city is going to be watching the battle of Alberta or the American election—or both. It's impossible to imagine a better time ..."

"Ash, there's no time to get ready. To pack, to figure out ..."

"What do you really *need* to take with you? Toothpaste, a toothbrush? A change of clothes, rain gear, a flashlight? Nothing that can't be packed in half an hour. I can tell you what you absolutely need: to get Bonbon across that border. Where they'll call him human. Where they'll let him be free. You need to have your passport, you need to have your driver's licence. If this house were on fire right now, would you need to have anything else?"

"I need my ... I need ... I need a lot of things. But a lot of those things I don't have anyways. I never had. You're right, Ash. I don't need nothing. I need love, I guess. Like we all do, and Bonbon needs love, and maybe we'll all get more of that wherever we're going to end up." Her face had crumpled a little, but now she started to revive. "Bonbon and me. That's a sort of love right there, isn't it? Maybe it's the most important sort of love, when you think about ... But *you*—what about you, Ash? Do you even have a passport? You don't have any reason to go to America except to ..."

"Which is why I'm not going. I'll paddle with you to the border —to just before the border. And then we'll pull into shore for a moment, and I'll get out, and the two of you will ..."

"Ash, I don't know the first thing about canoeing. When I was growing up I never even knew anyone who went to summer camp. I don't even know how to ..."

"It won't matter if you can't steer, if you can't do anything. I've checked the map thoroughly. There's no rapids marked anywhere on that stretch of the river; there won't be anything dangerous. Where I'll get out is right near the border. All you'll have to do is let the boat drift with the current across the border and towards the shore, as the river makes a turn; you should be able to grab hold when you get near the shore. And if you can't grab on to a branch or anything, you can get your feet wet. Hop into the water and pull the boat in to shore that way. The water won't be deep; I promise." Of course I couldn't promise any such thing, but I was pretty sure that the Coldwater River stayed shallow almost all the way to where it joined up with the Missouri.

"There's a little bridge only fifty yards or so into Montana, where a road crosses. A range road. I wouldn't think it's travelled much, but someone will come along eventually. You'll find a way out; you'll find a new life, Luce—you and Bonbon together."

Luce had started to cry softly, and there was a little catch in her voice as she tried to speak. "Everything's always too good to be true. Everything good, I mean. If you ..." She stopped until she could start again. "Would you want to come with us? I mean, if you could?"

"I don't know what I want, Luce. I mean, of course I want to be with you and Bonbon. But I don't know how it could work. The three of us, and me not being ..."

"You'd be an illegal. That's what they call them when they come from the other direction. They speak Spanish."

"And I don't, and I don't want to spend my life, like, with no proper papers and working on berry farms and in slaughterhouses. I'll stay here, I guess. I'll stop working in the animal prison. I'll go to university. I'll get a job. I'll get a life."

∾ That's what I told Lucinda, and it's part of what I told myself too. The other part? It was like I was about to be ripped open. *You can't leave him now*, the other half told me. *Luce won't be able to take care of him, and he won't be able to take care of himself either, and there is nothing you want more in your heart than to be with the two of them.* I suppose I forced the one half of me to take over. I could control myself; I could make it happen.

∾ I concentrated on walking at a normal pace as I got close to the entrance. I carried my uniform bag in my left hand—the bag that all staff are supposed to use if we're taking our uniforms offsite to clean them. *I just left work but then I realized I forgot something so I had to come back*—that was my story. Did I know the security guard on duty? I peered through the glass of the door to the foyer. Yes, I'd met him before, more than once. Kent? Ken? Something like that.

The central door to the main foyer, which extended right across the wide front of the building, was always open until midnight—receptions for members or for groups that rented the space often went late. But tonight everything was quiet; the cavernous space with its high ceilings extended to the east and west doors in semi darkness. At intervals, five hallways led from the foyer back into the body of the building. Along each of the hallways access to the zoo and the research facility was blocked by more doors. From the inside you could exit through any one of them by pushing it open with the security bar; from the outside you needed a key.

Kent—I'll call him Kent—was sitting on a stool at the security checkpoint. He looked at me, but only barely; his eyes kept flicking back and forth between me and the screen of the tablet he'd set up in front of him. Mainly they were on the screen. I discovered much later that there'd been an email telling people to keep a lookout for me; he must have not even opened it.

"I thought you only worked mornings," he said to the screen.

"Afternoons too, sometimes. And the odd evening the past while—but I'm done for the day. I just came back because I forgot something; I need to ..." There was a roar from the little screen he had parked in front of him. "Who's ahead?" I asked; I wanted him focused as much as possible on that little screen.

"Trump. Trump by two points. They just announced he took Florida. That was the crowd at Orlando you just heard—his campaign headquarters for the state. It's unbelievable."

"You're not watching the hockey?"

"It's still intermission; they're about to start the second period. Tied at one. On the play, Edmonton should be winning. Price has been amazing."

"Price?"

"Yeah, you know. Carey Price. Even people who aren't hockey fans know about ..."

"Right. The goalie. The goalie who was traded." It came back to me: it'd even made the national news when it happened—Canada's all-world goaltender traded from the Canadiens to the Flames.

"Did you know he's Indian? Native, whatever."

"I didn't know that."

"I mean, his father's white; it was only his mother who was, whatyacallit."

"First Nations. Indigenous."

"Yeah. She was actually a chief of this tribe, they were just saying. Anyways, ..."

"Look, I just need to get back into the compound for a minute. I left a ring in there."

"A ring?"

"Yeah, a ring my boyfriend gave me. I take it off if I'm mucking out the compound or anything like that. I don't know, it just doesn't feel right to have it on when I'm doing anything dirty." I could tell he wasn't really listening. "But this time I forgot to put it back on. I'm pretty sure I know where it is ..." I left the sentence hanging. After hours, no worker was allowed back into any of the animal compounds once they'd gone off shift. Ken or Kent or whatever his name was would know that as well as anyone.

"No, I'd better get it for you. But can you just wait a couple of minutes until they ..."

"The thing is, I'm, like, meeting my boyfriend at a party and I'm late already. He'll be so mad if he sees I'm not wearing it. But the game's on again, I can see—I don't want to take you away from that. Just give me the key for one minute—I'll be right back. And I won't say a thing!"

"I don't know. I guess maybe.... You know we're not supposed to ..." There was a huge roar from the screen. "Yeah! Two to one! Way to go, Johnny!" He barely looked at me as he pulled the key from his pocket and held it out in my direction. "Be as quick as you can, OK?" As soon as I was through the door I slipped the ring I had in my pocket over a finger. I turned right at the first side passage, walked quickly over to the hallway farthest to the east, and then back towards the foyer until I reached the security door. I eased it open a crack, slipped a wedge under it to hold it ajar by the tiniest amount, and rushed back the way I'd come. My heart was pounding; I was sure that if I were more than a minute he'd begin to wonder what was happening and come back to check on me.

But once again Kent barely looked at me; I dropped the key on the counter beside him, and let my hand linger for just a moment. He could see that one of the fingers on that hand now had a ring on it.

"Got it, eh?"

"Just where I thought it would be. Still 2-1? And Trump still ahead?"

"You got it. Enjoy your party."

"Thanks—you enjoy the game!" Did he notice that I started heading not across the foyer to the central doors I'd come in by, but down the foyer towards the east exit? Staff often used the east exit, which shortened the walk to the parking lot and the bus loop by a few steps for those who knew just where they were going; with any luck he would think nothing of it.

As I approached the last hallway I glanced over my shoulder. He was half turned away from me, glued to the screen. I ducked into the hallway. Everything was going just as I'd hoped.

* * *

Bonbon Gerson

I lay alone long last, but I was not be able make sleep happen. I was keep think what they did me, and what they would do me again. Next time Ashley could not be able to stop them. All the times I was fearing.

Then was she there. Ash was with me and with arms all round me. But Ash not speak like other the times. Her words were all the quick, the jumble. I was hear *gate* and *game* and *quick*, and also *close*—no, *clothes*—yes, *clothes, put them on, hurry!* she was say. Then opens bag.

In Ash uniform bag was not Ash uniform.

"They'll probably be too large; I wasn't sure what size," Ash said me as I was start to pull clothes all over me. Example, long underwear. Also thick sweatpants, thick sweatshirt, thick sweater, thick zipper-jacket too. And the thick socks, the slip-on shoes. I was fumbled as I quick pulled and pulled. "Don't worry about doing up the jacket—just come. Hurry, hurry!"

I was have no idea what the happening. But I could be able feel little spark.

"We're leaving—we're leaving now. And quiet, you have to keep *quiet*. Your mother's waiting by the river. We're springing you loose, Bonbon. We're taking you to America. Now. Tonight. Down the river to the border. You're going to be free." My heart was begin run away, little loops and little jumps. What could I be able do except follow her?

"The east hallway," she said me. I was follow her sure. "Turn here," she said. I was follow her sure. There was door that was been prop open one tiny bit. Ever so quiet, she was push push it more open. All her walk steps soft; I was walk like her sure. Then we was come to a corner. "The main hallway," she whispered me. "The guard is that way; he will be watching his screen, not us. If we're lucky," she whispered me again. I was not look back. I was look only where Ash was look, where Ash was start to move, she was start to move down hallway all dim, towards a long away door.

The sign was said "Exit"; Ash mouthed the red word, but not saying in sound. I stepped ever quiet, right behind Ash. Mouth in heart. Was this the yes, all the lucky? Ash was towards the door and then push push, Ash to the next door and then push push, and then was air, Ash and me and air, outside air.

And cross flat grass, and cross flat road, all quiet was every thing.

But then we were saw something—a shadow move on path. "Down!" Ash was tell me, and we dropped flat flat to the ground. "It's one of the keepers," she whispered me. "From the chimps' compound. But sometimes he's on night patrol for the whole east side of the zoo." We waited, both flat. Would he be turn where the path was a fork, just ahead us? If he was not turn he would be walk right past us; he would be see us, sure. I was press my arms and my legs to ground, my head to ground. It was hard, and there were pebbles, but Ash and me we kept so still, all so still. Then I was think of the pebbles and I was move my mouth ever so little. I was suck up one pebble. I was turn my head just a little little, and I was get the pebble in position. I was make no sound as the pebble was leave my mouth. Then was the *ping* as pebble it bounced off a tree some place away, maybe twenty the feet away. It was beyond where the path was a fork. Quick the keeper's head was turn. Slow he was start to walk towards where his ear was hear the *ping*. I was put other pebble in my mouth. The second *ping* was maybe fifteen the feet more far beyond. The keeper was peer in darkness as he walked farther long the path, towards the place of second *ping*. Ash was turn and signal me; in a flash we was moving again, ever so low and ever so quiet, until we was be able hide behind thickery, far side of where was fork in path. Another small time was pass, and then the keeper was shrug his shoulders at trees where were the pings had been before. He was turn back, and was took the path we was been crouched beside, small small time before. He walked on, slow. Ash was turn me again when the keeper out sight; even in dark I was be able see smile. *That was brilliant!*, she whispered me, and then Ash show me my way once more.

And we was cross more grass, more flat grass, then curve grass. Ash and me was run no-noise down hill. All quiet and all the green things they was dark dark, and in the far I could be able see a different dark, a dark that moved flat. A river.

* * *

Lucinda Gerson

How long had I been waiting on the shore? Shouldn't Ash have been back by now? I didn't even try to see the time—we'd agreed there wouldn't be any light. No light from the time we'd touched the shore and got out of the boat until we were off again and out of sight.

Getting out of the boat—now, that had been something. You think getting in and out of a goddam canoe is easy? When you're trying at the same time to hold on to a branch of a bush and the branch is so thin it's basically a goddam twig? And the boat is totally tippy and the current is moving at I-don't-know-how-many goddam miles an hour, and the current is trying its goddam best to pull you away from the shore, et cetera, et cetera. So yeah, I did get a soaker, *ha ha*, but it's not very funny when one of your feet is soaking wet and it's nighttime in November and it's getting fucking colder by the minute.

Ash had disappeared into the darkness. As soon as she headed up the hill my foot had started to go numb, so's I didn't hardly think nothing of it. Then there was silence, and sky, and the sound of the river—I couldn't hear nothing else. Time was passing, I guess, but time don't make no sound.

If it all went right, Ash would have Bonbon with her. It'd be just Ash if it all went wrong.

If it all went *really* wrong she might not be able to come back to the boat at all. I knew that, we'd talked about that; I should just leave the boat by the water if it all went wrong. I'd find my own way back, and I guess we'd find some way to live out the whole of our own effing lives, et cetera, et cetera.

Scared? Of course I was scared. The big things in life? You get one shot and that's it. If you're lucky. Some people don't get no shot at all, they just get their beer and no chaser, *ha ha*, if you can't laugh what can you do? This was our shot, this was our chance. This was Bonbon's chance, and I guess it was my chance too. I'd never really thought about that side of it. I hadn't any goddam idea about that side of it, really. I'd hardly had time to pack; what the hell was I going to do when I got over that border? When *we* got over that border. Where were we going to live? How was I going to find work? And what could Bonbon do? Would there be special school for a kid who couldn't say anything, couldn't understand anything? Could he work? How was I going to take care of little-Bonbon-who-wasn't-so-damn-little-anymore? Fucked if I knew. It was a dark night, there wasn't hardly no moon at all. It was our one shot. Sometimes you just know you have to goddam go for it.

What could be holding them up? It was, like, forever since Ash had headed up the hill. It had to be close to nine o'clock, anyways, maybe a little after. And we were thirty miles from the border, thirty miles as the river curves, but you can see on the map it doesn't curve much between Clearwater and the border. You better believe I'd looked at a map this time!

Ash had said we should be able to go five miles an hour, paddling with the current. Maybe six, even six and a half if the wind was behind us. I could do the math, couldn't I? That meant at least six hours on the water, maybe seven, maybe even more. Six goddam hours with this freezing foot. And we'd have to take breaks sometimes. Add in time for breaks and we wouldn't be over the border until sometime between four and five in the morning. That was, if everything Ash said was right.

∾ It was so damn dark. I remember thinking that, as I looked at the water and at how dark the water was. The whole night was dark. You could see all the stars but the moon was just about gone. Like I say, it was a strange night. You could just make out the white shapes of the pelicans, the ones you can always see out on the sandbar in the middle of the river, right there before it curves south. Ten, eleven pelicans were there that night. Maybe more. Whenever I'd see them there I'd wonder if it was the same kind of pelican that lived way down in Florida and New Orleans and all them places. Some day I was going to see the Mississippi, all the way to the mouth. Maybe we could fly all that way, Bonbon and me. Maybe. I don't know what all I was thinking.

Sometimes it's best not to know what you're thinking. Two of the pelicans took off. I turned, and then I could suddenly see moving shapes on the hillside. The one behind had a funny sort of loping motion—I actually remember seeing him as a strange shape, before I knew it was my Bonbon. And then they were with me and it was all hugging and *I can't believe it!* and all that and I really couldn't, I couldn't believe it, he was really there, they'd made it out, and quick whispers and then *quiet!*, and then a paddle banging against the metal of the boat, and I was fumbling with the rope at the front while Ash did the rope at the back. *Painter*, why the hell would they call it that? Funny the things you never think of, until you do. Even when something important is happening, even if it might be the most important thing in your whole goddam life.

"I've got it," she was saying. "I've got it, Luce." She sort of pushed me aside. She was good with knots, she'd been to summer camp and all that. But I didn't mind, really I didn't. "You're in front, Luce. Bonbon, you're in the middle," she said. As if he can understand, I thought, but what did I know? Then I saw she was pointing for him as well, and showing him how to hold the paddle, what all to do. We wobbled a little when I got in but not too bad, and then Ash slipped in to the boat at the back as she pushed off. I could feel the current beneath the boat, and I dug my paddle into the water and pulled just like she'd showed me. We were off.

19.

Ashley Rouleau

I've been down that stretch of river again and again since that night —at least once every two or three years. I guess I can say I know it well, but everything was all new to me then—to all three of us. At first it was the current and the darkness, that was all—dark shapes against darker shapes, and all of it shifting with the water. From where I pushed us out into the current the river turns sharply south almost immediately; it carries on more or less in a southerly direction all the way to the border. If it's nighttime, there's always a glow in the sky to the east—the Deerfoot Freeway, off in the distance. For a while the freeway runs parallel to the river, but well back of the water, and high up—you can never see it from below, even in broad daylight. But you can hear the odd whine of a motorcycle, and the sounds of pick-up trucks with roughened mufflers, gunning it in the passing lane, and always the steady drone of the eighteen-wheelers. Everyone was watching either the hockey game or the election results that night, but truckers aren't everyone.

To the west there was nothing to be heard—the parkland and the birds in their sanctuary go quiet at night, and in behind, the houses of Inglewood go quiet too. It must be two or three miles farther downriver before the glow of the expressway fades, and another mile or two until the glow of the city itself starts to fade. You know then that if you could climb the steep cliffs that rise from the riverbank on both sides you'd look out over grassland and darkened farms, a single light twinkling here and there, wild animals hidden in the dark underbrush, farm animals hidden in their dark sheds. And the dark of the prairie deepening far into the distance into the different dark of a prairie sky.

For a long time we were silent, all three of us, tense and silent. Gradually a calmer stillness began to steal over us, with the rhythm of our paddles breaking the water. Bonbon's paddle would bang a little against the gunwale from time to time, but soon he started to find a rhythm.

Within a half hour, though, Bonbon's strokes were becoming less and less steady, and he had begun to stab his paddle at the water. Worse, he had begun to shift his weight with alarming frequency. And sometimes he would lean over and peer into the dark water. I had to say something; I spoke as slowly, and as simply, and as clearly as I could.

"I have to tell you some things about canoeing. It's all new to you, I know. First thing: try not to poke at the water—you want to *pull* your paddle through the water. It will work better, and we'll get there much sooner. Second thing: it's very important not to shift your weight suddenly. You do that, and the boat's likely to tip over. You can stop paddling and rest when you need to, and you can move a little if you are not comfortable. But tell me before you shift your body. Then I can adjust—I can shift a bit in the other direction to keep us balanced."

"You told me all this already, Ash," said Luce. "Sure, it's all new to me, but you said I was doing fine before we stopped. And I *wasn't* poking at the water; I was pulling hard, just like you showed me. I want to get there just as much as you do."

"Luce, I was saying it for Bonbon. It's Bonbon who doesn't know anything about how to do this. You're doing fine." I could hear myself speaking much more quietly, even though Luce was farther away from me, at the front of the boat. She started to turn her head towards me, but she was careful not to shift her weight. I could tell what was coming.

"For *Bonbon*? He can't understand, Ash. You know that as well as I do."

"I think he can, Luce. I think he can." And then I saw her look at Bonbon, look at his face, and I knew that she knew.

I started to speak again, very slowly, very clearly. "Bonbon, if you can hear me—if you can understand what I am saying to you—nod your head." Bonbon had stopped paddling. Luce had stopped paddling. She was looking at him, hard. We were drifting with the current. She could see him nod. Was it a little less dark than it had been? He nodded again. And then once more.

"I don't believe it. I don't fucking believe it. All this time you've been pretending you can't understand a thing. And really ..."

"I eer oo. I eer oo ud."

"*I hear you*, is what he's saying, Luce. He can hear you good—hear you perfectly well, he says." Now her weight did shift. It shifted so much and so quickly that for a moment I thought we might tip. Whatever happened, we had to keep our heads; we had to keep moving down the river.

* * *

Bethany Farrier

[Following is the transcript of the recorded comments of Bethany Farrier when asked to recount what occurred during her security checks on the night of Tuesday, November 8, 2016.]

So my job is like a watcher, right? A night watcher? I go round and I check that there's no trouble, no animals running amok, no one's broken into the place, all of that. I'm security. I guess I'd be a night watchman if I was a man, but I'm not, right? You wouldn't want a night watchwoman, would you? It'd sound stupid. Anyways, I don't just watch: I know something about the animals too. I had some special training when I started? So if a giraffe has diarrhoea or anything like that, or a lion's foaming at the mouth, like, I can let them know. They're always on call, like. The veterinarians?

So this one night, I remember it because of a few reasons. It was the night they held their election, right? In the States? You know, with Donald Trump and Hillary Clinton? It was as dark as I've ever seen it. I don't suppose he had anything to do with that, Donald Trump I mean? And not the Russians either, that's a joke? I would have voted for Hillary if I'd have been American, I don't believe she killed those kids like everybody said, you remember?

So I was doing my nine o'clock round, it finished just after ten? It must have been close to ten when I checked on the bonzees and on Bonbon. You know, the hybrid? Everything seemed fine with all them. The bonzees for sure: they were all sleeping? And I could see into Bonbon's enclosure. I didn't go right in, I only have to do that once a night or if I think something's wrong, right? And nothing seemed wrong: I could see where his cover was all bunched up, like, the same way it's always bunched up. I mean when he's lying under it?

That's about all I can say about that, I guess. Except I found out about what had been happening in the election when I talked to Kent. At the front desk? He's security too. He told me all about Trump and Hillary, he'd been watching it all. On his computer, right?

* * *

Bonbon Gerson

I was my first time to float, my first time to have feel of the soft and strong under me, and always always the moving. In the dark was quiet, and in the water sparkles, and then I was think I had know beautiful for my first time.

The quiet was quiet still, for the long time. Then Ash began to say me soft, say me how I could be able pull better my paddle, and I was try to do the right. And Lucy was say, *Ash, he can't understand a thing.* But then she was knowing: I was not be the dumb Bonbon any the more.

When I was say the words, *I can hear you, I can hear you good,* Lucy she turned and her face was twisted all sad, and I was think all the things she was done since I was born, *I am thanking you* were words I was thinking, *I am sorry.*

But then sudden was Lucy more the anger than the sad. Example, she kept again and again with her say, *I don't effing believe it!* and *how could you not have effing talked to me?* And again and again, *My own effing child, for fuck's sake.* Ash was try tell her how much difficult was it for me, and how much I was wanted to tell her I was able to say words. I was nod *yes,* and after while the tight tight inside me was a little less, but then I was start crying, and tears were cover my face and not be able to stop. So I could not be able to speak or to paddle right but I kept trying to paddle and we kept on, we kept moving down the river in dark, *we should keep paddling,* Ash said, voice hard, *we should keep paddling no matter what,* and Lucinda kept turning her head round as was talking, head to me, and all time talking, *I'll keep effing paddling, you better believe I'll keep effing paddling, I'll get us to Montana before you effing know it,* and when she was saying those things she was pull her paddle the water so hard, the boat was jouncing at the every stroke.

For the long times she kept with her hard pulls, short grunts each pull. Finally she start to pull more slow. We all pull steady then, all three the one. Then all was quiet once the more, with our quiet pulling and the quiet float of us, and the dark water dark hills. *That must be McCrimmon's Landing,* Ash was say, *we must be about halfway there. Not too much more.* But it was seem a long more. Some of the times my paddle was bang the boat side a little, mistake. Maybe Lucy was still angry but she was not say, except sometimes was mutter under her breaths. I was hear her mutters but then not even that. Just the paddles and the water, dark.

* * *

Ashley Rouleau

For a long time it was not a comfortable silence. I tried to think of words that might help to bring them together again—Luce and Bonbon, I mean.

"Has anyone talked to you ever about borders, Bonbon?" I waited for him to shake his head.

"A border is, like, an edge. An end and a beginning. A between." It didn't matter really if I got this right. What mattered was to keep putting words between Bonbon and Luce, keep giving them time to forgive each other.

"A border is sort of imagined," I went on, "but it's sort of real too." I wanted Bonbon to say something, but it was Luce who answered.

"You're effing right it's real. Without no border, Bonbon, we wouldn't have no effing problem. It doesn't get more real than that."

"Luce is right, Bonbon. Your mother's right. It is real—all too real, sometimes. But it's also made up. People make up where one part of the world ends, and where another part begins. But here's what it means to you," I carried on. "The border we're going to— on the other side of that made-up line, the law says you are a person. A human person. One hundred percent. With all the rights a human person has."

Luce was in the dark at the front of the boat; what was she thinking? Her voice came back soft; I couldn't tell if she was crying. "It's true. It has to be true." Then she caught her breath, and it sounded as if she were crying. But it was dark, and she faced forward again, still paddling hard. I could hear fast water ahead.

* * *

Lucinda Gerson

It tore me apart, I can tell you that much. To think that he had been able to fucking talk, and he'd never said a goddam thing to his own effing mother. I couldn't stop fucking thinking about it. Couldn't fucking stop thinking about it. Whatever.

It was so dark, and so cold. We had to keep moving and I had to keep my paddle pulling through the water even though my arms were numb and the water was freezing. And you couldn't keep your fingers from running through it, 'cause you couldn't hardly see where the water began, it was that dark. I told myself I wouldn't think of any of that—the cold and the numbness and Bonbon not saying a goddam thing to his own goddam mother were some of the things I wouldn't think of.

After a while I started to think of how it had all happened, how everything had happened over all the years since I'd had the stupid idea that I'd go visit Susie in the goddam Congo. Fifteen goddam years.

The river kept bending back and forth, and everything I was thinking kept bending back and forth. I thought of Bonbon again, of Bonbon with his words, but I didn't think of me this time— sometimes we've all got to stop thinking *me, me, me,* you know what I mean? Instead I thought of how he fooled all those asshole researchers, fooled them year after effing year. And I thought how hard that must have been, and how great it was that he'd pulled it off. And I told him that, I told him right to his face, I turned and I said *I guess you fooled them pretty good, Bonbon, all those asshole researchers,* and I looked at him and I smiled and he did that strange sort of face-widening thing that's like a smile, only it's his, and he said *yeah,* which sounded just about like I'd say it, and I said it right back to him, *yeah*, and I could see Ash was smiling too; *Yeah!*—she said it too.

And suddenly I could see how this changed everything. For Bonbon. If he could talk and if he could understand, he could be normal. I mean, *normal*. He could go to school, he could find a girl-friend. Or a boyfriend, whatever he likes, you can do anything with anyone nowadays, I guess, so long as you don't hurt nobody. He could grow up normal. I mean, more or less.

So I was thinking all that, but then I started to think maybe the canoe wasn't going so straight, maybe we were slipping sideways a bit. I'll say this for Ash, she knows how to handle a canoe, but I was going to ask her if we needed to go this close to shore, we were get-ting close to a whole pile of rocks along the side of the river. But I didn't say anything 'cause when I looked back again I could see how hard she was working to try to make the boat go more to the left. She was huffing and puffing and she had her paddle way out wide to the right, stretching her muscles to sweep the water as she tried to turn us back to straight, *paddle hard, Bonbon* she said, *I need more power to turn us a bit to the left,* and then I could hear the water ahead, and I could see the white tops of waves against the dark water, I'd never been down a river but I knew what rapids were. That's what we were going to be in the middle of in about thirty seconds.

"We'll be OK," Ash panted, "we'll be OK. We can't let the cur-rent sweep us up against the rocks but we *have* to go down this side of the river."

"But the middle ..." I started to say. There were no big waves in the middle of the river; it looked a hell of a lot safer than the big waves we were headed towards.

"It's too shallow there. That's why there are just those ripples in the middle—no big waves. All the water's being pushed to this side of the river. Bonbon, Luce, I want you both to be ready to back paddle."

"Backpaddle?" I said, and "aggaddle? said Bonbon.

"Shit!"—that was what Ash said, and she said it real loud. It's about the only time I've heard her swear.

* * *

Ashley Rouleau

I couldn't believe how stupid I'd been. Why hadn't I shown Luce how to do this? There weren't supposed to be any rapids between Clearwater and the border; that was why. But of course all the information on the websites I'd checked was from people who were, like, *I went down the river this past July*—not November, when the water was always much lower. Rivers always change when the water's low; I knew that, and I knew I should have given Luce some white water training just in case.

"Instead of putting your paddle into the water in front of you and pulling back, you put your paddle into the water *behind* you, and you push *forward*. That way we'll be able to ride the big waves without slicing through them—without taking on water. If we're lucky. Try it now: put the paddle in behind you, then push it forward. Back paddle!" These were not rapids filled with rocks; they were nothing but standing waves, water forced into high waves as it squeezed through the narrow channel between the shallows on the left and the rocks by the shore on the right. Nothing but standing waves—but they were, what?—four feet high? Five? From crest to trough, closer to five. It was an open canoe, with not more than eight inches of freeboard. "Harder, harder! Bonbon, watch Lucinda —yes, yes, you've got it!"

We were starting into the heavy waves now, climbing up and then careening down into the trough. That was the danger point— the moment when we'd be most likely to ship water, just as we entered the next wave and started to climb again. And now the current was skewing us sideways, the bow starting to swing left. I couldn't let that happen; if we went broadside we would be under in a second. I leaned over wide to the left, pulling with everything I had to keep the stern from swinging right, trying not to think of what would happen if we went under in this cold, *pull hard, pull hard, back paddle!* I shouted, and then *that's it, that's it,* I could feel the force of us all pulling back against the current, feel the boat slowing, feel us straightening as we hit the next wave. *Hard again, hard, back paddle!.* Bonbon was small but he was strong. We went down into a trough and slewed a little sideways but then we were straight again, *we shipped a little water that time, but it's all right, it's all right,* I bellowed. Now it needed a hard draw stroke on the right to keep the stern from swinging the other way, *steady, steady,* and up again, *we shipped a little more but only a little, we'll be all right, all right now, one more big wave, just one more, back paddle hard!* And they did—they did, and slowly we were up to the top, the water splashing over the bow as we crested it, and down into the last trough. The canoe shivered for a moment as it hit the water hard. Had Luce shifted her weight? She had, but not so much as to tip us. The next wave was only half as big and then we were through, nothing but fast water ahead of us. Would it be like this now all the way to the border? Best not to think—we were through, that was what mattered. *It's all right,* I said, *it's all right,* and now I wasn't shouting and it really was all right, really.

For a minute or two no one spoke. Finally Luce said, *we couldn't have died anyway, could we? I mean, not with our life-jackets on and everything?* No, I lied, *no chance. Not with our lifejackets on.*

20.

Dr. Cyril Carlson

I was like everyone else the night of November 8—I was watching television. I don't give a shit about sports, but I'm a political junkie; of course I was going to watch the election results come in. I'd gone out to Jimmy's—that place on 17th that's so crowded no one goes there any more, as Yogi Berra used to say. As soon as I arrived I wished I hadn't gone there. Normally I'd stay home on a night like that but my old friend Trevor Larson had twisted my arm; we'd watched George W. Bush get elected in 2000 and Trevor said it'd be good luck to get together for this one too, *how many times can we get together and have a chance to see our guy win it all?*—all along he'd really believed the Donald would win. Back when Dubya won, we'd hung out at the Ship and Anchor, but we were both of us a little old for that place now. And it had become a little too liberal for us, I'd have to say—more like a pub in Vancouver or Seattle than anywhere in Alberta. We figured there'd be a few more like-minded souls at Jimmy's. We were right about that, but it was just way too loud and too crowded. People kept walking in front of us or standing up in front of the televisions, and half the time you couldn't see any of the screen at all. Trevor wanted to talk more than he wanted to listen, and he was like just about everybody else—they were all talking over the commentators. I remember some drunk leaning into me, *You wanna see a crazy conservative take power? This is our chance, eh? You like crazy?* I told him *yeah, I like crazy,* and I guess I do. It's not something I could ever be myself, and I wouldn't want to live in the same house with it, but yeah, I like it. I like it a lot. Not crazy like some guy getting drunk and talking too much, but crazy like some guy who likes power and you know he's right wing, but at the same time you never know quite what he might do. You feel he could do *anything*. I sort of liked that—I still sort of like that.

I hardly heard my cell phone when it rang but I could feel it vibrating. "Carlson here," I said, and wondered if they could hear me. Probably not. "I'm sorry it's so loud here," I added. "I'll try to get outside." All I could hear on the other end of the line was the one word—*gone*, the voice kept saying. *Gone*. It was Sol's voice; Sol was the senior security person on duty that night. "Speak up!" I told him, I might have even sworn at him, I can't remember. But it was no good. Finally I pushed my way outside and then I could make out the rest of what he was saying. *Bonbon. There's no sign of him. There's nothing broken, no fences cut. But he's gone. Gone.*

Jesus, I thought. *Jesus Fucking H. Christ.* I pressed the damn thing harder into my ear. I could still hardly hear. But I was on the move. Back to our table to get my coat and to throw a fifty in the direction of Trevor—good Scotch isn't cheap at Jimmy's. "Something's come up," I yelled. "Gotta go. You cheer him on for both of us!" I didn't wait for an answer but I could hear him calling *Cy! What the hell?* behind me as I headed for the door. Outside it was crisp, cold. The election wasn't over but the game was; crowds were spilling onto the street. My car was blocks away. "I'll be at the office as soon as I can," I told Sol. "And yes, I can drive perfectly well." I was answering my own question, not his. Two lousy drinks, that's all I had. Not even two; I must have left ten bucks worth of McCallan's in the glass. "You stay there; I'll be with you in twenty minutes. But send somebody now to the Gerson place." *To where?* he asked. We don't have the brightest security staff. "Lucinda Gerson," I told him, and I could tell from the silence on the line that he still didn't get it. "The hybrid—Lucinda Gerson is his fucking mother." You had to be blunt with these people; you couldn't screw around.

"You think they'll be hiding out there?"

"I think they'll be headed for the border, both of them. If we're lucky there'll be something at the Gerson place that will tell us where they're headed—which roads, which border crossing. Or what flights—but I don't think they'll fly."

"Should we call the police?" he asked.

"I'm going to do that right now. But I want you to check in with them too. And I want you to be with them at the office by the time I get there—I don't want any time wasted. We've got to get the little fucker before he crosses the border."

Yeah, that's what I called him: *the little fucker.* And I meant every word.

* * *

Lucinda Gerson

"Well that was pretty effing scary," I remember saying. I tried to keep a steady stroke as I turned my head and looked round at Bonbon for a second. "Pretty fucking scary." Why I had to say it again with the swear word I'll never know. "But it's going to be all right. We're going to cross the border, and everything is going to be all right." Maybe I figured if I kept telling him those things I'd start to believe them myself. He didn't answer but I think he was sort of smiling, so I figured I'd better keep on talking. "And you and me, we're going to start making a new life." 'Course I couldn't be talking like that without thinking again down deep, *How the hell are we going to do that?* Where was I going to get anyone at a Price Chopper or a Safeway in goddam Montana to take me on? Or effing New Orleans, for that matter. They'd have someone they knew already that they'd want to hire, someone no one was ever going to call an ape fucker.

Where was I going to find someplace for us both to *live*? I could feel my gut start to go all tight again, just like it had been in the rapids. You can't let your kids see how scared you are, can you?

"Are you worried?" I asked him. "I bet you're worried. And sure, there's one big fat whacking load of things to be worried about. But we're not going to go there. We're just not. You and me, we're going to figure things out. We're going to America, Bonbon. America—land of the free. It's going to be alright."

He still wasn't saying anything. What does a kid need to hear from a parent? I mean, a kid who can understand what you're saying to him. Love. That's what everyone says, right? Kids need to hear they're loved. Guess that makes us all kids, doesn't it, ha ha?

"I'm your mother, Bonbon. I'm where you came from, and you got to trust me. And I love you. I've loved you for as long as there's been a you. Since even before then. Detroit. You don't remember there, but it's where you were born. Where I borned you, and I loved you there and I loved you all the years they kept you locked up, and I'm going to love you in Montana or wherever the fuck we end up."

"I o." That was all he said—*I o.*

"You owe? No, you don't owe me anything. You ..." Then I got it. Know! You *know.* That's what you said, *I know.*

"Es." For a second it didn't seem like there was anything else to say. Then he asked me one more thing, I wasn't sure what he said, but like a lot of other times in my life when I couldn't hear stuff I went ahead and pretended I understood. "They're nice in America," I told him, "a lot of them are nice people. Some people say everyone is out for themself in America, but that's not right, most of them aren't like that." Maybe I lied, I don't know. I told him in America people cared for others just as much as they did anywhere else. Maybe more. Maybe a lot more. I told him he would be happy there. Not just free, but happy.

Of course I told him that. What parent wouldn't tell their kid exactly that? What parent is gonna tell their kid that life might not have a fairy tale ending after all?

And then I started singing that song, *All I want is to be free, and where that river flows, that's where I want to be; flow, river flow.* I don't know if I was singing it for Bonbon or I was singing it for me or I was singing it for everyone, but I sang it over and over, quiet like, as the three of us paddled on in the darkness.

* * *

Dr. Cyril Carlson

There were two officers with Sol and Bethany when I arrived. They looked a little unsure of themselves—the officers, I mean. I guess a manhunt for a hybrid wasn't in their normal line of work; well, they had better make it in their line of work, I thought. I saw at once that I'd have to take control of the questioning. Sol and Bethany looked plenty unsure of themselves too. They had reason; I guess they understood they wouldn't be likely to have a job the next morning.

"When exactly was Bonbon last seen?"

Two voices spoke together:

"Bethany says she ..." / "I saw him at ten o'clock? Didn't I say that? I always check him and the bonzees and the bonobos right about then every night?"

"We're asking you, Bethany. Not the other way round."

"I looked into his enclosure? Just like always? And he was there, like always, I saw him. Just like he's supposed to be?"

"And the front desk man ...?" I asked Sol, not Bethany.

"He says no one could have gotten past without him seeing them."

"And you don't believe him?"

"When I went over there he had the game on. Everybody's been watching the game, Cy. Or else what's happening in the States—you know that."

"When you're on the job, Sol, you are not supposed to ... You know perfectly well that you're supposed … —But I'm going to leave that for now. What you're saying is, they might have been gone for two, three hours."

"They?" one of them asked. Not the brightest officer the world has ever seen.

"He didn't do this on his own, officer. You think a bonzee can pick locks?"

"There was a bonobo once that managed to …" That was Sol. He never had any sense of what was appropriate. Never.

"Bonbon did *not* fucking do this on his own, Sol. Excuse the language, officers, but I know something about how animals be-have, what they can do and what they can't. Ashley Rouleau is behind this. That black girl. Her and Bonbon's mother, the wacko who started everything by having it off with an ape in the Congo." No, I was not mincing words—and I don't regret it one bit.

"We know for sure that Bonbon ate the food he was brought. That was at six?" Fucking Bethany and her up-speak.

"So they could have crossed the border already?"

"We're pretty sure that hasn't happened, sir." Now it was one of the officers talking. The one who hadn't already proved himself stupid. "Customs and Immigration have been on full alert ever since they got the call from you folks. He hasn't crossed—not since just after we got the call, anyway. And they're 99% sure, based on the description, that no one crossed before that. The only possible way they could have crossed would have been the NEXUS lane—if they had driven through the bypass lane for people who've been pre-cleared. We've had that lane blocked off for some time now; we're checking everyone. But a couple of hours ago? Before we got the call? Yeah, they could have gotten through."

"What about the airport? You've got a watch on at the airport?"

"They'd have to use passports to get onto any plane—and if you're trying that route there'd be no crouching low in the back seat for the hybrid. Or hiding in the truck. He'd need a passport, and a passport is one thing he doesn't have. I don't see how they could do it by air—even if we hadn't been sounding the alarm."

"What about the smaller roads?"

"Every crossing from the coast to the far side of Saskatchewan / North Dakota—they're all on full alert. Manitoba / Minnesota and Ontario / Michigan crossings will go on full alert tomorrow if we still haven't picked them up by then. Even the crossings that usually shut down at nine o'clock are being kept open in case they show up. Every crossing will be fully staffed all night."

"So we wait."

"Yes sir. We wait. I can't see any way they could get through, sir."

"There better not be any way. This is Alberta, right? We're still 80 percent white here and we're still—what?—maybe 90 percent middle class and mainstream. And these three? One is a lower class woman in her thirties who is—how do I put it?—the opposite of mainstream. The opposite of everything. The second is a young black woman who sounds like she came from some fancy part of Toronto. And the third is only half human—and looks it! They can't hide; they can't get away from what they are!"

"No sir. I don't think they can."

* * *

Bonbon Gerson

How we know the border? That was my words, but I knew how they heard me: *ow ee o ...?* A few weeks later I could be able to make words almost like how whole humans they make words. But not then, in the at first. My mouth was not easy to sound the hard letters. And Lucy? Lucy was turn towards me and I was see in her face—to hear me was hard.

Ash knew what I was say her: "Luce, I'm pretty sure he's asking us how we'll know when we get to the border. It's a good question."

"There won't be some sort of fence across the river?"

"Or some sort of wall? Not likely, I don't think. But some sort of cable across the river—there might be that. Or at least a sign-post—*you are entering the United States of America; do not cross the border unless* ... That sort of thing. Yeah, I think there will be some sign. And I think we'll see it in less than an hour."

* * *

Lucinda Gerson

"You know where this river ends up, Bonbon?" Sometimes I don't know why I say things. I just do. And even more that night, when it was so dark and so cold and so different. "In New Orleans. They say it's the most fun of any city in the whole world. And the most beautiful too." I turned and I could see him making that strange little sort-of smile. "You're going to be free now; we can go where we want, do what we want, say what we want. I'll teach you to say anything you fucking want." Then I thought about it for a moment. "I mean just *anything you want*. Not *fucking*. I guess I better teach you not to say *fucking*. And teach myself. Around you, anyway. Now that I know you can understand everything I effing say."

"Ut's effing?" The bonzees did it all the time; did he really not know the word for it?

"Effing is what Ever and Only and Jasper and all of them spend half their effing time doing."

"I u eep aying?" *Why you keep saying* the word? I knew that was what he was asking. Ashley didn't have to tell me. But how do you answer a question like that? I didn't say anything. Not right away.

"*Why do you keep saying it?* I think that's what he's asking," said Ash. "Is that right, Bonbon?"

"Es."

"He's asking why you keep saying *effing* and *fucking*."

"Why the ... Why do we do anything? Bonbon, humans have somehow set up the world so that we make sex seem like the most important thing. We get to thinking we want it more than anything else. Even money. Even goodness. And we've gotten it all tied up with money, and with power, I mean even more than it would be anyway, just with all the testosterone and that. So we say *He fucked me over* when we mean *He took advantage*, and we say *Fuck you* when we mean *Go away*, and we say ... We use it for a lot if things." I didn't know where I was going with this. "And people who don't have any power, sometimes they use it more than anyone. Maybe so we feel like we do have a little more power, I don't know.

"And then there's sex itself. Maybe bonzees get too much of it, but a lot of humans don't get enough of it, I can tell you that. Everywhere there's sexy advertisements and sexy clothes and sexy songs, we get sexy everything. Except sex. A lot of us don't get much sex, and when we do it's the one thing in the world that isn't sexy. It's some guy groping you and pushing his way inside you and you're supposed to like it. So maybe we get angry about that too, and maybe we start putting the words where they don't belong. And somehow that makes the other words seem stronger too, makes it seem like they mean more than they do.

"But it's not great, Bonbon. I know it's not great. I shouldn't be putting those words into every eff ... into every sentence. Ha! I almost said *every effing sentence*, didn't I? I had to stop myself! I have to stop myself. You can't be saying shi ... you can't be saying stuff like that around kids. And maybe we shouldn't be saying those words at all. You and me, we're going to learn how to talk, aren't we, Bonbon?"

"I an eech u."

Ashley started laughing behind me. *What did he say?* I had to ask her.

"*I can teach you.* He says he can teach you not to say those words."

I had to stop and think about that one.

I kept paddling as I was thinking; we all kept paddling right through everything. Paddling hard. "I don't know, Bonbon. Maybe you *can* help. People always say you should let your children help you. All right then. You get on my case if you hear me saying any of those bad words. I'm giving them up, all of them. Starting now."

Then I realized that wasn't everything I needed to say.

"You know there's this nasty old bully who might become President tonight? He swears all the time, he says he grabs women by the ... I don't even want to tell you what he says, and then he says it's all a joke. I bet he's never used the word *fuck* in a sexy way with someone he loves, used it with love in it, used it to mean, like, the pleasure people do with each other. And not something nasty that one person does to another person. There are so many people who don't care for anyone else except themselves, they'll screw anyone— yeah, there's another word you'll have to teach me not to say, but that's what they do, whether it's in an office or over their grand-mother's will or on a mattress or bent over the hood of a car, it's all screwing for them, it's people being nasty to other people, not think-ing of anyone 'cept themselves. How do people get to be that way?"

✳ ✳ ✳

Bonbon Gerson

Lucy who was my mother, when she was start to talk of the loving and the fuck-loving, I was thinking me not of words but of who I be fuck-loving. How was that happen different, the fuck-loving with a human?

Was Lucy and me to be living in same place? If Lucy had a fuck-lover, was she be letting me watch? Human people they are not like others to watch, I was think. Not like bonzee people. And I was both the peoples.

"I have remember this, yes," was my words. "I have remember what you say. You are stop saying the fuck-saying, and you are doing the stop for me. The giving up."

Then I was think of all the givings up, and of what Lucy was said other ways. Of her work the Safeway, and in Sunderland of her work the Price Chopper. I was sudden think Lucy would give all that up too, would stop all her jobs of work.

"Your Bonbon will be the help to you," I said her. "You are be famous—Lucy who made the half/half. I have no want for famous, but they will happen it to me, they will be wanting screen talk with mother that did the love-fucking, mother that did the making of me. All the money is America. They will be giving you the money, and then you will not be needing the Safeway."

"It's true," Ash said. "Bonbon's right. Luce, they'll want you on all the talk shows, your picture will be, like, everywhere. And there will be money in all of it. If you want it," she added. "You won't have to worry about money, you can ..."

"I can forget I'm goddam working class—that'll be it, won't it? I can sit around and—what am I supposed to *do* if I'm effing rich?"

It was time me start to teach her.

"Very," I said her. "*Very* rich."

"Erry?" She was still not understand my sounds that had the human meanings. "Erry itch?"

"Rich," Ash said her. "*Very rich*. That's what Bonbon said. And maybe you can be, if you want. But only if you want," she was add say. "And only if we get the two of you across the border."

* * *

Dr. Cyril Carlson

Yes, I'd said we would simply have to wait. But for three hours I couldn't keep off my cell phone. I kept phoning the police—police

headquarters, the highway detachments, the police who were keeping a watch on the house that Lucinda and Ashley had been sharing. I kept phoning the Canadian border posts, the American border
posts, trying to get anyone I could think of to be on alert. No one
would tell me a single fucking thing.

Could the three of them really have escaped by air? No, it was
impossible. Might they have gone in the opposite direction—headed north, thinking they could lie low somewhere for a few weeks
until the fuss died down, and then go south and quietly make their
way across the border? Yes, that was certainly possible. I phoned
Edmonton, Red Deer, Drumheller—everywhere.

There would be no way to live this down if they made it over
the border; I knew that. My whole career would be defined by it; I
would be forever remembered as the one who'd let the hybrid escape, the one who had missed out on the research opportunity of a
lifetime, the one who—it didn't bear thinking about.

I stopped for a moment. I put the phone down. I turned the
lights down. I tried to calm down, but it was no use. I realized I'd
grown hoarse from trying to keep my voice down. I would force
myself to stay off the phone for five minutes. No, for ten. I began
to breathe deeply; I couldn't stop myself from pacing back and forth
across the office. But then I stopped by the window. I forced myself
to look up at the stars, and I remembered how my parents had tried
to teach me to think of them as a moral lesson, a way of reminding
us of how small we are in the universe. Human beings, I mean.
They'd thought that would humble me—instead, it made me more
determined than ever to make as large a mark on the universe as I
could. It would not be a small mark; I knew that much by now. But
I knew too that it could never be large enough. There was never
enough time.

They were all out tonight, the stars—there was not a cloud to
be seen. And hardly a moon at all. I threw open the window—cold,
but less cold than you'd expect for a clear night in November. A

beautiful night, if it weren't for everything that had happened. I looked out at the broad slope going down to the river, and the faint light of the expressway beyond the river, and the great shadowy trees on the other side of the river ...

The river! In a flash I was at the phone again. The police had speedboats as well as cars. And they had helicopters. Perhaps I was crazy, but then again perhaps I wasn't. It would be a hell of a lot easier for three people to escape that way than by air. Why hadn't I thought of this earlier? Why hadn't my staff thought of this earlier? Why hadn't the fucking police thought of it earlier? What was it—four AM? There was probably still time.

Lucinda Gerson

Ashley was puffing in and out with every stroke, paddling harder than ever. I tried to do the same—paddle harder, I mean—but my arms ached so bad I couldn't. It was so cold, but paddling harder, pulling harder didn't seem to make me any warmer. Ash found a way to keep talking, taking breaths every so often between strings of words. "Maybe if you live ... in a small town ... live in one small town after another ... If you're ready to move every time they find out who you are." She was still thinking of what would happen on the other side—how we could find a way to live like normal people.

"Maybe," I said, and I started taking breaths like Ash. "Or maybe we could ... go all the way ... down the river ... to New Orleans ... where everyone's strange ... That's what they say ... Everyone's different ... We can be like everyone, maybe."

* * *

Ashley Rouleau

We weren't at the border yet, but soon, very soon. As I felt within me how close it was, I felt a surge of—what can I call it? Triumph? Pride? I was feeling *I've done it!* even before we were at the border. It's a dangerous feeling. I knew I had always had what people call courage—I could jump into things in ways that other people would call brave; that had always come naturally to me. But this? It was the planning of it that really pleased me—the thinking-through. When I'd been really young my parents had always been, like, *you're so smart, but you're a scatter-brain!* Maybe that did used to be true; it wasn't now. I looked into the darkness, around the next big bend of the river, and then up to the tops of the cliffs, and to the stars. I kept paddling, hard.

And I watched Bonbon's back as he paddled, and what I could see of his body—his hairy neck where the clothes I had given him stopped, and his right hand as it pulled his paddle through the water. I watched how the whole hand went underwater when he did that, not just a finger or two like it was with most people. I thought of how cold he must have been feeling, for hours now, and how he hadn't complained, not even once. And I thought of how other people would see those long arms and that hairy neck. They wouldn't see Bonbon; they'd see an ape-man, and they'd gawk and they'd say things just like they had at the zoo.

Would I see him again after this long, strange night? You can't know things like that, and you can't be thinking all the time. I had to look out for rocks. I had to steer the boat. I wanted to hug him and tell him it would be all right. And I guess I wanted to tell him that I would always love him.

But I never said that. I kept paddling. Yes, there were tears in my eyes. No one turned around; no one saw.

* * *

Bonbon Gerson

So cold. I was not thinking ever we were be there. Not thinking ever be cross the border over—whenever, whatever the free. I was knowing someways they would stop us. I was having the fear—fear what they would do to Lucy and to Ash and to me when they catched us. The more far we were gone, the more far I was thinking, at the end we will no one be free.

But I was not say *go back*, and Ash she was say again, *we're*

219

almost there, and say again. We are wanting the fairy tales, wanting the fairy tales come truly. And always we are wanting the free.

***

Lucinda Gerson

Alright, so maybe Bonbon couldn't be normal. But maybe he could be close—he could be as normal as anyone who's a hybrid could be. It wasn't just growing up and going to school. If he learned to speak better he could get friends, he could get a job, he could travel on his own. Especially once all the fuss quieted down. The fuss always quiets down in the end—look at Teddy Kennedy and what he got away with, a few years was all it took and then he was running for president.

Alright, so Bonbon's never going to grow up to run for president. But who the hell knows, really? If that asshole with the hair could run for President, and maybe even effing win, *and* he never grew up, neither ... The sky's the goddam limit, isn't it?

And then it hit me: Bonbon could live on his own. All in a rush I thought *will he want to stay with me?* What if he *wants* to live on his own? And then I thought *they wouldn't let him, he's just a kid*, but then after that I thought *shit. It's Montana.* It's Montana, where anything goes. They let you have your own goddam gun at the age of three. They sure as shit weren't going to make someone wait until they were eighteen before they could choose to live on their own. Was it sixteen? Then I remembered—Ash and me had watched a feature all about it on TV, about how low the age is some places, some places like Montana, and how the age of majority's different from what they call the age of effing *emancipation*. That was the word—*emancipation*, and I remembered thinking, *how weird is that?* As if kids have been slaves right through their goddam childhoods and then, like, there's some Lincoln with an Emancipation

Proclamation, ha ha. But it wasn't no joke, it was real, it was when a child can decide to live on its own. Fourteen. Was it fourteen in Mon-fucking-tana? Bonbon was going to be fourteen in just a few days, and he was developing faster than any human. It was like he was half bonzee, ha ha. He was already looking like he was twenty, twenty-one even.

How many twenty-one year olds want to stay with their mothers, for fuck's sake?

Stop saying fuck, *Lucinda!* I mean, I wasn't saying it, I was only thinking it. But still.

Bonbon had said he would help me—help me with the *fucking*. That didn't come out right, did it? Help me with saying *fuck* and *fucking*. Help me *not* to say them. And he'd probably help me with other stuff too, and I'd help him. For awhile we'd get along. But really, how long would someone his age want to stay with their mother? I felt a sort of a tightening in my chest when I thought that. Around where my heart is, I guess. How the hell do you know just where your heart is?

That's it, Lucinda! I said to myself. *You can do it!*

Alright, so I knew that a lot of twenty-year-olds (if we say he's like a twenty-year-old) *do* want to live with their mothers. I knew that. Especially the guys, the guys who can't afford to live on their own and can't get a job to support themselves. Or are too proud to take the sort of job that they really could get—the sort of job that their mothers do all the time, and that women their age do all the time—check-out clerk or bank teller or cleaner. A lot of young guys are too proud to take those sorts of jobs. They'd rather lounge around their parents' place and sponge. And their mothers fall for it, keep cooking for them and doing their laundry, et cetera, et cetera. Who wants their kid to live with them just because the kid's too lazy to do what he should be doing? To do what he *wants* to do, deep down?

What did Bonbon want to do, deep down? What did I want to

do, deep down? That's when I had another couple thoughts: they hit me like a ton a bricks. How much did I want to live with Bonbon, if it was going to be like that? With a twenty-year-old, sure. But with a twenty-four-year-old? With a twenty-eight-year-old? When he was thirty? Thirty-five? I knew I wouldn't want that. I'd want him to be him, and me to be me. I'd want to visit him, and I'd sure as hell expect him to visit me. And I'd expect him to bring his girl-friend or boyfriend or whoever it was as well. But would I want to live with him day in, day out?

The time for that was just about gone. I could see that. Most parents have their kids' whole childhoods to remember. What I'd got to remember was—well, it wasn't what most parents have, was it? But you could say it was special, that was for sure. And what are you gonna do? You gotta roll with the punches, right? You gotta pick yourself up off the mat, pick yourself off the couch, whatever. And go get yourself another Bud from the fridge, ha ha.

Jesus it was cold.

It's a pretty short moment, isn't it? I mean, what mothers have with their children. Fathers too, if the fathers ever show up, ha ha. And then for a moment I thought of Bei, and it wasn't funny, I just hoped he was all right, that his life—I don't know what-all I hoped, but I hoped it hard. Susie might be able to tell me what had happened to him, that is, if I ever got in touch with Susie again. I'd looked her up, I knew she was married, two kids, house in the suburbs, et cet-era, et cetera. Whatever.

It's a stupid cliché, but it's true isn't it? Everyone says it can feel like forever when kids keep you up all night, the crying and the rocking and the … But I missed all that, didn't I? Missed a helluva lot of it, anyway, with all those years of four hours a day. There was just a big hole in life where something normal should have been. *But who wants normal, anyway?* I was asking myself that, and then suddenly I could hear someone answering *I do! I do!* Was I saying it out loud? I tried to keep quiet but for a couple seconds I could hear little choking sounds coming out of my mouth. Anyways, sometimes you have to just wipe the goddam tears off your face and shut the fuck up, and that's what I did, in that crazy boat on that crazy dark river, trying to find goddam America. Trying to get to the place where America began, ha ha.

* * *

Ashley Rouleau

"Bonbon, Luce, look—there it is! Ahead ... Way down there. No, to the left, just before the river curves out of sight. Ten o'clock. You see?"

"Ah an see!" / "Yes, I can see it!" They spoke together.

"Iz a zine."

"A sign with something in the corner ... —it must be the American flag."

"And look beyond it—another fifty yards downstream."

"Another sign, a flag on that one too. They've laid out the goddam welcome mat.

"*Do not cross this border without prior clearance from the Department of Immigration.*"

"But there's no fence, there's no ..."

"Oh wall."

"Or wall! You're so right, Bonbon. There is no fence, there is no wall. Just clear water from here to the border. Another couple of hundred yards and ..."

"America."

* * *

Bonbon Gerson

Was it? Was it? Now when, now when, paddle hard, paddle hard. No more the putting on table, the strap down. Now could be fairy tale coming truly. So cold, but start light in sky. Every thing was almost, the border line, the free. I was keep paddling, whole me was paddle hard, was no go back, was fairy tale coming truly, the end. The real, the now, the free.

* * *

Ashley Rouleau

But it was not America yet. Less than fifty yards ahead there was one more barrier, stretching almost all the way across the river. You could see in the beginnings of the morning light how the water went pale brown, almost right the way across. Shallows. Another sand-bar. How much water was flowing over it—two inches? Three? Was that enough clearance? We would have to plough forward and do our best to clear it—and be ready to get out and get wet and drag the boat across the shallows if we couldn't float through. The alternative? Risk the narrow passage far off to the right by the western shore, where almost all the water in the river was pressed into a narrow chute—a chute no more than ten feet across, with standing waves as high as the ones we'd barely made it through earlier. But these were worse; almost exactly in the middle of the chute you could just make out the shape of a huge boulder. Hit that and any boat would crumple in a second.

"You see that? We can't go anywhere near that chute! Luce, Bonbon, you may have to get into the water …"

"Yeah. We can do that."

I knew it could be dangerous anytime a novice got in or out of a canoe. You could make a wrong move in so many different ways, and end up flipping the boat, injuring yourself. If it could be done, I wanted them to stay inside the boat.

"We'll see if we can power our way across the bar. It might not be as shallow as it looks. If..."

"What's that?"

"I say it might not be as shallow as it looks. If we ..." But Luce was still shaking her head as if she couldn't hear me. And then I heard it too. A whine in the distance, a faraway whine but you could hear it getting closer.

"A motorboat? At this hour? What the ..."

"A police boat, Luce. It has to be, I think. They patrol the river and—no! They're not patrolling; they're coming for us. Paddle hard, paddle hard! They can't get to us if we're on the other side of that sandbar! Bonbon, no, not back-paddle—*fore*-paddle. Yes, yes, hard. Forward! Hard!" The paddles dug in on both sides—as deep as we could. "Faster! Harder, pull together, ten more strokes, come on, *One!*" Behind us the whine had become a roar, but then suddenly it died back; they must have seen the sandbar too."

"*Two! Three! Four!*" Now we could hear a megaphone, a voice coming over the water. I don't know how close they were; I didn't look back. "*Seven! Eight! Nine!*"

"This is the police! Do not attempt to cross that sandbar. Do not attempt to cross the border. Pull your oars out of the water."

I snorted. Oars! How clueless could they be? We would hit ground in just a few seconds—if we were going to hit ground at all. Maybe we could clear the bar, speed right over, right through.

"*Ten! Eleven! Twelve!*"

"You are under arrest! Repeat: you are under arrest!"

"They're not going to get you, Bonbon. We're not going to let them get you. The border's right there, and you're getting over it, we're getting over that sandbar, over that border, *Fourteen! Fifteen! Sixteen!*" Now, suddenly, it was not just the police boat; there was a humming whirr above the whine of the police boat's outboard; the whirr came rapidly closer, and settled into a steady roar; it was directly above us and I heard Bonbon cry *No! No!* He started to cover his head with his hands, his paddle angled strangely behind him.

"Come on!" I yelled, "We can't stop. Paddle! *Nineteen! Twenty! Twenty-one!*"

"Stop where you are. Do not attempt to take your craft any farther! Repeat: stop where you are!" But Bonbon was paddling again, Luce pulled harder than ever, everything was driving us forward. The shallows were right there, the sandbar, and we were still moving through the water, we were almost through, *we're going to make it over!* I tried to shout above the whirr of the copter, *we're going to make it through!*

And then suddenly a hard screech against the bottom of the boat, another screech, and we jerked to a halt. Our bow still floated free—it was through—but the stern was heavier, and it had stuck fast in the gravel and sand a few inches below the surface of the water. I could feel the police boat floating closer, its engine on idle now, closer, closer, and the megaphone again—

"This is your last warning. Do not attempt to go farther. Do not attempt to cross the border ..."

I was out of the canoe now, feet in the water, pushing the canoe forward with all my strength. Luce started to stand up as I began to haul, *I'll help!*, she said, *I can help!* and she turned just as I jerked the boat forward and she started to fall back towards me, *Luce!* I yelled, *keep low, the boat's coming free, it's coming free! Keep low, hang on to your paddle ...*

* * *

Lucinda Gerson

I effing tried. I really did. My left foot twisted as I turned, and it swung out over the side and the boat started pitching back and forth, left to right and back again, I thought we were going to tip, and I was falling towards the back of the boat and the current was catching the bow and starting to pull the boat forward as it was still pitching side to side, and then my one foot was in the water and then my other foot twisted and my whole body twisted and I fell back against Ash like the heavy goddam weight I am. The boat shot forward out from under me, and suddenly Ash and me we were both of us half on sand and half under water. The boat pitched wildly again as it moved away from us but it did not tip, it was being pulled by the current, could we get to it? Ash and me were tangled up together, we tried to pull free of each other and she stumbled one way and fell sideways and I stumbled and splashed in the other direction, and then we staggered to our feet and that was all we could do, we were that far away. We stood on the sandbar in a few inches of water, in the goddam cold, with the goddam police boat and helicopter whirling above, and everything loud and screeching, and everything over.

I looked out at him, at my Bonbon. The light was growing and even from far off I could see him looking back at me, *Lucy!* he called, he called as if he would never see me again, and he grew smaller and smaller until he looked smaller than he was when he was small, and I could hear Ash swear, and then she said *But he's going to make it, Luce. He's going to make it!*, and I couldn't say anything, everything was tightening inside me again and all I could do was look after him. I tried to shout but I couldn't, and he grew smaller and smaller and his voice went faint and I had no voice at all. And my ankle hurt so bad but I didn't feel it, the river was taking him away, the goddam river was taking him away.

* * *

Jennifer Bhakta

[Following is a transcript of the responses of Officer Jennifer Bhakta to questions put to her during a phone

conversation with Dr. Cyril Carlson, Wednesday, 9
November, 2016.]

"No, Dr. Carlson, we can't get to him directly from here. There's a
sandbar, the water's too shallow, we have to turn back and find the
channel on the other side of the river where there's enough depth to
get through. We're backing the boat up now, we're turning ... But I
don't think we have time to ..."

"Wait, wait. We can't get through that side either ... There's
rocks, sir ... No, right in the middle of the channel, huge boulders ...

"It's not a question of taking a chance, sir, it would be a 100%
certainty. This boat would be ripped apart if we tried it ..."

"No, I don't think the copter will be able to stop him either, sir.
It can't land in the water, it could rescue him if ..."

"That's right, he's very close to the border now ..."

"No, we're not allowed to pursue beyond ..."

"Yes, the hybrid is the only one in the boat. The others are on
the sandbar ... That's right, we should be able to pick them up in a
few moments ..."

"I can't say for sure whether charges will be laid, no, that's not
my ..."

"Yes, I hear you, Dr. Carlson. Sir, at this point there's nothing
I can do. Unless that canoe goes aground again, it will be across the
border in half a minute—even less. And there's no other sandbar in
front of him, there's lots of clearance for a craft that small and light.
In fact, the current seems to be moving the boat quite quickly, it's
spinning, but it's moving downstream at quite a clip ..."

"There's no call for that kind of language, Dr. Carlson. I appreciate that this is a difficult situation for you, sir. It's difficult for
all of us, but I ..."

"Sir, strictly speaking, I shouldn't even be talking to you. You
should be going through my superi ... Yes sir, I know you've spoken
to him already and I ..."

"Sir, I'm afraid I'm going to have to end this call. You're breaking up and ..."

***

Bonbon Gerson

There was no thinking. There was the loud above and all round, and cold, and the water. And Ash was gone, and Lucy was gone, Lucy that was my always name for everything at the beginnings, and then I could not see them for time as the boat was go round and go round, and was only the river and the loud, I was knowing they were want stop me, sky machine men, they were want take me to Carlson and the table and the straps hold me down. My paddle I pushed it, I pulled it, was try get away Carlson, was try not lose Ash, was try not lose Lucy, was try not lose love, still round I went, and round, and went, *what was if? what was then?* I was alone, was I gone over the line? Over the line what no one can touch, no one can see? Was I free?

afterword

So far as the story of Bonbon's early years is concerned, there is little I can add to the collection of excerpts I have gathered here—and this, it seems to me, is the natural point for such a volume to end. Any narrative that tries to piece together his later life (and that of his mother, and that of Ashley Rouleau) must be a whole other story—one that is forced at key points to rely on conjecture and guesswork as much as on any body of established fact. So I leave Bonbon here, with Lucinda and Ash growing smaller and smaller behind him, and with the river pulling him onwards, out of reach, across a line that none of them could see, to a place that none of them really knew.

Acknowledgements

I'm deeply indebted to a number of people who have read and commented on all or part of this book at different stages along the way—and who have helped to make it much better than it would have been had I tried to do everything on my own. I would like to thank in particular Beth Humphries, Jackie Kaiser, Naomi LePan, Maureen Okun, Emelia Quinn, Julie Roorda, Peter Singer, Deborah Willis, and Laura Wright.

About the Author

Don LePan has spent most of his adult life working as a book publisher; he is the founder and CEO of the academic publishing house Broadview Press. He has also worked as a taxi driver, a hospital cleaner, and a secondary school teacher. He holds a BA from Carleton University, an MA from Sussex University, and was awarded an honorary doctorate by Trent University in 2004 for his contributions to academic publishing. LePan is also a painter (a solo exhibition of his work was held in Brooklyn in 2008). *Lucy and Bonbon* is his third novel; his first, *Animals*, was praised by J.M. Coetzee as "a powerful piece of writing, and a disturbing call to conscience." Born in Washington, DC and raised in Ontario, LePan spent many years as a resident of Calgary, Alberta, and has lived for briefer periods in New Orleans, Louisiana; Lewes, Sussex; and Murewa, Zimbabwe. Since 2009 his home has been Nanaimo, British Columbia.